THE ONE
WOMAN

A STORY OF MODERN UTOPIA

THOMAS DIXON, JR.

1ˢᵗ WORLD
LIBRARY
Literary Society

The One Woman

Thomas Dixon Jr.

© 1st World Library – Literary Society, 2006
PO Box 2211
Fairfield, IA 52556
www.1stworldlibrary.org
First Edition

LCCN: 2006930802

Softcover ISBN: 1-4218-2203-2
Hardcover ISBN: 1-4218-2103-6
eBook ISBN: 1-4218-2303-9

Purchase *"The One Woman"*
as a traditional bound book at:
www.1stWorldLibrary.org/purchase.asp?ISBN=1-4218-2203-2

1st World Library Literary Society is a nonprofit
organization dedicated to promoting literacy by:

- Creating a free internet library accessible from any computer worldwide.
- Hosting writing competitions and offering book publishing scholarships.

Readers interested in supporting literacy
through sponsorship, donations or
membership please contact:
literacy@1stworldlibrary.org
Check us out at: www.1stworldlibrary.ORG
and start downloading free ebooks today.

The One Woman
contributed by Tim, Ed & Rodney
in support of
1st World Library Literary Society

DEDICATED TO THE MEMORY OF MY
MOTHER (1834-1902)
TO WHOSE SCOTCH LOVE OF ROMANTIC
LITERATURE I OWE THE HERITAGE OF
ETERNAL YOUTH

CONTENTS

LEADING CHARACTERS OF THE STORY

Scene: New York-Time: The Present

RUTH GORDON . . . The One Woman

REV. FRANK GORDON . . A Social Dreamer

KATE RANSOM . . . The Other Woman

MARK OVERMAN . . . .A Banker

MORRIS KING . . Ruth's Old Sweetheart

ARNOLD VAN METER . . A Shorthorn Deacon

BARRINGER . . Assistant District Attorney

CHAPTER I

THE MAN AND THE WOMAN

"Quick - a glass of water!" A man sprang to his feet, beckoning to an usher.

When he reached the seat, the woman had recovered by a supreme effort of will and sat erect, her face flushed with anger at her own weakness.

"Thank you, I am quite well now," she said with dignity.

The man settled back and the usher returned to his place and stood watching her out of the corners of his eyes, fascinated by her beauty.

The church was packed that night with more than two thousand people. The air was hot and foul. The old brick building, jammed in the middle of a block, faced the street with its big bare gable. The ushers were so used to people fainting that they kept water and smelling-salts handy in the anterooms. The Reverend Frank Gordon no longer paused or noticed these interruptions. He had accepted the truth that, while God builds the churches, the devil gets the job to heat, light and ventilate them.

The preacher had not noticed this excitement under the gallery, but had gone steadily on in an even monotone very unusual to his fiery temperament.

A half-dozen reporters yawned and drummed on their fingers with their pencils. The rumour of a brewing church trouble had been published, but he had not referred to it in the morning, and evidently was not going to do so to-night.

Toward the close of his sermon he recovered from the stupor with which he had been struggling and ended with something of his usual fervour.

He was a man of powerful physique, wide chest and broad shoulders, a tall athlete, six feet four, of Viking mould, hair blond and waving, steel-gray eyes, a strong aquiline nose and frank, serious face.

He had been called from a town in southern Indiana to the Pilgrim Congregational Church in New York when, on its last legs, it was about to sell out and move uptown. He had created a sensation, and in six months the building could not hold the crowds which struggled to hear him.

His voice was one of great range and its direct personal tone put him in touch with every hearer. Before they knew it his accents quivered with emotion that swept the heart. Emotional thinking was his trait. He could thrill his crowd with a sudden burst of eloquence, but he loved to use the deep vibrant subtones of his voice so charged with feeling that he melted the people into tears. His face, flashing and trembling, smiling and clouding with hidden fires of passion, held every eye riveted. His gestures were few and seemed the resistless burst of enormous reserve power - an impression made stronger by his great hairy blue-veined hands and the way he stood on his big, broad feet. He spoke in impassioned moments with the rush of lightning, and yet each word fell clean-cut and penetrating.

An idealist and dreamer, in love with life, colour, form, music and beauty, he had the dash and brilliancy, the warmth and enthusiasm of a born leader of men. The impulsive champion of the people, the friend of the weak, he had become the patriot prophet of a larger democracy.

A passion for music, and a fad for precious stones, especially pearls and opals, which he carried in his pockets and handled with the tenderness of a lover, were his hobbies. He had in a marked degree the peculiar power of attracting children and animals, and all women liked him instinctively from the first.

But to-night he was not himself. After a brief prayer at the close of the sermon he dismissed the crowd with the announcement of an after-meeting for those personally interested in religion.

As the people poured out through the open doors the unceasing roar of the great city's life swept in drowning the soft strains of the organ - the jar and whir of wheels, the wheeze of brakes, the tremor of machinery, the rumble of cab, the clatter of hoof-beat, the cry of child and hackman, the haunting murmur of millions like the moan of the sea borne on breezes winged with the odours of saloon and kitchen, stable and sewer - the crash of a storm of brute forces on the senses, tearing the nerves, crushing the spirit, bruising the soul, and strangling the memory of a sane life.

Gordon frowned and shivered as he sat waiting for the crowd to go, and a look of depression swept his face.

These after-meetings for personal appeal were a regular feature of his ministry. He held them every Sunday evening, no matter how tired he was or how hopeless the effort might seem. When the doors were closed about a hundred people had gathered in the centre of the church near the front.

He rose from his chair behind the altar-rail with an evident effort to throw off his weariness. He had laid aside his pulpit robe, a tribute to ritualism that this church had dragooned him into accepting.

"My friends," he began slowly and softly, with his hands folded behind him, "first a few words of testimony from any who can witness to the miracle of the Spirit in our daily life.

We are crushed sometimes with the brutal weight of matter, and yet over all the Spirit broods and gives light and life. Who can bear witness to this miracle?"

"I can!" cried a man, who rose trembling with deep feeling.

His high, well-moulded forehead showed the heritage of intellectual power. His eyes, soft and tender as a woman's, had in their depths the record of a great sorrow.

Taking his watch out of his pocket, he looked at it a moment, and, as the tears began to steal down his face, spoke in a tremulous voice.

"Seven years, four months, three days and six hours ago the Spirit of God came to my poor lost soul and found it in a dirty saloon on the East Side. I was dead - dead to shame, dead to honour, dead to love, dead to the memory of life. I was so low I found scant welcome in hell's own port, the saloon. They knew me and dreaded to see me. I had served time in prison, and when I drank I was an ugly customer for the bravest policeman to meet alone.

"Ragged, dirty, blear-eyed, besotted, I was seated on a whisky barrel wondering how I could beat the barkeeper out of a drink, when a sweet-faced boy came up and handed me a card of this church's services.

"I don't know how it happened, but all of a sudden it came over me - where I was, and what I was, and what I once had been - a boy with a face like that, with a Christian father and mother who loved me as their own life, and then how I had gone down, down in drink from ditch to ditch and gutter to gutter to the bottomless pit.

"I jumped down off that whisky barrel and washed my face. That night I found this church, and the Spirit of God, here in one of these after-meetings, led my soul to the foot of the cross of Jesus Christ. I looked up into His beautiful face - the fairest among ten thousand - the one altogether lovable, and I heard Him say, as to the thief of old, 'This day shalt thou be with me in Paradise.'

"From that day, hour and minute I've been a living man, a miracle of grace and love. I have not touched a drop of liquor since, and these hands, which had not earned an honest cent for years, have handled thousands of dollars of other people's money and not one penny has ever stuck to them. I am the living witness that God's spirit can raise man from the dead, and Jesus Christ keep him unto life!"

He sat down, crying.

Gordon lifted his hand and said, "Let us bow our heads a moment in silent prayer while every heart opens the door to the Spirit."

At the close of the service he passed the man who had spoken and pressed his hand.

"Ah, Edwards, old boy, you knew I needed that to-night. God bless you!"

Jerry Edwards smiled and nodded.

"A lady wishes to speak to you in the study, sir," the sexton said to him.

He looked around for his wife to tell her to wait, but she had gone.

His study opened immediately into the auditorium at the foot of the pulpit stairs. As he entered, a young woman of extra-ordinary beauty, elegantly and quietly dressed, advanced to meet him and shook his hand in a friendly, earnest way.

"Doctor, I've waited patiently to-night to see you," she said. "I've been coming to hear you for six months, and yet I have never told you how much good you have done me; and I specially wish to tell you how sorry I am that my stupid weakness to-night interrupted you. I think I came near fainting. It was so close and hot - and, pardon me if I say it - I suddenly got the insane idea that you were about to faint in the pulpit."

"Well, that is strange," interrupted Gordon, looking at her with deepening interest. "You have the gift of the sympathetic listener. I noticed no disturbance, but I did come near fainting. I have had a hard day - one of fierce nerve-strain."

She looked at him curiously.

"Then I don't feel so badly, now that I know my idea was not incipient insanity," she said, smiling. "I've quite made up my mind to send back to Kentucky for my forgotten church-letter. I've seen all fashionable society in New York can offer and I am weary of its vacuity. I've been disillusioned of a girl's silly dreams, but there are some beautiful ones in my heart I've held. I can't tell you how your church and work have thrilled and interested me. I have never heard such sermons and prayers as yours. You give to the old faiths new and beautiful meaning. Every word you have spoken has seemed to me a divine call."

"And you cannot know how cheering such a message is to me to-night," he thoughtfully replied, studying her carefully.

"I never could summon courage to come up and speak to you before, but your sermon this morning swept me off my feet. It was so simple, so heartfelt, so sincere, and yet so close in its touch of life, I felt that you had opened your very soul for me to see my own in its experiences. It will be a turning point in my life."

She spoke with a quiet seriousness, and Gordon felt that he had never seen a face of such exquisite grace.

With a promise that he would call to see her within the week, she left.

He stood for a moment gazing at her name, "Miss Kate Ransom," on the card she gave him, his mind aglow with the consciousness of her remarkable beauty, the famous Kentucky type, and yet a distinct variation.

Her figure was full and magnificent in the ripe glory of youth, a delicate face, the blonde's colour, thick, waving auburn hair that seemed brown till the light blazed through its deep red tints, violet-blue eyes, cordial and smiling, at once mysterious, magic, friendly, gravely candid. Her skin was smooth as a babe's, with the delicate creamy satin of the blonde flashing the scarlet tints of every emotion. Her lips were cherry-red, and as she listened they half parted with a lazy suggestion of tenderness and love; while the face was one of refined mentality, as unconscious as a child's of its splendid beauty.

Her gait was proud and careless, telling of perfect health and stores of untouched vital powers, a movement of the body at once strong, luxurious, insolently languid, rhythmic and full of dumb music. It was when she moved that she expressed the consciousness of power, a gleam of cruelty, a challenge that was to man an added charm.

"What a woman!" he exclaimed aloud, as he drew on his coat. "The kind of a woman who enraptures the senses, drugs the brain and conscience of the man who responds to her call - the woman about whom men have never been able to compromise, but have always killed one another!"

His wife opened the door for him in silence.

"Who was that woman, Frank?" she asked at length, her long, dark lashes blinking rapidly.

"What woman, Ruth?"

"The beauty I saw glide softly into your study."

Gordon smiled as he sank into a chair in the library.

"Miss Kate Ransom, a stranger I never met before."

"You seem a magnet for strange women, and your church their Mecca."

"Yes, and strange men. God knows New York, with its dead and deserted churches, needs such a Mecca."

"You promised to call, of course?"

"Certainly; it's my business. The Church needs every friend and every dollar to be had on Manhattan Island."

"And the distinguished young pastor of the Pilgrim Church needs the smiles of all beautiful women. His wife is a little faded with worry and care for his children, while crowds hang on his eloquence and silly women sigh into his handsome face. Ah, Frank, before we came to New York you had eyes only for me. The city, the crowd and the flattery of fools have turned your head. You are letting go of all things you once held. Now the Bible is 'literature.' You are sighing for the freedom of a 'larger life.' Where will it end? I wonder if you have weighed marriage in the balances and found it wanting?"

Gordon rose with a sigh, walked slowly to the window and looked down on the city lying below. Their little home was perched on the cliffs of Washington Heights.

The smile had died from his handsome face and his tall figure was stooped with exhaustion. He raised one hand and brushed back a stray lock from his forehead, across which a frown had slowly settled.

"By all means keep your hair adjusted," his wife continued sarcastically. "The women are all in love with that blond hair.

And it is so effective in the pulpit. If you were not six feet four it might be effeminate, but I assure you it is the secret of your strength. I trust you will be wiser than Samson."

Gordon smiled.

"You have quit the old faiths," she continued rapidly, "and gone to preaching Christian Socialism. You have driven the best members of the church away, and made the press your enemy. That mob which hails you a god will turn and curse you. You will never build your marble dream out of such stuff. Both your sermons to-day will make your trustees more hostile. There was no Bible in them - only personalities and rank Socialism. I saw that woman in front of me drinking it all in as the inspired gospel."

Gordon winced and his brow clouded.

"I gave up everything for you - home, talents, friends," she went on. "Now that I am thirty-one, it is the new face that charms."

"You did give up a very particular friend for me," Gordon remarked teasingly. "I only learned recently that you were once engaged to Mr. Morris King, your faithful attorney, and that you threw him over for an athletic parson with blond hair and a smile, yet I have never chided you about this little secret. Mr. King is still a romantic bachelor. He has not been initiated into the joys of a Sunday sermon at 10 P. M., with his wife in the pulpit. He has much to live for."

Her lips quivered and her eyes grew dim.

"Come, come, my dear; you know that I love you and that I am faithful to you. But such words and scenes as these may destroy the tenderest love at last. Words, even, are deeds."

"How philosophical! Quite like one of the epigrams of your chum, Mark Overman, of whose cruel tongue you're so fond. I wonder you don't make Mr. Overman a deacon in the new order of your church."

Gordon sank back into the chair and thoughtfully shaded his brow with his hand, his face drawn into deep lines of weariness.

When she saw the look of pain in his face her eyes softened.

"What I fear of you, Frank, is not your intention, but your performance. You mean well, but you never could resist a pretty woman."

"In a sense, no. If I could, I never would have married."

The faintest suggestion of a smile played about her eyes and then faded.

"I wonder what pretty speeches you said to the stranger to-night? You have such charming manners with a woman."

He looked at her appealingly and she stared at him without reply.

"For God's sake, Ruth, end this scene. If you only knew how tired I am to-night - tired in body, in heart and soul. I think the past week has been the most trying of my whole life. It opened with a newspaper attack on me inspired by Van Meter. You know how sensitive I am to such criticism.

"Saturday came without a moment for preparation for the great crowds I knew would be present to-day after that attack on me. Instead of work yesterday, a procession of people, hungry and suffering, were at the door from morning until night. All their burdens they poured out to me; All their wrongs and grievances against God and man became mine.

"On Saturday night the trustee meeting was held to discuss our building project. Van Meter led the opposition with skill.

When I poured out my soul's dream to them of a great temple of marble, a flaming centre of Christian Democracy instead of the old brick barn we call a church - a temple that would flash its glory from the sky above the sordid materialism that is crushing the lives and hearts of men, telling in marble song of God, of immortality, of faith and hope and love - they stared at me in contempt until I felt the blood freeze in my veins. When I drew a picture of its great auditorium thronged with thousands of eager faces, Van Meter coolly interrupted me with the remark:

"'We don't want such trash elbowing our old parishioners out of their pews. We've had too much of it already. With all your mob, the pew-rents have fallen off.'

"My first impulse was that of Christ when he took a whip in the temple. I wanted to knock him down. Instead, I rushed out of the house and left him victorious.

"I waked this morning with the burden of all this week's horror choking me, waked to the consciousness that in a few hours thousands of faces would be looking up to me with hungry souls to be fed. Well, I had nothing to give them except my own heart's blood, and so to-day I tore my heart open for them to devour it. True, I didn't preach the Bible except as its truth had passed into my own soul's experiences. When I preach such sermons I always quit with the sense of utter helplessness, exhaustion and failure. Could my bitterest enemy read my heart in that hour he would cry out for pity.

"I never so felt the crushing burden of all that crowd of people as to-day. I've heard so much of their sorrows and struggles the past week. I felt that the city was a great beast in some vast arena of time, that I was alone, naked and unarmed, on the sands, struggling with it for the life of the people, while my enemies looked on. As never before, I heard the rush of its half-crazed millions, its crash and roar, saw its fierce brutality, its lust, its cruelty, its senseless scramble for pleasure, its indifference to truth, its millions of to-day but a symbol of the millions gone before and the trampling millions to come, and I felt I was a failure. I felt that I was pitching straws against a hurricane, only to find them blown back into my face. I came down out of that pulpit with the weariness of a thousand years crushing my tired body and soul, feeling that I could never speak again, or struggle against the tide any more - that I was broken, bruised and done for all time, and I came home feeling so -"

He paused a moment and a sigh caught his voice. His wife's face had softened and a tear was quivering on her long eyelashes.

"I came home thus worn out to-night hoping for a word of cheer, yet knowing it would be days before I could recover from the sheer nerve-agony I had endured. What a reception you have given me! And for what? A beautiful woman stopped to tell me my message had not been in vain, that it had made for her a light on life's way, and that the prayers in which I had tried to realise as my own, the people's thoughts and hopes and fears had been a revelation to her, and because I smiled -"

His wife was again staring at him with the glitter of jealousy. He saw it and ceased to speak.

He suddenly sprang to his feet and walked to the door. Taking down his hat and light overcoat from the rack, he said, as though to himself:

"We will spend the night under different roofs."

As he passed toward the door there was a faint cry fiom within scarcely louder than a whisper, tense with agony and pitiful in its pleading accents;

"Frank, dear, please come back!"

But when she summoned strength to rush to the door, crying

with terror she had never known before "Frank! Frank!" he had turned the corner and disappeared.

CHAPTER II

VISIONS IN THE NIGHT

Gordon walked rapidly with the quick stride of the trained athlete. Walking was a pet exercise.

His mind was now in a whirl of fury. He had never before given away to passion in a quarrel with his wife. They had been married twelve years, and, up to the birth of their boy, four years before, had lived as happily as possible for two people of strong wills. Discord had slowly grown as his fame increased. His wife was now jealous of almost every woman who spoke to him.

They had quarreled before, but he had always kept a clear head and laughed her out of countenance. These quarrels had ended with tears and kisses and were forgotten until the next.

To-night somehow every thrust found his most sensitive spots. He wondered why? Dimly conscious of a curious interest in the woman who had spoken so sweetly to him at the close of his service, he wondered if his wife divined the fact by some subtle power their long association had developed and sharpened.

His enthusiasm for the Socialistic ideal was fast becoming an absorbing passion, and was destined to lead him into strange company.

His wife felt this, resented it, and, becoming more and more conservative, the gulf between them daily widened and deepened.

He cared nothing for her ridicule of his blond locks. He wore them half in defiance of conventionality and half in whimsical love for the picture of a beautiful mother from whom he had inherited them.

"What could have possessed her to-night?" he slowly muttered as he emerged from Central Park and swung into Fifth Avenue. "Am I really losing my grasp of truth because I am giving up traditional dogmas? Has God given to her soul the power to look inside my heart and find its secret thoughts? Why does she keep asking me if I have lost faith in marriage? Never in word or deed have I hinted at such a thing."

And yet the memory of that beautiful woman, with a voice like liquid music, friendly, soothing, reassuring, kept echoing through his soul.

As the tumult of passion died in the glow of the walk in the open air he became conscious of the life of the city again. The avenue was a blaze of light. Its miles of electric torches flashed like stars in the milky way.

He passed under dozens of awnings before palatial homes in front of which stood lines of carriages. The old Dutch and English ancestors of these people were once faithful observers of the Sabbath. Now they went to church in the mornings as a form of good society and held their receptions in the evenings. Some of them employed professional vaudeville artists to enliven their Sunday social bouts.

New York, proud imperial Queen of the Night, seemed just waking to her real life, a strange new life in human history - a life that had put darkness to flight, snuffed out the light of moon and star, laughed at sleep, twin sister of Death, and challenged the soul of man to live without one refuge of silence or shadow.

And yet the warmth and glow, the splendour and beauty of it all stirred his imagination and appealed to his love.

At length he stood before the old church that had been the arena of his struggles and triumphs for the past ten years, and was destined to be for him the scene of a drama more thrilling than any he had known or dreamed in the past.

He passed into the auditorium, ascended the pulpit, and sat down in the armchair where but a few hours before he had held the gaze of thousands. The electric lights glimmering through the windows of the gable showed the empty pews in sharp outline.

"I wonder if they know when they go they sometimes leave my soul as empty and as lonely as those vacant pews? I give, give, give forever of thought, sympathy and life and never receive, until sometimes my heart cries to a passing dog for help!

"I'd build here to God a temple whose sheer beauty and glory would stop every huckster on the street, lift his eyes to heaven and melt his soul into tears. It must - it shall come to pass!"

He sat there for nearly two hours, dreaming of his plans of uplifting the city, and through the city as a centre reaching the Nation and its millions with pen and tongue of fire. Gradually the sense of isolation from self enveloped him, and the thought of human service challenged the highest reach of his powers.

He opened the face of his watch and felt the hands, a habit he had formed of telling the time in the dark. It was one o'clock.

He thought of his wife and their quarrel. He had forgotten it in larger thoughts, and his heart suddenly went out in pity to her. He had not meant what he said. He loved her in spite of all harsh words and bitter scenes. She was the mother of his two lovely children, a girl of ten and a boy of four. The idea of a night apart from her, he, and theirs came with a painful shock. He felt his strength and was ashamed that he had left her so cruelly. He hurried to the Twenty-third Street elevated station and boarded a car for his home.

When his wife recovered from the first horror of his leaving, she was angry. With a nervous laugh she went into the nursery, kissed the sleeping chil-dren and went to bed. She tossed the first hour, thinking of the quarrel and many sharp thrusts she might have given him. Perhaps she would renew the attack when he came in and attempted to make up. The clock struck eleven and she sprang up, walked to her window and looked out.

A great new fear began to brood over her soul.

"No, no, he could not have meant it - he is not a brute!" she cried, as she began to nervously clasp her hands and turn her wedding ring over and over again on her tapering finger, until it seemed a band of fire to her fevered nerves.

As she stood by the window in her scarlet silk robe she made a sharp contrast in person to the woman whose shadow had fallen to-night across her life. She was a petite brunette of distant Spanish ancestry, a Spottswood from old Tidewater Virginia. To the tenderest motherhood she combined a passionate temper with intense jealousy. The anxious face was crowned with raven hair. Her eyes were dark and stormy, and so large that in their shining surface the shadows of the long lashes could be seen.

Her nature, for all its fiery passions, was refined, shy and tremulous. A dimple in her chin and a small sensitive mouth gave her an expression at once timid and childlike. Her footstep had feline grace, delicacy and distinction. She had a figure almost perfect, erect, lithe, with small hands and feet and tiny wrists. Her voice was a soft contralto, caress-ing and full of feeling, with a touch of the languor and delicate sensuousness of the Old South. About her personality there was a haunting charm, vivid and spiritual, the breath of a soul capable of the highest heroism if once aroused.

At twelve o'clock she relighted the gas and went downstairs to stand at the parlour window to scan more clearly every face that might pass, and - yes, she would be honest with herself now - to spring into his arms the moment he entered, smother him with kisses and beg him to forgive the bitter words she had spoken in anger.

She was sure he would come in a moment. He must have gone on one of his long walks. She could see the elevated cars on their long trestle, count the stations, and guess how many minutes it would take him to climb the hill and rush up the steps. Over and over she did this, and now it was one o'clock and he had not come.

What if he had been stricken suddenly with mortal illness! His face had looked so weary and drawn. She began to cry incoherently, and sank on her knees.

"Lord, forgive me. I am weak and selfish, and I was wicked to-night. Hear the cry of my heart. Bring him to me quickly, or I shall die!"

As the sobs choked her into silence, she sprang to her feet, both hands on her lips to keep back a scream of joy, for she had heard his footstep on the stoop.

The latch clicked, and he was in the hall.

There was a flash of red silk and two white arms were around his neck, her form convulsed with a joy she could not control or try to conceal.

He soothed her as a child, and, as he kissed her tenderly, felt her lips swollen and wet with the salt tears of hours of weeping.

"You will not remember the foolish things I said to-night, dear?" she pleaded. "There, there, I'll blot them out with kisses - one for every harsh word, and one more for love's own sake. But you must promise me, Frank, never to leave me like that again." A sob caught her voice, and her head drooped.

"You may curse me, strike me, do anything but that. Oh, the loneliness, the agony and horror of those hours when I realised you were gone in anger and might not come back to-night - dear, it was too cruel. Such wild thoughts swept my heart! You do forgive me?"

He stooped and kissed her.

"Why ask it, Ruth?"

"I know I am selfish and fretful and wilful," she said, with a sigh. "I was only a spoiled child of nineteen when you took me by storm, body and soul. You remember, on our wedding day, when I looked up into your handsome face and the sense of responsibility and joy crushed me for a moment, I cried and begged you, who were so brave and strong, to teach me if I should fail in the least thing? And you promised, dear, so sweetly and tenderly. Do you remember?"

"Yes, I remember," he slowly answered.

"And now, somehow, you seem to have drawn away from me as though the task had wearied you. Come back closer! When I am foolish you must be wise. You can make of me what you will. You know I am afraid of this Socialism. It seems to open gulfs between us. You read and read, while I can only wait and love. You cannot know the silent agony of that waiting for I know not what tragedy in our lives. Frank, teach and lead me - I will follow. I love you with a love that is deathless. If you will be a Socialist, make me one. Show me there is nothing to fear. I've thought marriage meant only self-sacrifice for one's beloved. I've tried to give my very life to you and the children. If I'm making a mistake, show me."

"I will try, Ruth."

She ran her tapering fingers through his hair, smiled and sighed.

"How beautiful you are, my dear! I know it is a sin to love any man so. One should only love God like this."

CHAPTER III

THE BANKER AND HIS FAD

When Gordon woke next morning from a fitful sleep he was stupid and blue and had a headache. His wife had not slept at all, but was cheerful, tender and solicitous.

"Ruth, I can't go down to the ministers' meeting this morning," he said wearily. "I must take a day off in the country. I'll lose both soul and body if I don't take one day's rest in seven. I didn't tell you last night that I came near fainting in the pulpit during the evening sermon."

She slipped her hand in his, looking up reproachfully at him out of her dark eyes.

"Why didn't you tell me that, Frank?"

"I thought you had enough troubles last night. I'll run out on Long Island and spend the day with Overman. You needn't frown. You are strangely mistaken in him. I know you hate his brutal frankness, and he is anything but a Christian, but we are old college chums, and he's the clearest-headed personal friend I have. I need his advice about my fight with Van Meter. Overman is a venomous critic of my Social dreams. I've often wondered at your dislike of him, when he so thoroughly echoes your feelings."

She was silent a moment, and gravely said: "Take a good day's rest, then, and come back refreshed. I'll try to like even Mr. Overman, if he will help you. I'm going to turn over a new leaf this morning."

He laughed, kissed her, and hurried to catch the train for Babylon, where Overman lived in his great country home.

Mark Overman was a bacholer of forty, noted for the fact that he had but one eye and was so homely it was a joke. His friends said he was so ugly it was fascinating, and he was constantly laughing about it himself. He was a Wall Street banker, several times a millionaire, famed for his wit, his wide reading, his brutally cynical views of society, and his ridicule of modern philanthropy and Socialistic dreams.

He was a man of average height with the heavy-set, bulldog body, face and neck, broad, powerful hands and big feet. He had an enormous nose, shaggy eyebrows and a bristling black moustache. But the one striking peculiarity about him was his missing right eye. The large heavy eyelid was drooped and closed tightly over the sightless socket, which seemed to have sunk deep into his head. This cavern on one side of his face gave to the other eye a strange power. When he looked at you, it gleamed a fierce steady blaze like the electric headlight of an engine. How he lost that eye was a secret he guarded with grim silence, and no one was ever known to ask him twice.

Though five years older, he was Gordon's classmate at Wabash College.

Overman had always scorned the suggestion of an artificial eye. He swore he would never stick a piece of glass in his head to deceive fools. He used to tell Gordon that he was the only one-eyed man in New York who had the money to buy a glass eye and didn't do it.

"I prefer life's grim little joke to stand as it is," he said, as he snapped his big jaws together and twisted the muscles of his mouth into a sneer. He had a habit, when he closed an emphatic speech, of twisting the muscles of his mouth in that way. When animated in talk, he was the incarnation of disobedience, defiance, scorn, success.

Two things he held in special pride - hatred for women and a passionate love for game-cocks. He allowed no woman on his place in any capacity, and, by the sounds day and night, he kept at least a thousand roosters. He would drop the profoundest discussion of philosophy or economics at the mention of a chicken, and with a tender smile plunge into an endless eulogy of his pets.

Gordon found him in a chicken yard fitting gaffs on two cocks.

"Caught in the act!" he cried.

"Well, who cares? They've got to fight it out. It's in 'em. They're full brothers, too. Hatched the same day. They never scrapped in their lives till yesterday, when I brought a new pullet and put her in the neighbouring yard. They both tried to make love to her through the wire fence at the same time, and they were so busy crowing and strutting and showing off to this pullet they ran into each other and began to fight. Now one must die, and I'm just fixing these little steel points on for them so the function can be performed decently. I'm a man of fine feelings."

"You're a brute when you let them kill one another with gaffs."

"Nonsense. The fighting instinct is elemental in all animal life - two-legged and four-legged. Animals fight as inevitably as they breathe. You can trace the progress of man by the evolution of his weapons - the stone, the spear, the bow and arrow, the sword, the gun."

"Well, you're not going to have the fight this morning. Put up those inventions of the devil and come into the house."

"All right. You're a parson; I'll not allow them to fight. I'll just chop the head off of one and let you eat him for dinner." Overman grinned, and pierced Gordon with his gleaming eye.

"It would be more sensible than the exhibition of brutality you were preparing."

"Not from the rooster's point of view, or mine. I love chickens. If I tried to eat one it would choke me. But I can see your mouth watering now, looking at that fat young pullet over there, dreaming of the dinner hour when you expect to smash her beautiful white breast between your cannibal jaws. Funny men, preachers!"

Gordon laughed. "After all, you may be right. Our deepest culture is about skin deep. Scratch any of us with the right tool and you'll find a savage."

They strolled into the library and sat down. It was the largest and best-furnished room in the house. Its lofty ceiling was frescoed in sectional panels by a great artist. Its walls were covered as high as the arm could reach with loaded book-shelves, and alcove doors opened every ten feet into rooms stored with special treasures of subjects on which he was interested. Masterpieces of painting hung on the walls over the cases, while luxurious chairs and lounges in heavy leather were scattered about the room among the tables, desks and filing cabinets. At one end of the room blazed an open wood fire of cord wood full four feet in length. Beside the chimney windows opened with entrancing views of the Great South Bay and the distant beaches of Fire Island. Across the huge oak mantel he had carved the sentence:

"I AM AN OLD MAN NOW; I'VE HAD LOTS OF TROUBLE, AND MOST OF IT NEVER HAPPENED."

"Frank, old boy, you look as though you had been pulled through a small-sized auger hole yesterday. How is the work going?"

"All right. But Van Meter puzzles me. I want your advice about him. You've come in contact with him in Wall Street and know him. He is the one man power in my church - the senior deacon and chairman of the Board of Trustees of the Society. In spite of all my eloquence and the crowds that throng the building, he has set the whole Board against me. He is really trying to oust me from the pastorate of the church. Shall I take the bull by the horns now and throw him and his Mammon-worshiping satellites out, or try to work such material into my future plans? Give me your advice as a cool-headed outsider."

Overman was silent a moment.

"Well, Frank, now you've put the question squarely, I'm going to be candid. I'm alarmed about you. The strain on your nerves is too great. This maggot of Socialism in your brain is the trouble. It is the mark of mental and moral breakdown, the fleeing from self-reliant individual life into the herd for help. You call it 'brotherhood,' the 'solidarity of the race.' Sentimental mush. It's a stampede back to the animal herd out of which a powerful manhood has been evolved. This idea is destroying your will, your brain, your religion, and will finally sap the moral fiber of your character. It is the greatest sentimentalist."

Gordon grunted.

"It's funny how you have the faculty of putting the opposition in terms of its last absurdity."

"Grunt if you like; I'm in dead earnest. You want to put on the brakes. You've struck the down grade. Socialism takes the temper out of the steel fiber of character. It makes a man flabby. It is the earmark of racial degeneracy. The man of letters who is poisoned by it never writes another line worth reading; the preacher who tampers with it ends a materialist or atheist; the philanthropist bitten by it, from just a plain fool, develops a madman; while the home-builder turns free-lover and rake under its teachings."

"You're a beauty to grieve over the loss to the world of home-builders!" Gordon cried, with scorn.

"Maybe my grief is a little strained - but really, Frank, I hate women, not because I don't feel the need of their love -"

He drew the muscles of his big mouth together and looked thoughtfully out of the window with his single piercing eye.

"No; for the first time on that point I'll make an honest, clean confession to you. I hate women because I'm afraid of them. I have a face that can stop an eight-day clock if I look at it hard enough; and yet beneath this hideous mask there's a poor coward's soul that worships beauty and hungers for love! I don't allow women in this house because I can't stand the rustle of their drapery. I don't want one of them to get her claws into me. They can see through me in a minute. Women have an X-ray in their eyes. They can look through a brick wall, without going to see what's on the other side. A man learns a thing is true by a painful process of reasoning. A woman knows a thing is so - because! She knows it thoroughly, too, from top to bottom. Whenever a woman looks at me I can feel her taking an X-ray photograph of the marrow of my bones."

He wheeled suddenly and fixed his eye on Gordon.

"I'll bet you had another quarrel with your wife last night?"

"How do you know?"

"Tell by your hangdog look. You look like an old Shanghai rooster that a little game-cock has knocked down and trampled on for half an hour before letting him up."

"We did have some words."

Thomas Dixon

"Exactly; and I can tell you what about. Your wife is growing more nervous over the tendency of your religion and your thinking. You can't fool her about it. She knows you are drifting where she can never follow. She knows instinctively that Socialism is the return to the animal herd and that the family will be trampled to death beneath its hoofs."

"Come, Mark, you're crazy. The Brotherhood of Man and the Solidarity of the Race can have such meaning only to a lunatic."

"Don't you know that the triumph of Socialism will destroy the monogamic family?" Overman asked sharply.

"Rubbish."

"Strange, how you sentimentalists slop over things. You have allowed second-hand Socialistic catch words to change your methods of work and thought and revolutionize your character, and yet you have never seriously tried to go to the bottom of it. Come into this room a minute."

They went into an alcove room.

"Here I have more than a thousand volumes of Socialistic literature. I've read it all with more or less thoroughness. When I look at the titles of these books I feel as though I've eaten tons of sawdust. You are preaching this stuff as the gospel, and yet you don't know what your masters are really trying to do."

"I know that there can be no true home life until the shadow of want has been lifted," said the preacher emphatically. "The aim of Socialism is to bring to pass this dream of heaven on earth."

"Just so. But you've never defined what the dream will be like when it comes. Your masters have. Let me read some choice bits to you from these big-brained, clear-eyed men who created your movement. I like these men because they scorn humbug.

Defiance, disobedience, contempt for thing that is, consumes them."

He drew from the shelves a lot of books, threw them on a table, and took up a volume.

"This from Fourier: 'Monogamy and private property are the main characteristics of Civilisation. They are the breastworks behind which the army of the rich crouch and from which they sally to rob the poor. The individual family is the unit of all faulty societies divided by opposing interests.'

"And this choice bit from William Morris: 'Marriage under existing conditions is absurd. The family, about which so much twaddle is talked, is hateful. A new development of the family will take place, as the basis not of a predetermined lifelong business arrangement to be formally held to irrespective of conditions, but on mutual inclination and affection, an association terminable at the will of either party.'"

Overman fixed his eye on Gordon for a moment, laid his hand on his arm and asked:

"Now, honestly, Frank, confess to me you never read one of those sentences in your life?"

"No, I never did."

"I was sure of it. Listen again; this from Robert Owen: 'In the new Moral World the irrational names of husband, wife, parent and child will be heard no more. Children will undoubtedly be the property of the whole community.'

"But perhaps the idea has been best expressed by Mr. Grant Allen. Hear his clean-cut statement: 'No man, indeed, is truly civilised till he can say in all sincerity to every woman of all the women he loves, to every woman of all the women who love him: "Give me what you can of your love and yourself; but never strive for my sake to deny any love, to strangle any impulse that pants for breath within you. Give me what you can, while you can, without grudging, but the moment you feel you love me no more, don't do injustice to your own prospective children by giving them a father whom you no longer respect, or admire, or yearn for." When men and women can both alike say this, the world will be civilised. Until they can say it truly, the world will be as now, a jarring battle-field of monopolist instincts.'

"Then this gem from another of the frousy-headed - Karl Pearson: 'In a Socialist form of government the sex relation would vary according to the feelings and wants of individuals.'

"Observe in all these long-haired philosophers how closely the idea of private property is linked with the family. That is why the moment you attack private property in your pulpit your wife knows instinctively that you are attacking the basis of her life and home. Private property had its origin in the family. The family is the source of all monopolistic instincts, and your reign of moonshine brotherhood can never be brought to pass until you destroy monogamic marriage."

"But my dream is of an ideal marriage and home life," cried the preacher.

"Yes, and that is why you make me furious. You don't know the origin or meaning of this Socialistic dream and yet you are preaching it every Sunday, inflaming the minds of that crowd. I don't blame your wife. She sees in her soul the rock on which you must wreck your ship sooner or later. The herd and the mating pair cannot co-exist as dominant forces. This is why Socialism never converts a woman except through some - individual man. Woman's maternal instinct created monogamic marriage. The only women who become Socialists directly are the sexless, the defectives and the oversexed, who can always be depended on to make the herd a lively place for its fighting male members. What have you to say to this?"

Overman turned his head sideways and pierced Gordon again

with his single eye.

"Well, I confess you've given me something to think about, and I'm going to the bottom of the subject. You've opened vistas of great ideas. It's the question of the century, the thought that is sweeping life before it. While I've been listening to you, more and more I've seen the need of consecration to the leading and teaching of the people who are being swept by millions into this movement. But you haven't told me what to do with Van Meter."

"Yes, I have, The trouble, I tell you, is with you, not Van Meter. He's a little man, but he's just the size of a deacon in a modern church in New York. Win him over and work with him. He's your only hope. Van Meter knows his business as a deacon and trustee. You are off the track."

"But how can I ever reconcile Van Meter's commercialism with any living religion?"

Overman frowned and shrugged his shoulders.

"Religion? Man, you haven't religion! Religion is the worship of a Superior Being, fear of His power, submission to His commands, inability to discuss theoretically the formulas of faith, the desire to spread the faith, and the habit of considering as enemies all who do not accept it. You can't pass examination on any of these points. Your idea of God is the First Cause. You do not really worship or fear anything. You submit blindly to nothing. You have written an interrogation point before every dogma. You have ceased to be missionary and become humanitarian. As a priest you're a joke. Van Meter is a better deacon than you are a priest. I don't blame him. He must put you out, or be put out of business sooner or later. Your passion for reforming the world, your 'enthusiasm for humanity,' are things apart from worship and absolutely antagonistic to it."

"But not antagonistic to the mission of Christ."

"Granted. But the Christianity of Christ is one thing and modern Christianity another thing. The ancient Church, you must remember, absorbed Paganism. Van Meter's religion is, I grant you, a pretty stiff mixture of Paganism and Christianity, but historically he is in line with the Church and you are out of line with it. I'd do one of two things - use Van Meter for all he is worth, or get out of his church and let him alone. It's his. He and his kind built it. You are an interloper."

"Perhaps so," Gordon mused.

"You know my opinion of your dream of social salvation. I say let the fit survive and the weak go to the wall. If you could save all the floating trash that so moves your pity, you would only lower the standard of humanity. Hell is the furnace made to consume such worthless rubbish. You are even apologising for hell because you can't stand the odour of burning flesh. I like the old God of Israel better than the ghost you moderns have set up. Honestly, Frank, you have never treated Van Meter decently. He's a small man, but he is in dead earnest, and he is historically a Christian. I don't know what the devil you are, and I don't believe you know yourself. Go to Van Meter, have a plain business talk with him, and see if you can't come to an understanding."

"That's the only sensible thing you've said to me."

"And the only immoral thing; for if you and Van Meter ever agree you will both do some tall lying."

"I think I'll take your advice and see him, anyhow."

CHAPTER IV

THE SHORTHORN DEACON

Gordon and Overman came into town on the four o'clock express. They sat down in opposite seats near the centre of the car.

Neither of them noticed Van Meter, who also lived at Babylon in the summer, board the train as it pulled out of the station. He was a pompous little man, short and red-faced, with gray side whiskers and bald head. His eyes were sharp and beady and shined like shoe-buttons. Piety and thrift were written all over him. As a deacon he passed the bread and wine at the Lord's Table on Sunday, with his black eyes half closed, dreaming of cornering the bread market of the world on Monday. For him New York was the centre of the universe, and the Stock Exchange was the centre of New York. The rest of this earth was provincial, tributary soil. He had gone abroad, but rarely ventured beyond Philadelphia or Coney Island on this side. He was the presiding officer of the Stock Exchange and the President of the Metropolitan Bible and Tract Society. He took himself very seriously.

As they got out of the car at Long Island City, Gordon said to him:

"Deacon, I wish to have a talk with you tomorrow. Shall I call at your home or office?"

"Come down to the office at two o'clock; I'll be out at night," Van Meter answered briskly.

The next day Gordon walked from the church down Fourth Avenue to Union Square and down Broadway to the Battery. It was a glorious day in early spring. The air had in it yet the cool breath of winter, but the electric thrill of coming life was in the soft breezes that came from the South, where flowers were already blooming and birds singing. The hucksters were selling sweet violets and the cry of the strawberry man echoed along the side streets.

Fourth Avenue was piled with builders' material. The old brick homes were crumbling and steel-ribbed monsters climbing into the sky from their sites.

"Progress everywhere but in the churches," muttered Gordon. "The Church alone seems dead in New York."

Broadway was one vast river of humanity. As far as the eye could reach the throng engulfed the pavements and overflowed into the streets between the curbs, mingling with the mass of cars, cabs, trucks and wagons. On either side towered the interminable miles of business houses whose nerves and arteries reach to the limits of the known world, savage and civilised. Behind those fronts sat the engineers of industry with their hands on the throttles of the world's machinery, their keen eyes and ears alert to every sound of danger in the ceaseless roar around them.

Shadowy and far away seemed the Spirit world from those hurrying, rushing, cursing, struggling men. And yet the earth was quivering beneath them with the shock of spiritual forces. The age of miracles was only dawning.

He felt like climbing to the tower of one of those great temples of trade and shouting to the throng to lift up their heads from the stones below and beyond the line of towering steel and granite see the Glory of God. And as he thought how little that crowd would heed it if he did, he felt himself in the grip of Titanic forces of Nature sweeping through time and eternity, and that he was but an atom tossed by their fury.

As he passed the City Hall his eye rested on the towering castles of the metropolitan newspapers. He could feel in the air the throb of their presses, the whir of their wheels within wheels telling the story of a day's life, wet with tears of hope and love, or poisoned with slander and falsehood, their minarets and domes the flaming signs in the sky of a new power in history, a menace to the life of the ancient Church and its priesthood. Was this power a threat to human liberty, or the highest expression of its hope? Only the future would reveal. What silent forces crouched behind those towers with their throbbing cylinders the world could only guess as yet.

He walked past old Castle Garden where so many weary feet have landed and found hope.

His heart filled with patriotic pride. Far out in the harbour stood Liberty Enlightening the World, lifting her torch among the stars, her face calm and majestic, gazing serenely out to sea.

"Land of faith and hope - my country!" he exclaimed. "Here the commonest man has risen from the dust and proved himself a king. Home of the broken-hearted, the tyrant-cursed, the bruised, the oppressed, within thy magic gates the miracle of life has been renewed!"

He looked out on the great emerald harbour gleaming in the sunlight, its sky-line white with clouds and penciled with the pennant-tipped masts of a thousand ships flying the flags of every nation of the earth. His soul was flooded again with the sense of the city's imperial splendour, stretching out her hand to grasp the financial scepter of the world, already the second city of the earth, a kingdom mightier than Caesar ruled and richer than Croesus dreamed.

He came back to Wall Street, and, as he turned into the

narrow lane, felt its power shadow his imagination.

"After all," he muttered, "Van Meter is not far wrong in his idea of the omnipotence of this street."

The Deacon's office was plainly furnished. He was seated at an old-fashioned mahogany desk, evidently a relic of his Knickerbocker past. Born in New York sixty years before, he was popularly reckoned a multimillionaire, though his wealth was overestimated. Compared to the big-brained, eagle-eyed men who had come from the West and mastered Wall Street, Van Meter was really a pygmy.

He greeted Gordon politely.

"Delighted to welcome you, Doctor, to my office. This is the first call you have ever honoured me with downtown."

"I've been to your home often, Deacon."

"But somehow you've always been shy of Wall Street," said Van Meter, expansively. "I suppose you look on us down here somewhat as the old-time preacher regarded the saloon-keeper. You should know us better. This alley is the jugular vein of the nation, and the Stock Exchange its heart. We have a President and Congress at Washington, and some very handsome buildings there. It is supposed to be the capital of the republic. A political myth! Here is the capital. The money centre is the seat of government. The Southern Confederacy failed, not for lack of soldiers or generals of military genius, but because it had no money."

Van Meter's stature grew taller and his eyes larger as Gordon felt the truth of his words.

"Well, Deacon, I wish to know you better. I'm afraid I've not always been fair to you as the senior officer of the church and one of its oldest members."

"I haven't worried over it," he replied quickly.

"I know you in your home life," Gordon continued. "You are a faithful and tender husband and father. If you were to die tomorrow, your servants would stand sobbing at the doorway when I entered. You are one of the kindest men in your individual life."

"Thanks. I hardly thought you would say so much."

"Then you have misjudged me. The only criticism I've ever made of you has been as a part of our social and economic order. This is a question, it seems to me, we might differ about and still be friends. Now, I wish you to tell me honestly, face to face, why you object to me as the pastor of your church?"

"You wish me to be perfectly frank?" he asked, with his black eyes twinkling.

"Perfectly so. You couldn't say anything that would anger me. I am too much in earnest."

"Well, to begin with, you don't preach the simple gospel."

"No; but I do preach the gospel of Christ."

"Your reference to the strike amongst the women shirt-makers in New York drove one of the richest men out of our church."

"Yes; I saw him jump up and go out during the service. The women were making shirts for his house at thirty-five cents a dozen, finding their own thread and using their own machines. I said if I found one of those shirts in my house I'd put it in the fire with a pair of tongs, and I would. I'd be afraid to touch a seam lest I felt the throb of a woman's bruised fingers in it."

The Deacon softly stroked his whiskers.

"It was an unfortunate remark. He contributed $500 a year to the church. He has gone where the simple gospel of Christ is preached."

"Yes, so simple that he can sleep through it and know that it will never touch his life," Gordon said with a sneer. "What's the use to talk about mustard plaster? I say apply it to the place that hurts."

"You preach Evolution. I don't like the idea that man is descended from a monkey."

"The weight of scholarship sustains the theory."

"Well, my idea is, if it's true, the less said about it the better. And then you lack dignity out of the pulpit."

"Even so, Deacon, the most dignified man I ever saw was a dead man - a dead New Yorker. What we need in the church is life."

"But you have departed from the faith of our fathers."

"Perhaps," Gordon said, with a twinkle in his eye, "if you mean our famous fathers who 'landed first on their knees and then on the aborigines.'"

Van Meter ignored the remark.

"You said one day that in America we had but two classes, the masses and the asses. That sentence cost the church a thousand dollars in pew-rents. I think such assertions blasphemous."

"Well, it's true."

"I don't think so; and if it were, it don't pay to say such things."

"Am I only to preach the truths that pay?"

"We hired you to preach the simple gospel of Christ."

"Pardon me, Deacon; I am not your hired man. I chose this church as the instrument through which I could best give my message to the world. I answer to God, not to you. The salary you pay me is not the wage of a hireling. My support comes from the free offerings laid on God's altar."

"We call them pew-rents. You are trying to abolish this system, as old as our life, and allow a mob of strangers to push and crowd our old members out of their pews."

"I believe the system of renting pews un-Christian and immoral-a mark of social caste."

"And that's why I think you're a little crazy. Even your best friends say you're daft on some things."

"So did Christ's."

The Deacon's face clouded and his black eyes flashed.

"From denouncing private pews you have begun to denounce private property. Our church is becoming a Socialist rendezvous and you a firebrand." "Deacon, you have allowed your commercial habits to master your thinking, your religion and your character. In your home, you are a good man. In Wall Street," he smiled, "pardon me, you are a highwayman, and you carry the ideals and methods of the Street into your duties as a churchman."

"Pretty far apart for a pastor and deacon, then, don't you think?"

"You ran the preacher away who preceded me, too," mused Gordon.

The Deacon's eyes danced at this acknowledgment of his power.

"He was a little slow for New York. You are rather swift."

Gordon rose and looked down good-naturedly on the shining bald head as he took his leave.

"I suppose we will have to fight it out?"

"It looks that way. My kindest regards to Mrs. Gordon."

CHAPTER V

THE CRY OF THE CITY

Kate Ransom entered the church with enthusiasm. Even Van Meter, learning that she lived on Gramercy Park and was a woman of wealth, congratulated Gordon on the event.

She organized a working-girls' club and became its presiding genius. Her beauty and genial ways won every girl with whom she came in contact. Her club became at once a force in Gordon's work, absolutely loyal to his slightest wish. She formed a corps of visitors and asked to be allowed to help in his pastoral work.

"Before we begin," she said, "let me be your assistant for a day. I wish to see the city as you see it, that I can direct my girls with intelligence."

On the day fixed, she acted as usher for his callers at the church.

The President of his boys' club was admitted first to tell him a saloon had been opened next door to their building in spite of their protest to the Board of Excise.

Gordon frowned.

"It's no use to waste breath on the Board. They know that saloon is within the forbidden number of feet from our church. But as the Governor of New York has recently said, 'Give me the vote of the saloons; I don't mind the churches,' go down to this lawyer and tell him to insist on an indictment of Crook, the Chairman of the Board, for the violation of his oath of office."

"It's no use, sir," said Anderson, his assistant. "I've been to see him. He tells me there were three indictments for penitentiary offenses pending against Crook when the Mayor promoted him to be Chairman of the Board. Three courts have pronounced him guilty, but the new Legislature is going to pass an ex-post facto law to relieve him of his term in prison."

"Then try him with one more indictment and include the whole Board of Excise this time. We will let them know we are alive."

Kate ushered in a slatternly little woman, dirty, ugly, cross-eyed and her face red from weeping. "Please, Doctor, come quick. They've got Dan. They knocked him in the head, dragged him down the stairs and flung him in the wagon. He's in jail, and they say they'll have him in Sing Sing in a week. He ain't done a thing. You're the only friend we've got in the world."

"On what charge did they arrest him, Mrs. Hogan?"

"Just a lot o' policemen charged on him with billies!"

"But why did they do it?"

"It's the policeman on the beat who's got a grudge agin him. He swore he'd land him in Sing Sing. And if you can't stop him, he'll do it."

Gordon wrote a note to a lawyer and handed it to her.

"Go to this lawyer and tell him to take the case."

"Dan's a friend of mine," he explained to Kate. "I've taken him out of the hospital three times from delirium tremens, and found work for him a dozen times. But he can't hold his job. Everything seems against him.

"'It's me face, Doctor,' he tells me in despair. 'When they see me they won't stand me. Me wife's cross-eyed, or she'd 'a' never married me. I was tin years prowlin' up an' down the earth seekin' a woman. But I couldn't catch one. She'd 'a' got away from me if she could 'a' seed straight.'"

Kate laughed and ushered in a young woman with blond hair and an ill-fitting dress. She walked as in a dream, and there was a strange look in her eye.

"I hope you are feeling better to-day, Miss Alice."

She made no reply, but seated herself wearily, while Gordon drew a cheque for fifty dollars and handed it to her. She placed it mechanically in her purse.

"I hope you are making progress in your art now that you have a comfortable studio," he said kindly.

"I want to see him," she replied in a low voice.

"But I can't give you his address, When he came to me, conscience stricken, and told me that you were wandering about the streets of New York ill and half starved, and placed this fund at my disposal, he stipulated that he would pay it only so long as you let him alone. You promised me last month to stop writing letters to the general post-office."

"I can't help it. I love him. I don't want this money; I want him."

"But you know he is married."

"He said he'd get a divorce. I love him. I'll be his servant, his dog - if he will only see me and speak to me. Tell me where to find him. I believe all men are friends to one another."

Kate, waiting behind the curtain which cut off Gordon's desk, could hear distinctly.

When the young woman emerged she led her into the adjoining room, and there was the sound of a kiss at the door as she left.

An aged father and mother came, dressed in their best clothes, and very timid.

"We have a great sorrow, Doctor," the father began tremulously. "We are strangers in New York. We hate to trouble you. But we heard you preach, and you seemed to get so close to our hearts we felt we had known you all our lives."

He paused and the mother began to brush the tears from her eyes.

"Our boy is a medical student here. We were proud of him - all we had dreamed and never seen, all we had hoped to be and never been in life, we expected to see in him. We skimped and saved and gave him an education. Sometimes we didn't have much to eat at home, but we didn't care. Did we, Ma?"

The mother shook her head.

"Then we mortgaged the farm and sent him here to study three years and be a great doctor."

He paused, bent low and covered his face with his hands.

"And now, sir, he's taken to drink, and they tell us at the college he won't get his diploma! And we thought, after we heard you, maybe you could see him, get hold of him, and help us save him. He's all we've got. The rest are dead."

Gordon looked away and his lips quivered.

"You'll help us, Doctor?"

"I'll do the best I can for you, my friends. It's such a sad old story in this town that one gets hardened to it till we see it in some fresh revelation of anguish like yours."

He took the name and address and the old man and woman went out, softly crying.

A widow came to tell him of an assault on her twelve-year-old daughter.

"And because the brute is a rich man on an avenue," she sobbed, "they've turned him loose with a fine. I'm poor and ignorant, and I'm not a member of your church, but all the people are talking about you in our neighbourhood, and told me you were a friend of the weak, and I'm here."

He called his assistant in.

"Anderson, do you know anything of this case? How could such a thing be?"

"I've looked into it. It's just as she tells you. The man was arraigned before a police magistrate, who had no power to try such a case. He was allowed to plead under an assumed name-John Stevens, of Newark, New Jersey, fined and discharged. I informed the city editor of the Herald of the case; he detailed a reporter, who wrote it up. He left out the man's real name. Nothing has come of it. Our courts have become so debased, God only knows what they will do next. We have a police judge now who is the owner of five disreputable dives, which he runs every day and Sunday. He sits down on the bench on Monday and discharges the cases against his saloons. We've another, who was drunk in the gutter, with two warrants out for his arrest, when the Boss made him a judge. What can we expect from such courts?"

He sent her away with the premise to consult the best legal talent.

A little frousle-headed woman, carrying a bag full of documents, then explained to him that she was the inventor of a process for preserving dead bodies, meats and eggs by treating them with the purifying ozone of the air, and wished him to organise a company, make her president, and act as her secretary.

"It's the greatest invention ever conceived by the human mind," she explained, as she spread out scores of letters and testimonials from men who had tested it, and many who had signed anything to get rid of her.

"Madam, if your process can only be applied to the city government of New York you will deserve a monument higher than the Statue of Liberty. But I'm afraid there's not enough ozone in the atmosphere."

He had to call help to get her out, and then she only went after she got the loan of five dollars to tide her over the week.

A theological student with an open hatchet face, from the western plains, on his way to Moody's school at Northfield, asked for money to get there.

"I had a-plenty," he explained, "but I met a man who asked me to change a bill for him. He got the change, but I'm looking for him to get the bill. I don't know, to save my life, how he got away. I still have his umbrella that he asked me to hold."

Gordon smiled and loaned him the money.

"I don't ask you for any references. You are the real thing, my boy."

A woman in mourning, whom he recognised immediately

from her published pictures, asked him to champion the cause of her son, who was under sentence of death.

Gordon readily recalled the case as a famous one. He had followed it with some care and was sure from the evidence that the young man was guilty.

For a half hour she poured out her mother's soul to him in piteous accents.

"My dear madam," he said at last, "I cannot possibly undertake such work."

"Then who will save him? I've tramped the streets of New York for six months and appealed to every man of power. Your voice raised in protest against this shameful and unjust death will turn the tide of public opinion and save him. You can't refuse me!"

"I must refuse," he answered firmly.

She turned pale, and her mouth twitched nervously. He looked into her white face with a great pity and a feeling of horror swept his heart. The pathos and the agony of the tragedy filled him with strange foreboding. In his imagination he could hear the click of handcuffs on his own wrists and feel the steel of prison bars on his own hands as he peered through the grating toward the gate of Death.

But he was firm in his refusal, and she left with words of bitterness and reproach.

After a long procession of people, sick, and most of them out of work, he was surprised to see one of his own deacons approach with a look of dejection.

"Why, Ludlow, what ails you?"

"Sorry to trouble you, Pastor, but I've lost my place. You see,

I'm more than fifty years old, and though I've worked for my firm twenty years, they laid me off for a younger man. I'm ruined unless I can get work. I've four people dependent on me. I've come to ask you to see the Manager of the new department store and get me a place. I've been there three times, but I can't get to the Manager."

"I'll do it to-day, Deacon. Let me know when you need anything."

After two hours of this work, he left, with Kate Ransom, for his round of visits.

She looked at him as he started smilingly from the church.

"And you have gone through with this every day for ten years?"

"Of course."

"While I have been around the corner laughing and dancing with a lot of idiots. And you seem as cheerful as though you had been listening to ravishing music!"

"Yes, I must be cheerful."

"How do you endure it? Yet it fascinates me, this life - in touch with drama more thrilling than poets dream. It seems to me I'm just beginning to live. I am very grateful to you."

He looked into her face, smiling.

"The gratitude is on my side. You are going to be more popular than the pastor."

"I'm sure you will not be jealous."

"Hardly, as long as I hear the extravagant things you are telling your girls about loyalty to the leader."

She blushed and turned her violet eyes frankly on him.

"I believe in loyalty."

He answered with a look of gratitude.

"We must go first to that store for Ludlow. He's the best deacon in the church, a staunch friend, a loyal, tireless worker."

Gordon waited patiently at the store a half hour and succeeded in reaching the Manager. As they left, he said to Kate:

"Did you see that crowd of two hundred men waiting at his door?"

"Yes; what were they doing there?"

"Waiting their turn to see the Manager. They will come back to-morrow, and next day and next day, just like that. I felt mean to sneak in ahead of them by a private door because my card could open it. The Manager gave me a note to the head of the department Ludlow wishes to enter and asked him to suspend the rule against men fifty years of age and give my man a trial. In return for this favour he coolly asked me to deliver a lecture before his employees that will cost me a week's work. I had to do it. The head of the department who read the note told me to send Ludlow to see him, but he scowled at me as though he would like to tear my eyes out. He will put him on and discharge him in a month for some frivolous offense."

They boarded a Broadway car and got off at City Hall Park.

"Where are you going down here?" she asked.

"To a building that collapsed yesterday and killed thirty working people. That house was condemned fifteen years ago by the Inspector. But its owner was a friend of the Boss, and it stood till it fell and killed those people."

The street was blocked by the fire department playing their streams on the smouldering ruins, while gangs of men worked cleaning away the rubbish and searching for dead bodies.

A crowd of relatives and friends were pressing close to the ropes. Many of them had stood there all night, crazed with grief, wringing their hands, hoping and praying they might find some token of love left of those dear to them, and yet hoping against hope that they might find nothing and that their beloved would appear, saved by some miracle.

Gordon had promised a mother whose daughter was missing to help her in the search. She did not know where her own child worked. She only knew it was downtown near the City Hall. A building had fallen in, and she had not come home.

Just as they approached the ruins a body was found and brought to the enclosure for identification. The mother recognized her daughter by an earring. She flung herself across the black-charred trunk with a shriek that rang clear and soul-piercing above the roar and thunder of the city's life at high tide. Above the rumble of car, the rattle of wagon, the jar of machinery, the tramp and murmur of millions the awful cry pierced the sky.

Kate put her hand on Gordon's arm and pressed her red lips together, shivering. "O dear! O dear! what a cry! I can't go any closer. I'll wait for you out at the edge of the crowd."

He pushed into the throng, lifted the woman, spoke a few words of tenderness to her, and told her he would call at her home later.

As he was about to leave, a tall, delicate man working among the ruins reeled and sank in a faint. When he revived, he quit his job and went home without a word.

"What was the matter with that man?" Gordon asked the foreman of the wrecking company.

"Starved, to tell you the truth. He came here yesterday and begged for a job. He looked so pale and sick I couldn't refuse him. He fainted the first hour and went home. He came back this morning and begged me to try him again. I did, but you see he is too weak. He told me his family was starving."

He joined Kate and they crossed the City Hall Square and walked down Centre Street to the Tombs prison.

She was pale and quiet, glancing at him now and then.

"I've an engagement at the Tombs," he told her, "with a lady to whom I used to make innocent love in our youth in a college town. I got a note from her yesterday, written in the clear, beautiful hand I recognised from the memory of little perfumed things she used to send me. You don't know what a queer sick feeling came over me when I recognised from the street number that she was in prison. I haven't seen her in fifteen years. She was the village belle and made what was supposed to be a brilliant marriage."

They entered the grim old prison, that looked like an Egyptian temple, with its huge slanting walls of granite squatting low on Centre Street like a big pot-bellied spider, watching with one eye the brilliant insects of wealth on Broadway and with the other the gray vermin swarming under the Bridge and along the river.

Kate put her hand on Gordon's arm and drew closer as they passed down its gloomy corridor to the warden's office.

She tried to smile, but by the twitching at the corners of her full lips he could see she was nearer to crying. Again, as her body touched his, he felt the warmth and glow of her beauty, her blue eyes, cordial and grave, her waving auburn hair with its glowing fires, her step luxurious and rhythmic, and. now as her hand trembled, instead of the gleam of cruelty and conscious power, the timid appeal to the strength of the man.

She looked at him and lowered her eyes, and then flashed them up straight into his face with a smile.

"I'm not afraid!" she said impulsively.

"Of course not."

His steel-gray eyes looked into hers, and they both laughed.

Gordon asked the warden's permission to see the woman whose letter had brought him and also the young man who had returned from Sing Sing for a new trial.

"What is the charge against the woman?" he asked.

"Shoplifting, sir. She's been here before and begged off. But they are going to send her up this time. I'll allow her to see you in the reception room."

She came in, with a poor attempt at dignity, and then collapsed into whining but hopeful lying. She was dressed in an old sunburnt frock. Her hair was tousled, her shoes untied, and a corset-string was hanging outside her skirt. Her front teeth were out, and the red blotches on her face told the story of drink and drugs.

"Doctor, it's all a mistake. I swear to you I am innocent. You don't know how it humiliates me for you to see me like this - you, who knew me in the old days at home, when I was rich and petted and loved. And now I haven't a friend in the world. My husband left me. If you will tell them to let me off, they will do it for your sake. I swear to you I will leave New York, go back to my old home and try to begin life over again." She buried her face in her hands.

"What shall I do?" he whispered to Kate. "She is lying. She will never leave New York."

"Promise her - promise her; I'll try to do something for her."

They passed inside, along Murderers' Row, and stopped before the cell in which stood the man waiting his new trial. He poured out his story again, and as Gordon looked sadly through the bars at his face the certainty of his guilt gave the lie to every fair word.

As his glib tongue rattled on, Gordon's mind was farther and farther away. He was thinking of that grim sentence from the old Bible, "Sin when it is full grown bringeth forth death." And again this problem of sin, the wilful and persistent violation of known law, threw its shadow for a moment over his dream of social brotherhood. The voice of the man angered him. He frowned, bade him good-by and left.

And as he passed out, he felt, in spite of the charm of Kate's companionship, the shadow of that veiled mother by his side, and heard the bitter cries of her broken heart, until the sin and shame of the man seemed his own. The pity and pathos of it all haunted and filled him with vague forebodings. - "Now for something more cheerful," he said, as they passed out of the Tombs and boarded an uptown car.

"A derrick at work in that wreck yesterday fell on a working-man. He has a wife and four children. We must see how he is getting on."

They got off on the Bowery, turned down a cross street toward the East River, threading their way through the masses of people jamming the sidewalks, and dodging missiles from dirty children screaming and romping at play.

"Mercy!" exclaimed Kate, "I thought Broadway and Fifth Avenue and the shopping districts crowded - but this is beyond belief! I didn't know there were so many people in the world."

"And what you see, just a drop in the ocean of humanity. There are miles and miles of these tenements in New York - square mile after square mile, packed from cellar to attic. We have a million and a half crowded behind these grim walls on this island alone."

"Surely not all so ugly and wretched as these?"

"Many worse. But don't let the outside deceive you. Back of these nightmares of scorched mud, festooned with shabby clothes, are thousands of brave loving men and women, living their lives cheerfully, not asking us for pity. Even in this squalor grow beautiful, innocent girls like flowers in a muckheap. When I see these children growing up thus into fair men and women with such sur-roundings, I know that every babe is born a child of God, not of the devil."

They climbed a dark stairway and knocked at the back door of a double-decker tenement.

A stout woman opened it, and they entered the tiny kitchen, so small that the table had to be pushed against the wall to pass it and the family of six could not all eat at one time because the table could not be pulled out into the room.

"How is John this afternoon, Mrs. McDonald?"

"We don't know, sir. The doctor's in there now. If he dies, God knows what we will do; and if he lives, a cripple, it'll be worse."

The doctor called them into the front room and whispered to Gordon:

"He's got to die, and I'm going to tell him. I'm glad you are here."

He took the man by the hand.

"Well, John, I'm sorry to say so to you, but you must know it. You can't live beyond the day."

The man drew himself upon his elbow, looked at the doctor in a dazed sort of way and then at his wife holding his crying baby in her arms, the other little ones clinging to her dress, and gasped:

"Did you say die? Here - now - to-day - die? And if I do, I leave my helpless ones to starve."

He paused, fingering the covering nervously, shut his jaws firmly and looked at the doctor.

"Almighty God! I can't die!" he growled through his teeth. "I will not die!"

"No, no, you sha'n't die, John. We'll help you to live!" his wife cried.

"Very well; if you keep on feeling that way you may live," said the doctor cheerfully. "We will hope for the best."

Kate's eyelids drooped as she stood watching this scene as in a dream. She took the woman by the hand as she left:

"I do hope he will live for your sake. I believe he will."

When they reached the street, the doctor said to her:

"Glad to welcome you, Miss Ransom, from the little world into the great one."

"Thank you. I begin to feel I have not been in the world at all before. Will he live, do you think?"

"If he holds that iron will with the grip he has on it now he'll pull through - and be a hopeless invalid for life. He will join the great army of industrial cripples - a havoc that makes war seem harmless. The wrecking corporation have already sent their lawyer and settled his case for eighty-five dollars cash: not enough to bury him. He thought it better than nothing."

The doctor hurried on to another patient.

It had grown quite dark. Gordon took Kate by the arm after the modern fashion, and they threaded their way through the crowds made denser by the return of the working people. She had removed her right glove in the house and did not replace it immediately. His big hand clasped her rounded, beautiful arm, and a thrill of emotion swept him at the consciousness of her nearness, her sympathy, her open admiration and sweet companionship in his work.

Again, as she walked with the quick, sinuous and graceful swing of her body, he was impressed with her perfect health and vital power. She had recovered her balance now, and when she spoke it was with contagious enthusiasm.

"I can never thank you enough for opening the door of a real world to me, Doctor," she declared, looking up at him soberly.

"And you have no idea what inspiration you have given the church - just at a time I need it, too," he answered warmly.

"I've been wondering what I did here for nine years, unconscious of this wonderful drama of love and shame, joy and sorrow about me. But what did he mean by an army of cripples greater than the havoc of war?"

"Victims of machinery. It's incredible to those who do not come in contact with it. The railroads alone kill and wound thirty-five thousand working-men every year: this is a small percentage of the grand total. More men are killed and wounded by machinery in America than were killed and wounded any year in the great Civil War, the bloodiest and most fatal struggle in history. We pay billions in pensions to our soldiers, but nothing is done about this. The social order that permits such atrocity must go down before the rising consciousness of human brotherhood. The employers ask, 'Am I my brother's keeper?' and forget that they are echoing the shriek of the first murderer over his victim's body."

"And I never thought of it before. How strange that so many people are in the world and never a part of it."

"You can begin to see the outlines of the problems before us. It will be years before you can realise the height and depth of need that calls here to-day for deeds more heroic than knights of old ever dreamed."

Again she looked at him with frank admiration.

"But the most wonderful thing I have seen to-day has been a man," she boldly said. "Your faith, your optimism, your dreams in the face of the awful facts of life, and with it a tenderness of sympathy I never thought in you, have been a revelation to me. I feel more and more ashamed of the years I have wasted."

She said this very tenderly, while Gordon unconsciously tightened the grip of his big hand on her arm, and then went on as though she had not spoken.

"What a call to an earnest life! New York City furnishes two-thirds of the convicts of the state. We have one murder and ten suicides every week. More than eighty thousand men and women are arrested here every year. Fifty thousand pass through that basilisk's den we saw to-day. We have a hundred thousand child workers out of whose tender flesh we are coining gold. Three hundred thousand of our women are hewers of wood and drawers of water, robbed of their divine right of love and motherhood. There are twenty thousand children and fifty thousand men and women homeless in our streets. I have seen more than five hundred of them fighting for the chance of sleeping on the bare planks of a dirty police lodging-house."

He felt her nerves quiver with sympathy and surprise.

"I never dreamed such things took place in New York."

"Yes, and those homeless children are the saddest tragedy. We haven't orphanages for them. When a house burns down that has a coal shute or an opening in it where a child can crawl, the firemen thrust their hooks in and pull out a bundle of charred rags and flesh - one of these homeless waifs. No father or mother that ever bent over a cradle, looked into a baby's face and felt its warm breath can realise that horror and not go mad. We don't realise it. We ignore it. We have four hundred churches. We open them a few hours every week. We have nine thousand saloons opened all day, most of the night, and Sunday too. We haven't orphanages, but we have these nine thousand factories where orphans are made. When our country friends come to see us we take them to see the saloons! Our shame is our glory. You have to-day seen some of the fruits."

"And yet you have faith?"

"Yes; I have eyes that see the invisible. In all this crash of brute forces I see beauty in ugliness, innocence in filth. Here one is put to the test. Here the great powers of Nature have gathered for their last assault and have challenged man's soul to answer for its life. Dark spiritual forces shriek their battle-cries over the din of matter. The swiftness of progress, crushing and enriching, the mad greed for gold, the worship of success - a success that sneers at duty, honour, love and patriotism - the filth and frivolity of our upper strata, the growth of hate and envy below, the restlessness of the masses, the waning of faith, the growth of despair, the triumph of brute force, the reign of the liar and huckster - all these are more real and threatening here, as beasts and reptiles increase in size as we near the tropics. We are nearing the tropics of civilisation. We must not forget that the flowers will be richer, wilder, more beautiful, and life capable of higher things."

They had reached her door, and he released her arm, soft, round and warm, with a sense of loss and regret.

"Yet with all its shadows and sorrows," he cried with enthusiasm, "I love this imperial city. It is the centre of our national life - its very beating heart. If we can make it clean, its bright blood will go back to the farthest village and country seat with life. I shall live to see its black tenements swept away, and homes for the people, clean, white and beautiful, rise in their places. I have a vision of its streets swept and garnished, of green parks full of happy children, of working-men coming to their homes with songs at night as men once sang because their work was glad. I haven't much to depend on just now in the church. But God lives. I have a growing group of loyal young dreamers, and you have come as an omen of greater things."

She smiled.

"I'll do my best not to disappoint you."

He shook hands with her, declining to go in, and, as she sprang swiftly and gracefully up the steps, his eyes lingered a moment on the rhythm of her movement and the glory of her splendid figure in sheer rapture for its perfect beauty.

As he turned homeward, he thrust his hand, yet warm with the touch of her bare arm, into his pocket, drew out two pearls, looked tenderly at them and felt their smooth, rounded forms. A longing for such companionship in work with his wife swept his soul.

CHAPTER VI

THE PUDDLE AND THE TADPOLE

When Gordon started home from his round of visits with Kate the wind had hauled to the north and it began to spit drops of snow. The cars were still crowded, the aisles full and the platforms jammed, though it was seven o'clock. He buttoned his coat about his neck and paced the station, waiting for a train in which he could find a seat.

"Bad omen for my trustee meeting to-night," he muttered. "This air feels like Van Meter's breath."

He allowed four trains to pass, and at last boarded one worse crowded than the first. With a sigh for the end of chivalry, he pushed his way through the dense mass packed at the doors, wedging his big form roughly among the women, to the centre of the car, and mechanically seized a strap. He was so used to this leather-strap habit that he held on with one hand and, while reading, unfolded and folded his paper with the other.

He climbed the hill to his home in the face of a howling snow-storm.

Ruth looked at him intently.

"I am sorry I couldn't get home earlier," he said, "I've had a hard day."

"But such pleasant help that you didn't mind it, I'm sure. I heard Miss Ransom was assisting you. I went to the church and found you had gone out with her. I hear she is becoming indispensable in your work."

"Come, Ruth, let's not have another silly quarrel."

"No; it's a waste of breath," she replied bitterly.

He slipped quietly out of the house after supper and hurried back to his study to collect his thoughts for the battle he knew he must wage with Van Meter. This one man had ruled the church with his rod of gold for twenty years. He had established a mission station on the East Side and gathered into it the undesirable people. He was the watchdog of the Prudential Committee guarding the door to membership.

This trustee meeting had for him a double interest. A panic in Wall Street had all but ruined Van Meter. He had attempted to corner the bread market. The wheat crop had been ruined by a hard winter, and the little black eyes, watching, believed the coup could be made.

The attempt was in concerted action through his associate houses in Chicago and St. Louis, and he had plunged as never before. The corner had failed. It was reported that he had made an assignment. This had proved a mistake. His long-established credit and his high personal standing in Wall Street had rallied money to his support and he had pulled out with the loss of three-fourths of his fortune.

Gordon wondered what the effect of this blow would be on his character and attitude toward the church's work. He was specially anxious to know the effect of the reverse on the imagination of the other members of the Board, who merely revolved in worshipful admiration around his millions.

He asked Van Meter to come to his study for a personal interview before the meeting. The Deacon was cool and polite, and his little eyes were shining with a distant luster.

"I was sorry, Deacon, to learn of your personal misfortunes."

Van Meter wet his dry lips with his tongue, looked Gordon squarely in the face and snapped:

"Were you the clergyman who made the statement concerning that corner reported yesterday in an evening paper?"

Gordon flushed, turned uneasily in his chair, and boldly replied:

"Yes, I was, and I repeat it to you. On every such attempt to coin money out of hunger and despair, I pray God's everlasting curse to fall. I am glad your corner failed. The world is larger than New York, and New York is larger than the Stock Exchange. Am I clear?"

"Quite so. With your permission I will return to the trustee meeting."

"Very well. I wish to make a statement to the Board when you are ready."

Gordon frowned, sat down and made some notes of the points he wished to urge.

He had often wondered at the impotence of the average preacher in New York. But as he felt the forces of materialism closing about him, and their steel grip on his heart, he began to know why New York is the preacher's graveyard. He had won his great audience. His voice had not been drowned in the roar of the breakers of this ocean of flesh, but he had met bitter disillusioning. As he looked into the faces of his Board of Trustees, dominated by that little bald-headed man, he felt the cruel force of Overman's sneer at the modern church as the home of the mean and the crippled and the sick. The appeal to the ideal seemed to stick in his throat.

He had thrilled at the struggle with the big city's rushing millions. Their stupendous indifference dared him to conquer or die, and he had conquered. He had seen these indifferent millions swallow cabinets, presidents, princes and kings, and rush on their way without a thought whether they lived or died. He had made himselfheard. But this power that worshiped a dollar and called it God, that controlled the finances of the church and sought to control its pastor and strangle his soul - this was the force slowly choking him to death unless he could conquer it.

The average preacher, when he landed in New York and faced the roar of its advancing ocean of materialism, fluttered hopelessly about for a year or two like a frightened sand-fiddler in the edge of the surf of a cyclone, was engulfed, and disappeared.

To conquer this sea and lift his voice in power above its thunder, and then be strangled in a little yellow puddle full of tadpoles, was more than his soul could endure.

"I'll not submit to it," he growled, with clenched fist.

When he entered the meeting, the dozen men were hanging on Van Meter's lips as on the inspired word of Moses.

"I was just telling the Board," he suavely explained, "that Mr. Wellford, on whom we must depend for such a building enterprise involving millions, has declared his hostility to the scheme. He is out of sympathy with the sensational methods of the Pilgrim Church."

"I'll inform the Board," said Gordon, as he advanced toward Van Meter and thrust his hands in his pockets, "that it's not true. I have seen Mr. Wellford, by his invitation, this week at his home. I laid our great plan before him. I found him a big man, a man who thinks big thoughts, and does big things. He told me frankly he was heartily in favour of it and would do his part the moment we were ready and other men of wealth would join in the movement. He simply declares that we must act first."

Van Meter pursed his lips and tried to lift his nose into a sneer.

"May I ask, Doctor, if it is your intention to demand a vote to-night on this building scheme?"

"It is."

"Then I suggest that we vote first and hear your speech afterward. Some of us may wish to go before you're done."

Gordon turned red with rage and started to sit down, but, wheeling, he again faced the chairman and glared at him.

"Pardon my business methods, Doctor," he went on, "but your visions are rather tiresome. We are old New Yorkers. We know what you are going to tell us of the dark problem of the city's corruption, the poverty of the poor, and so on. Every now and then we see such sacred fires burning in the heart of a country parson called to town. Yet, in spite of the splendour of these little fizzling pinwheels that light the cruelty and darkness of metropolitan life for a moment, New York has managed somehow to jog along."

Gordon's anger melted into a laugh as he watched the Deacon's face grow purple with fury as he fairly hissed the last sentence of his speech. He was not an impressive man in an attempted flight of eloquence, and the preacher's laughter quite unhorsed him.

"Gentlemen," Gordon said with quiet dignity, "I came here to-night to make an appeal. But, I'm no longer in the mood. I see in your faces the folly of it. I make an announcement to you. The Temple will be built, with or without you. I prefer your cooperation. I can do it with your united opposition. God lives, and the age of miracles is not passed."

"In behalf of the Board, I accept your challenge and await the miracle," retorted Van Meter. "You can pray till you're blue in the face and you will never get money enough to buy a lot on Fifth Avenue big enough to bury yourself, to say nothing of rearing a Solomon's Temple on it."

"We shall see," the young giant replied.

"This Board is tired of the circus business," Van Meter went on angrily. "You have transformed the church already into a menagerie. We don't want any more of your Soup-House Sarahs, Hallelujah Johns nor decorative bums testifying here to the power of miracles, while we wonder whether our overcoats will be on the rack when we recover from the spell of their eloquence. It's a big world, there's room for us all, but there's not room for any more new wrinkles in this church."

"Yes, it is a big world, Deacon, but there are some small potatoes in it. There's hope for a fool, he may be turned from his folly, but God Almighty can't put a gallon into a pint cup."

"We'll see who the small potato is before the day is done," Van Meter snorted.

Gordon continued, meditatively, without noticing the interruption:

"Of all the little things on this earth a little New Yorker is the smallest. I've met ignorance in the South, sullen pigheadedness in New England; I've measured the boundless cheek of the est, my native heath; but for self-satisfied stupidity, for littleness in the world of morals, I have seen nothing on earth, or under it, quite so small as a well-to-do New Yorker. He has little brains, or culture, and only the rudiments of common sense, but, being from New York, he assumes everything. Of God's big world, outside Wall Street, Broadway, Fifth Avenue, Central Park and Coney Island, he knows nothing; for he neither reads nor travels; and yet pronounces instant judgment on world movements of human thought and society."

And deliberately he put on his hat and left the room.

The net result of the meeting was a vote to reduce the pastor's salary a thousand dollars and add it to the music fund; and Van Meter hired two detectives to watch the minister.

CHAPTER VII

A STOLEN KISS

For several weeks after Gordon flung down the gauntlet to his Board of Trustees and began his battle for supremacy, his wife maintained a strange attitude of silence and reserve.

She had hired a nurse and resumed her study of music. Her contralto voice, one of great depth and sweetness, he had admired extravagantly in the days of their courtship, but she had ceased to sing of late years. He always listened to her lullaby to the children with fascination. The soft round notes from her delicate throat seemed full of magic and held him in a spell.

Before he left for his study one morning, she looked up into his face with yearning in her dark eyes.

"Come into the parlour, Frank; I will sing for you."

She took her seat at the piano, and her white tapering fingers ran lightly over the keys with deft, sure touch.

"What would you like to hear?" she asked timidly, from beneath her long lashes, with the old haunting charm in her manner.

"Tennyson's 'Break, break, break, on thy cold gray stones, O Sea!' No poet ever dreamed that song as you have sung

Thomas Dixon

it, Ruth."

Never did he hear her sing with such feeling. Her Voice, low, soft and caressing with the languid sensuousness of the South, quivered with tenderness, and then rose with the storm and broke in round, deep peals of passion until he could hear the roar of the surf and feel its white spray in his face. Her erect lithe figure, with the small white hands and wrists flashing over the keys, the petite anxious face with stormy eyes and raven hair, seemed the incarnate soul of the storm.

"Glorious, Ruth!" he cried, with boylike wonder.

And then she bent over the piano and burst into tears.

"Why, what ails you, my dear?"

"Oh, Frank, I'm selfish to leave the children to a nurse and study music."

"Nonsense. Self-sacrifice is rational only as it is the highest form of self-development. It is your duty to develop yourself. Self is the source of all knowledge and strength; books are its record; the world exists only through its eyes."

"I'm afraid of it. I wish to give all to you and the children, not to myself. I want you all to myself, and you are growing away from me. I know it, and it is breaking my heart."

He laughed at her fears, kissed her and went to his study.

Since his break with his Board, he had grown daily in power - power in himself and over his people. Conflict was always to him the trumpet call to heroic deeds. The knowledge that Van Meter was now his open enemy and that he was attempting to build a hostile faction within the church roused his soul to its depths. Thrown back thus upon himself and his appeal to the greater tribunal of the people, he preached as never before in his life. His sermons had the vigour and prophetic fire of the crusader. His crowds increased until it was necessary to ask for police aid to control the exits and entrances to the building. Long before the hour of service, a dense mass of men and women were packed against the doors.

Van Meter watched this growth of influence with wonder and disgust. He determined to leave no stone unturned that might put a stumbling-block in his way. His detectives had failed as yet to find any clue that might compromise him. Once they rushed to his office with the information that they had tracked him to a questionable house. The Deacon called up his son-in-law and asked excitedly for a reporter to write a thrilling piece of news. The reporter found that Gordon had called at the house, but in answer to a summons to see a dying girl.

Van Meter insisted upon the item being printed, but the young city editor scowled and threw it in the waste basket.

The Deacon at length discovered Ruth's jealousy and located the woman who was its object. A costly bouquet of flowers was placed on Gordon's desk in the study every morning, and an enormous one blossomed every Sunday morning and evening on the little table beside his chair in the pulpit. The sexton could not tell who paid the bills. A florist sent them.

The Deacon had been bitterly chagrined at the outcome of his movement in reducing the salary. At first the people heard it with amazement, and then, when Gordon informed a reporter of the fight in progress and it was published, they laughed, and a cheque was sent him for two thousand dollars to make good the deficit and add one thousand more.

The day after this advent he had a hard day's work. A procession of people drained him of every cent of money he could spare and every ounce of sympathy and shred of nerve force in his body.

He had tried the year before to establish a free employment bureau to relieve him of this strain. But the bureau added to his work. He had to close it. It had required the employment of five assistants, and even these could make little impression on the list of applicants who crowded the rooms and blocked the pavements from morning until night.

When the sick and hungry and out-of-works had been disposed of after a fashion, the miscellaneous crowd filed in.

An old college mate came in shivering in a dirty suit. He fumbled at his hat nervously until he caught Gordon's eye and saw him smile.

"Well, by the great hornspoon, Ned, you look like you've fallen into a well!"

"Worse'n that, Frank; I slipped clean into hell. I got with some fellows, went on a drunk, stayed a month and lost my place. I want you to loan me money to get to Baltimore, buy a decent suit of clothes, and I'll get another position. Yes, and I'll lift my head up and be a man."

Gordon sent out to the bank and got the money for him.

Another seedy one softly explained to him that he was a fellow countryman from Indiana. Gordon gave him a quarter.

A sobbing woman closely veiled he recognised as a bride he had married in the church after prayer meeting two weeks before.

"Doctor," she said in a whisper, "I've called to beg you please not to allow any one to know of my marriage. My husband turned out to be a burglar. He stole ten thousand dollars from an old lady who is one of our boarders, and skipped. He married me to get the run of the house. He tried to marry her first, though she was seventy-five years old, got in her room last night, stole the money, and now he's gone. I'm heart-broken!"

"What! because he's gone?"

"No; because I was a fool. I know he has a dozen wives. He was so handsome."

"Madam, I'm not very sorry for you. I tried to prevent you marrying him that night. I begged you to go back to Jersey City to your own church."

"You will keep it secret, Doctor?" she begged.

"I'll not publish it. But the certificate is on file in the Hall of Records. Any one can see it who wishes. It is beyond my control."

An old woman with bedraggled skirt, reddened eyes and a fat, motherly face timidly approached. She had been overlooked.

"Doctor, you're my last chance. I come up to New York to see my son-in-law, as grand a rascal as ever lived. He owes me a thousand dollars and won't pay it. We lost our crop down in Old Virginia. So I scraped up the money and got here to squeeze what he owed out of that rascal. Now he's turned me out into the street and moved where I can't find him. I'm starvin' to death. I ain't got a cent to go home; an' what's worse'n all, I got a letter this mornin' tellin' me my idiot boy's down sick an' cryin' for me. I'm the only one can do anything for him. He can't understand nobody else."

Her voice broke and she bit her lips to keep back the tears.

"I've begged all day. Everybody laughs at me. I heard you preach one Sunday. I knowed you wouldn't laugh at me. I want you to loan me twenty dollars to get home quick. I'll start the minute I can get to the train, an' I'll pay you back if I have to sell my feather beds. Now, will you do it?"

"Well, a more improbable story was never told a New Yorker, but something whispers to me you're telling the truth."

"You'll do it?"

"Yes."

She drew a deep breath, and cried with streaming eyes:

"Oh, Lord, have mercy on my poor soul, that I doubted You, and thought You had forsaken me!"

Gordon handed her the cheque.

"I'm going to kiss you!" she fairly screamed.

Before he could lift his hand or protest, she threw her arms around his neck and kissed him.

As he took her hands down from his shoulders and drew his face away from the mouldy-smelling old shawl, he looked toward the door, and Ruth stood in the entrance. Her eyes blazed with wrath, but as she saw the faded and bedraggled dress and moth-eaten shawl and looked into the tear-stained motherly old face she burst into hysterical laughter.

Gordon rose and escorted the woman to the door with courtesy.

"You will find the bank at the corner of Sixth Avenue and Twenty-third Street - the Garfield National. Write me how your son is when you reach home, and send me the money when you are able."

"I will. God bless you, sir," she answered with fervour.

When he returned to his study, Ruth was still hysterical, and he sat down without a word and began to write.

"Frank, I'm sorry to have been so rude," she said at length.

"Is that all?"

"No; I'm sorry I humiliated myself by spying on you."

She sat twisting her handkerchief, glancing at him timidly.

"And you can't understand how deeply you have wounded me by such an act, Ruth. I hope you have heard all that passed here this morning."

"It's strange how I always seem to be in the wrong. Frank, I am very sorry. You must forgive me. And I have another confession. I've been receiving anonymous letters about you for the past three weeks. I was too weak and cowardly to show them to you. It was one of these letters which caused me to come here this morning. And now I've wounded you, and alienated your heart from me more than ever. I feel I shall die."

She began to sob.

"Come, Ruth, you must conquer this insanity. Naturally you are bright, witty, cheerful and altogether charming. Jealousy reduces you to a lump of stupidity."

"You do forgive me?"

"Yes; and don't, for heaven's sake, do such a thing again. Ask me what you wish to know. I am not a liar; I will tell you the truth."

"But I don't want to hear it if it's cruel," she protested.

"The truth is best, gentle or cruel."

She kissed him impulsively and left.

He sat for an hour, tired, sore and brooding over this scene with his wife. He caught the perfume of the flowers on his desk, and in the tints of the roses saw the warm blushes of the woman who had sent them. Her voice was friendly and caressing and her speech, words of sweetest flattery - flattery

Thomas Dixon

that cleared the stupor from his brain and gave life and new faith in himself and his work; flattery that had in it a mysterious personal flavour that piqued his curiosity and fed his vanity. How clearly he recalled her - the superb figure, with rounded bust and arms full and magnificent, in the ripe glory of youth, her waving auburn hair so thick and long it could envelop half her body. Often he had watched the light blaze through its red tints while he talked to her of his dreams, her lips half parted with lazy tenderness and ready with gentle words. He recalled the rhythmic music of her walk, strong and insolent in its luxury of health. And he was grateful for the cheer she had brought into his life.

CHAPTER VIII

SWEET DANGER

Kate Ransom had attempted no close analysis of her absorbing interest in Gordon's work. The change in her life from weariness to thrilling interest had been its own justification. Wealth had robbed her of the mystery and charm of accident. The future was fixed; there could be no unknown. The men she had met in society were mere fops, or expert butlers who wrote books on etiquette. Life was a problem for them of what the tailors could do.

She had been isolated from humanity. Now she felt the red blood tingling to her finger tips. Her days were full of sweet surprises or sudden revelations of drama and tragedy, and her woman's soul responded with eager interest.

She had never loved. Such a woman could not love a tailor's dummy. Her nature was warm, rich and passionate, and she was consumed with longing for the moment of bliss when her whole being would so burn with sacrificial fire for her beloved that she could walk with him naked in winter snows, unconscious of cold.

Dress, the great mania of the empty minded, she had outgrown. She knew instinctively the colour and the style most becoming to her beauty, and she used these with the ease and assurance of an expert. She was proud of her beautiful face and figure and held them as divine gifts, the surest tokens of the fulfilment of her desires.

Her heart, rich in the ripened treasures of unspent mother-hood, brooded in tenderness over her new work - the tortures of half-starved mothers, their doomed babes, their idle fathers, and the misery of the poor and the fallen. This yearning to help she knew to be the cry within her own soul for peace. How to express this fullness of life Gordon was teaching her. Slowly and unconsciously she was clothing this powerful, athletic man with every attribute of her ideal. His steel-gray eyes seemed to pierce her very soul and say, "I understand you; come with me." His eloquence and emotional thinking were more and more to her the voice of a prophet seer. His face, that flashed and trembled, smiled and clouded with fires of smouldering passion, held her as in a spell. She knew this power was slowly tightening about her heart, yet she rejoiced in its very pain. When she greeted him, and he unconsciously held her soft hand in his big blue-veined grasp, a sense of restful joy came she knew not whence nor why.

Her enthusiasm in his work, her faith and cheering flattery were drawing him with resistless magnetism.

As the summer advanced the heat became so terrific and the suffering in the city so great that Gordon determined to stay at his post and take his vacation in the fall. Mrs. Ransom fussed and fumed over Kate's determination to stay, but there was no help for it.

July broke the record of forty years for heat. Scores were prostrated daily and dead horses blocked traffic at almost every hour. A drought threatened the water-supply, and night brought no relief to the millions who sweltered in the tenements.

The babies began to die by thousands - more than two thousand a week on Manhattan. Island alone. The city's wagons raked the little black coffins up and dumped them into the Potters' Field, one on top of the other, like so many dead flies. Down every tenement-walled street the white ribbons fluttered their tragic story from cellar to attic. At night tired mothers walked the pavements, hot and radiating heat, till the sun rose again, carrying their sick babies, or crowded the housetops, fanning them as they lay on their pallets, pale and still, fighting with Death the grim, silent battle.

Kate Ransom finally gave her entire time to these children. She fitted up a hotel in the mountains of Pennsylvania and kept it full. She chartered a steamer and took a thousand of them for a day up the Hudson as an experiment, and asked Gordon to go with them. They would have music, and a dinner spread under the trees of the park which stretched back from the water's edge into the towering hills.

He met them at the ferry slip from which the steamer sailed. Kate was already there, and the throng filled every inch of the floor space. She was moving about among them, while they gazed at her in admiration no words in their vocabulary could express. Her face was flushed with excitement, and her violet eyes, wide open, were sparkling with pleasure.

The man's eyes lingered on the scene, feeling that, for all her magnificently human body, no angel ever made a fairer vision.

He was struck with the silence of these children. As he looked closer it was only too plain they were not children. They were only little wizen-faced men and women, who had never learned to laugh or smile or play; little pinched faces with weak eyes that had never seen God's green fields; little dirty ears that had been bruised with a thousand beastly noises, but had never heard the murmur of beautiful waters in the depths of a forest. His heart went out to them in a great yearning pity as he recalled his own enchanted childhood.

His voice was soft with tears as he greeted Kate.

"A more pathetic sight than this crowd of silent children old earth never saw. But the shining figure in the centre lights the shadows with a touch of divine beauty."

"It does break one's heart to see such children, doesn't it?" she answered, looking at them tenderly and ignoring his pointed tribute to her beauty.

"Are we all ready?" Gordon cried.

"If you are. Is Mrs. Gordon not coming?"

"No; I couldn't persuade her. She took our chicks to the seashore."

As the boat moved swiftly up the great river in the fresh morning air and the breeze blowing down its channel strengthened, they sat together on the after deck and watched the dead souls of the little ones stir with life under the kiss of the wind and the caress of the music.

In the park they spread out in the whispering stillness of the woods. Nature breathed the sweet breath of her life into their hearts again and they began to twist their queer little faces and try to laugh. They called to one another and listened with mute wonder at the echo among the rock-ribbed hills. Gordon watched curiously in their faces the flash of the inherited memory of forest habits, choked and stunted and dormant in all city folks, and yet alive as long as the human heart beats. Within two hours they had grown noisy with play after a timid, clumsy fashion.

"Give them a week and they would learn to laugh!" Kate exclaimed.

But the man was now more interested in watching the woman than the children, as he saw her satin skin flush with pleasure and the creamy lace on her full bosom rise and fall.

They sat down on a rock beside a brook.

"What an inspiration to see this old yet ever new miracle of regeneration unfold under the magic touch of a woman's hand!"

"You mean a man's hand," she replied. "This would never have interested me except that you led me to see it."

"Then we've helped one another. I'm beginning to feel you are indispensable. I wonder if you, too, will leave us after awhile as so many pass on."

"No; this has become my very life," she soberly answered, looking down at the ground and then into his face with frank, open-eyed pleasure.

He was silent for several minutes and then softly laughed.

"What is it?" she cried.

"You could never guess."

She lifted her superb arms, showing bare to the elbow, and felt of the mass of auburn hair. "That load of red hay about to fall?"

"Don't be sacrilegious. No."

"Harness broken anywhere?" She felt of her belt, and ran her hands down the lines of her beautiful figure, eyeing him laughingly.

"I'll tell you," he said, sinking his voice to its lowest note of expressive feeling, while a whimsical smile played round the corners of his eyes. "Sitting here in the woods by your side on this glorious summer day, your eyes looked so blue in the creamy satin of your face, I suddenly thought I smelled the violets with which God mixed their colours."

"You think of such silly things," she said with mock severity.

"There's nothing silly about it. Beauty is an attribute of the divine. I worship it for its own sweet sake wherever I find it, in pearl or opal, dewdrop or flower, the stars, or a woman's face or form or eyes."

She lowered her head.

"Do you know the old legend of the opal?" he asked.

He took some stones from his pocket and held in the light an opal of rare luster.

"Isn't it beautiful?" she cried.

"And its story is as beautiful as its face. Listen: A sunbeam lingered under a leaf in the forest at sunset, loath to leave so fair a spot, until the moon suddenly rose. Enraptured with the shimmering beauty of a moonbeam, he stood entranced and trembling and could not go. In ecstasy they met, embraced and kissed. The sun sank and left him in her arms. The opal is the child of their love. In its fair face is forever mingled the silver of the rising moon and the golden glory of the sunset."

"I believe you made that up," she laughed.

"I wish I were poet enough."

"I had no idea you dreamed of such romantic nonsense."

"Yes, I dream many things. I had a funny dream about you the other night."

"Tell me what it was," she begged.

"I dare not."

"I thought you would dare anything."

"No; you see, dreams are such intimate, unconventional

mysteries. Dreams have no regard for law or custom The soul and the body seem equally free and without sin or shame. I have a curious feeling of awe about sleep and dreams. It's the surest evidence I have of immortality and the reality of a spiritual life. It is to me the prophecy of the ideal world, too, in which we will dare to live some day what we really are, without pretence or hypocrisy - live that deep secret inner life we try sometimes to hide from the eye of God."

"And you will not even give me a hint of this dream?"

"No. It was very foolish, but very charming and beautiful. It was in part a picture from that dream which made me laugh awhile ago about your eyes."

"I think it mean in you to tell me that much and no more."

"I would tell you if I dared. I may dare some day."

She was afraid to ask him after that, and yet something within cried for joy.

They rose, gathered the children for dinner, ands after three hours in the woods, returned to the city as the twilight softly fell over its ragged steel and granite sky-line.

"You must take tea with us to-night," she said, as they stepped from the boat.

His wife would not return for supper and he consented.

It was not the first time he had spent an hour at the table of the Ransom household. Mrs. Ransom deemed herself honoured by his visits, and his chats with the invalid father about books were bright spots in his life.

Kate had sent the stringed band from the boat to the house and stationed them in the conservatory opening into the dining-room. The tender strains of the music, the splash of a fountain mingled with the songs of birds in their cages, the gleam of silver and diamond flash of cut glass, gave Gordon's senses a soothing contrast to the wild beauty of the woods. His nature responded to art and luxury as quickly as to the sensuous voice of Nature in the glory of her summer's splendour.

There was something in this glittering beauty, cold and cruel, that appealed to him. He always felt at home in such surroundings. Beneath his idealism and love of humanity there was still hidden somewhere the nerve of an Epicurean.

When Kate appeared, dressed for tea, simply but richly, with her splendid neck and shoulders bare and little ringlets of hair curling about her face as though scorched by the warmth of the red blood below, he felt the picture complete.

She chatted with him before entering the dining-room.

Her manner was always flattering and frankly gracious, but to-night there was an added note of warmth and familiar comradeship. Never had he seen her so charming and so resistless. Always intensely conscious of her sex, she seemed to have the power to-night of communicating to the man before her that consciousness so intimately, so directly and yet so delicately that he was led captive.

With scarcely a spoken word their relationship leaped the space of years. The quiver of her eyelid, the dilation of a nostril, little inarticulate exclamations, the turn of her head, the rising and falling of her bosom, the flash of her violet eyes, the subtle perfume of her hair or the graceful movement of her magnificent form spoke the language of life deep and rhythmic which no words have ever expressed.

He went home, on fire with the dream of an ideal life and work with such a woman of supreme beauty.

CHAPTER IX

THE SPIDER

The passing of a year added immensely to the fame of the pastor of the Pilgrim Church. His sermons now reached twenty millions of people through the daily press every Monday morning. It had become necessary to issue tickets of admission to the members and admit them by a small door that was cut beside the large ones.

Van Meter had ceased to be of sufficient importance for serious notice. The growth of Gordon's influence within the year had been so rapid, he found he had set out to fight a flea with artillery.

The old man felt his eclipse with bitterness. He had quit talking much, but writhed in silent fury at the sight of this tall athlete with his conquering gray eyes and smooth, serious face. Yet he was a regular attendant. The preacher's eloquence, the vibrant tones of his voice, full of passion, or trembling with prophetic zeal, and the whole drama of a living militant church with this daring revolutionist at its head, risen from the grave of the old, fascinated him in spite of his hatred.

In the local development of the church Kate Ransom had become, next to the pastor, the most important factor. She had shown strong administrative talent, had organized kindergartens, night-schools for teaching domestic science to girls, established a reading-room, and opened a coffee house on the corner near the church, fitting it up with the magnificence of a saloon, with free lunch counter, music and singing. It was crowded with working-men and women every night.

Her work had brought her in daily contact with Gordon, and their comradeship had become so constant and so sweet that neither of them dared face the problem of its meaning.

To the woman the man had become little less than her God. Their daily life, its hopes, its poetry, its dreams of social and civic salvation, were enough in themselves: she did not analyse or question.

For the man, this fair woman, beautiful in face and form beyond the flight of his fancy, and loyal in the worship of his strength, as the soul of the strong man ever desires of his ideal woman, she had become a daily inspiration. And yet he had not acknowledged this even in a whisper of his soul.

In the meanwhile, his wife's interest in music had ceased, and she was rarely seen at the church on Sundays or at its weekday functions. She had withdrawn from its life and had settled into a state of somber resentment.

She would frequently sit through a meal eating little, speaking in monosyllables, her black eyes staring, wide open, and yet seeing nothing, looking past the things that bound her, back into the sunlit years of girlhood, or forward into the future whose shadow's chill she felt already on her soul. Often he found her at night seated by the window in the dark alone, looking down on the city below.

She had ceased to ask him of his work or plans and he no longer troubled her with their discussion. Their lives were separated by an ever-widening gulf.

Stimulated by a sermon he had preached in August of the previous summer, when the death-rate was at its highest, a wave of reform had swept over New York. In his sermon he had arraigned the city government in terms so trenchant and terrible the people had rallied as to a trumpet call to battle.

A resistless movement for the overthrow of a corrupt administration took the city by storm. Day and night with voice and pen, with all the fire and passion of his magnetic personality, he had led these assaults.

Complete success crowned the movement. The reform Mayor was elected by a large majority.

Ten months had passed and the net results were discouraging. Police scandals ran riot as of yore; gambling, drinking and the social evil flourished as before; and the press, that had valiantly and almost unanimously championed Reform, now exhausted upon it the vocabulary of abuse.

Gordon was disgusted and sickened and felt that one of his fairest dreams had been shattered forever.

The reaction from this reform programme had thrown him more than ever back upon his ideas of a Socialistic revolution which should destroy Commercialism itself, and he had become its enthusiastic champion.

Kate Ransom had followed his change of views with keenest sympathy. She had read every book after him and had responded to his every mood.

"No; we're on the wrong tack, with our half-way measures and our fitful charities," he said to her.

"We must go deeper. We must make the Fatherhood of God and the Brotherhood of Man our daily life, not merely a poetic theory.

"We have hundreds of beautiful-souled men and women giving their lives in sacrifice for the city's poor and fallen. They seem to make little impression on its ocean of misery. We are bailing out the sea with teaspoons."

"I feel you are right, as you always are," she responded, unconscious of the contradiction.

"The Brotherhood of Man and the Solidarity of the Race we must make vital realities. Greed, commercialism, competition and the monopolistic instincts are the cause of all this crime and misery and confusion. Love, not force, must rule the world."

"And you are the prophet to lead humanity into this Kingdom of Love," she said, her eyes enfolding him with their soft blue light.

"I fear I'm too great a coward for such a task. The man who does it must break with the past, become accursed for the truth's sake, defy social law and convention, breast the storm of the world's hate, die despised, and wait for a nobler generation to place his name on the roll of the world's heroes."

"It is your work," she cried with elation.

"It's a lonely way for the soul to travel."

"You will have one loyal follower the blackest hour of the darkest night that comes."

A curious smile played around her full lips, and he looked away, afraid to say anything.

"Yes, I know that," he softly answered. "And I'm more afraid for that very reason."

"I'm not afraid." Her voice rang clear and thrilling.

"I wonder if you know the meaning of such words; or if you are thinking of one thing and I of another?" he slowly asked.

"I dare to think many things I've never dared to say," she replied.

"A break must come sooner or later," he went on. "No man of my temperament and brain can live under the conditions here, feel the grip of this cruelty on the throat of humanity, read and think, and endure it."

"It seems to me a social revolution must come quickly."

"I wondered if you had felt that?" Gordon asked, as he leaned back in his chair and locked his powerful hands behind his head. "This presentiment of overwhelming change haunts me day and night and makes many things seem childish and futile.

"Ill and feverish from overwork one day last week, I stood by my window, looking down on the city, dreaming and listening to its cries for help, watching the sweep of the elevated trains coming and going, and I was overwhelmed with the immensity of its complex life. Our hurrying cars carry within the corporate limits daily more passengers than all the railroads of the western hemisphere. I thought of the rivers of human flesh that flow unceasingly through its streets and flood its market places. And these millions are but one wave of the ocean forever breaking on the shores of time, its tides everlasting, insistent, resistless, never pausing, behind them the pressure of the heaped centuries, and over them the lowering clouds of fresh storms soon to burst and add their tons."

He paused and closed his eyes as though to shut out the roar, while she listened with half-parted lips.

"And as I looked out the window I had a startling experience. I saw a huge dragon-like beast begin to crawl slowly down from the hills and stretch his big claws over the housetops of the city below. I was not asleep or in a trance, but wide awake, only a little feverish. With increasing horror I watched this monster stretch his enormous body, covered with scales, and short hair growing between the scales, on and on, until he covered the city and gathered its thousands of houses within his huge paws. His eyes were enormous and blood-red, his breath hot.

"I moved back, gasping with surprise and horror, to find it was only a spider crawling down his slender thread on the window close to my eye. It was a fevered delusion, but it haunted me for days, and haunts me still.

"I am growing in the conviction that the very foundations of morals are shifting, and that Religion, Society and Civilisation must readjust themselves or humanity sink into unspeakable degradation.

"Belief in the old religious authority is gone. Our church is thronged because of a peculiar personal power with which I am endowed. I could wield that power without a church, society, creed or Bible. Esthetic forces now draw people to non-ritualistic churches that once came for prayer and preaching. The preacher must secularise his sermon or talk to vacant pews. Historic Christianity has been destroyed by Criticism. A thousand wild Isms nourish in the twilight of this eclipse of Faith, while Materialism and the Pursuit of Pleasure strangle out spiritual hopes."

"And you are the seer called to lead out of this chaos," the woman whispered. "I know this from my own life. But for you I would be listening to idiotic platitudes, cultivating sham, my very soul 'crucified between a whimper and a smile.' I owe it to you that I am a woman - not a cross between an angel and an idiot."

The passion with which she said this, bending her beautiful face, flushed with emotion, so close to his that he caught the perfume of her mass of waving hair, went to the man's head like wine.

"Why not spring our building scheme on the people at once, without authority from the Board of Trustees, and make it the rallying cry of the new Humanity?" he cried eagerly.

"I believe it will succeed," she answered, her heart glowing with the consciousness of the intimacy of that little word "our" he had used.

She got pad and pencil, and Gordon dictated to her a plan for engaging every force of the church and its congregation and various societies in the project.

He fixed the Sunday on which to make the effort of his life in his appeal to the people of his congregation and the world for the million-dollar fund needed. It was eleven o'clock before they finished the discussion of the scheme, and aglow with enthusiasm he left for his home.

As he sat down in the car and lived over again his happiness of the past hours in this woman's companionship the paradox of his return in a few minutes to the arms of his wife struck him squarely in the face for the first time.

He could not plead a mistake in his first love. His romance was genuine. He had loved with all the fire of his youth. The passion which drew him to Ruth was mutual and resistless. Yet its ardour had cooled. He could not say it was his fault, not altogether hers. It seemed as inevitable in its decline as its onrush was resistless. Yet at the thought of this new woman he felt his heart beat with quicker stroke. He was older and stronger than the youth of the past, and the woman more mature in the ripened glory of beauty.

Yet he began to recall with infinite tenderness the love life with Ruth. Its memories were very real and very sweet. And the faces of his children haunted him with strange power. The idea of a divorce from Ruth and the loss of these children cut him with sharp pain.

Had he outgrown his first love? Could he continue to live with one woman if he loved another? Was not this the one unpardonable sin and shame? And yet to break that bond and form the other if he could meant the end of associations in which the fibers of his very life were wrought.

But was not this one of the burning problems of the new humanity, this freedom of the soul and body, this new birth into the liberty and love of a great Brotherhood? Was not sham and hypocrisy now the law of life, and was not Society perishing because of it?

Thus wrestling with the tragic dilemma he felt closing about him, he went past his station to the end of the line and had to take the down train back. It was past midnight when he reached his home.

CHAPTER X

THE BLACK CAT

When Van Meter heard of the scheme to appeal directly to the people to build the temple in defiance of the Board of Trustees, who were the legal managers of the church's property, he was thunderstruck.

When the Sunday arrived he came half an hour earlier than usual to watch every incident of the day with his little black eyes open their widest.

It was a crisp November morning. Recent rains had washed the streets clean, the wind was blowing fresh, the sky was cloudless and the sun lit in cool gleaming splendour every avenue and park of the great city.

The people had returned from their country places and the hotels were thronged with merchants and visitors from the four quarters of the earth.

An enormous crowd squeezed into every inch of space the police would allow to be filled in the church, and hundreds were turned away, unable to gain admission.

Gordon had spent the entire day and night before in an agony of preparation, and he had not left his study until two o'clock Sunday morning. He took his seat in the pulpit trembling with anxiety. The organ burst into the strains of the Doxology and the crowd rose. He stood with folded hands looking over the sea of faces, and his heart began to ache with an agony of suspense and fear of failure.

The singing ceased, and every head bent as he lifted his big hand, with its blue veins standing out like a net of steel wires, and pronounced a brief invocation.

When he read the hymn, the people felt in his voice the shock of a storm of pent-up emotion. He read it slowly, beautifully, and with exquisite tenderness.

While they sang he sat with his elbow on the little table on which stood a vase of roses, his face resting thoughtfully on his left hand, studying the people, his soul on fire with the sense of their infinite needs.

Crouching low in his seat under the left gallery, he saw a man who had confessed a great wrong and was searching for peace.

At a post on the right, in a seat where he had been accustomed to see a working-girl for the past two years, a stranger sat. The girl was found dead in her room the week before. She had lost her place because she wore shabby clothes, and she wore shabby clothes because she had been sending her earnings to her home in Connecticut, supporting an aged father, mother and a worthless brother.

The rich, the poor, the old, the young, the outcast, the publican and sinner, the strange woman and the sweet face of innocent girlhood were there looking up at him for guidance and help.

But outnumbering all were massed rows of clean-faced young men whom his enthusiasm had drawn resistlessly. His heart went out to them in yearning sympathy, fighting their battles in the morning of life with the powers and princes of the spirit world for the mastery of the soul.

He felt the sledge-hammer blow of their united heart-beat strike his brain with the pain of a bludgeon.

The agony of fear was now upon him. He saw Van Meter sitting in the central tier of seats watching him sharply out of his little half-closed eyes, the incarnate sign of the mortal enmity of organised wealth, and he must appeal for money.

His great crowd had infinite needs, but much money they did not have. He thought with hope of the twenty millions of people who read his sermons on Monday morning, and of a dozen big-hearted men of wealth he knew in the city, and he was cheered.

He had prepared a most powerful sermon on the text, "The common people heard Him gladly." He felt they could not resist his appeal. And yet in spite of himself his gaze would wander back to Van Meter, drawn by his black eyes as by the charm of an adder.

The Deacon was wondering, as he watched him, what could possibly be the outcome of this daring insanity. He had been fooled so often by the power of this athletic dreamer, he feared to predict the end, though he felt certain what it would be.

The services were unusually impressive. Special music had been prepared by the choir and rendered magnificently. Gordon read the hymns and Scripture with a feeling so intense the people were thrilled. His prayer had been simple and heartfelt, and had melted scores of people to tears.

He rose and faced the crowd with the keenest sense of solemnity. The hour was propitious; he could feel the hearts of the people beat responsive to his slightest tone, word or gesture.

As he swept rapidly through his introduction and into his theme he knew he was holding these thousands of breathless listeners in the hollow of his hand. He could feel their heartstrings quiver as he touched them with tenderness or struck them with some mighty thought.

His soul was singing with triumph, when suddenly a ripple of laughter ran along the front tier of the gallery, and a hundred heads were turned upward to see what the disturbance meant.

Had a bolt of lightning struck his spinal column he could not have been more shocked.

He repeated mechanically the last sentence in a dazed sort of way, and a louder ripple of laughter ran the entire length of both galleries and echoed through the main floor.

He stopped, fumbled at his notes, and turned red. The people before him were smiling and craning their necks to see more plainly something on the wide platform of the pulpit.

He suddenly got the insane idea that a fiend had thrust his head in the door behind him and was mocking and grinning.

He turned and looked, and there sat an impudent little black cat with big yellow eyes.

She had been sitting on her haunches blinking at him when he raised his voice or gestured, and the crowd has never yet gathered on this earth in the temple of Baal or Jehovah that can resist a cat accompaniment to the functions of a priest.

When Gordon looked the little cat full in the face, she liked him at once, and in the softest, friendliest treble said:

"Meow!"

And the crowd burst into incontrollable laughter.

At first the full import of the situation did not reach his mind, he was so stunned with surprise. He stood looking at the cat in helpless stupor, and blushing red. And then the sickening certainty crushed him that the day was lost; that it was beyond the power of human genius, or the reach of the spirit of God, to remove that cat and regain control of his audience.

He turned sick with anger and humiliation, and his big bear-like hands clasped his sheet of notes and slowly crushed them.

He continued to look at the cat and she cocked her head to one side, opened her yellow eyes wider and, slowly, in grieved accents said:

"M-e-o-w!"

Which unmistakably meant, "I'm very sorry you don't like me as well as I do you."

Again the crowd laughed.

Gordon stepped backward and bent slowly over the cat. She did not look very bright, but she was too shrewd for that movement.

The crowd watched breathlessly. He grasped at her.

She sprang quickly to one side, bowed her back, bushed her tail, and scampered across the platform crying:

"Pist! pist!" and ran up the column that supported the end of the gallery.

The preacher's empty hand struck the bare floor, and the crowd was convulsed.

A young man sitting in the gallery near the column caught the cat as she climbed over the rail, ran to a window and was about to throw her down to the pavement twenty feet below.

Gordon lifted his hand and cried:

"Don't do that, young man - don't hurt her; bring her here."

It had, suddenly occurred to the preacher as he watched Van Meter bending low in his pew overcome with laughter, that he had stooped to this contemptible trick to defeat him and make the solemnest hour of life ridiculous. He knew the Deacon had come to the church earlier than usual. He was sure he had done it.

A curious smile began to play about his lips, and a cold glitter came into his steel-gray eyes.

He took the cat in his arms and stroked her gently. She purred and rubbed her face against his and moved her feet up and down, sheathing and unsheathing her claws in his robe with evident delight.

The crowd grew still. Instinctively they knew that something big was happening in the soul of the man they were watching.

"This little cat, my friends," he said, "is an innocent actor in a tragedy this morning, but she is the agent of one who is not innocent."

He fixed his gaze on Van Meter, who stirred with uneasy amazement.

"They say that cats sometimes incarnate the souls of dead men. This one is the soul of a living man, my good friend, Deacon Arnold Van Meter, who had her brought here this morning."

The Deacon turned red, drew his head down as though he would pull it within his shoulders, and shrank from the gaze of the crowd.

Gordon handed the cat back to the young man, whispered something to him, and he disappeared.

Then, walking up to the pulpit, he snatched off its crimson

cloth and threw it behind him. He ran his big muscular hands into the throat of his robe, ripped it open, tore it from his arms, crushed it into a shapeless mass and threw it on the floor.

He snatched up the golden lectern pulpit, hurled it back into the comer, and moved the little table with its vase of roses into its place. He did this quickly, without a word or an exclamation to break the awful stillness with which the crowd watched him.

They knew that a tremendous drama was being enacted before them. So intense was the excitement the people on the back tiers of the galleries sprang impulsively to their feet and stood on the pews.

Van Meter's eyes danced with wild amazement as he straightened himself up, sure Gordon had gone mad. But when he advanced to the edge of the platform, looking a foot taller in his long black Prince Albert coat, folded his giant arms across his breast, the nostrils of his great aquiline nose dilated, his lips quivering, and looked straight into Van Meter's face, the Deacon saw there was dangerous method in his madness.

His eyes blazing with pent-up passion, he began in deliberate tones an extempore address.

In a moment the air was charged with the thrill of his powerful personality wrought to the highest tension of emotional power.

"My friends," he began, "there are moments in our experience when we live a lifetime - moments when the hair of our heads turns gray, a soul dies within a laving body, or a dead one rises, shakes off its grave clothes, and lifts its head in the sunlight.

"From this hour I am a free man. I will live what I am, and speak what I feel to be the truth. The truth shall be its own justification. I will wear no robes, mumble no ceremonies, call no man Rabbi, and permit no man to call me Rabbi. I proclaim the universal priesthood of believers.

"While I am your pastor the Kitchen Mission in which we have gathered the poor on the East Side will be closed at the hour of service, and all God's children shall enter this house because it is their Father's!"

Van Meter shrank back in his pew as a ripple of applause ran round the galleries.

"If men ask a sign to-day whether the Church of the living God exists in New York, what is our answer?

"Look about you. New York is the centre of the commerce, society, art, literature and politics of the Western World. Her port, in which fly the flags of every nation, is the gateway of two worlds. The feet of four millions daily press her pavements. Her walls frame the furnace in which are being tried by fire the faiths, hopes and dreams of the centuries past and to come. In mere volume of population she is the equal of three great Atlantic states: Virginia, North and South Carolina. One man alone of her millions of citizens possesses wealth greater than the valuation of all the property of the State of North Carolina, the cradle of American democracy, containing fifty thousand square miles and supporting a population of a million six hundred thousand.

"In the roar of this modern Babylon beats the fevered heart of modern civilisation. He who wins that heart holds the key to the century. Imperial Rome, mistress of the world, was a pygmy compared to this.

"And what are we doing?

"Our Protestant churches have thirty-five thousand men and one hundred thousand women enrolled out of two millions on Manhattan Island. Our invested capital is one hundred million dollars, our annual gifts four millions, and we fail to hold one-half the children born in our own homes.

"As a remedy for this the Trustees proposed to me to sell out and move uptown to vacant lots! They say the people have gone. They have come - come in such numbers and with such problems, churches have fled before the avalanche of humanity.

"Within a stone's throw of this church are districts in which ten men and women sleep in one room twelve feet square. New York is the most crowded city in the world. London has seven people to a house; we have sixteen. In two houses were found the other day one hundred and thirty-six children. Death stalks through these crowded alleys with scythe ever swinging.

"Shall we, too, desert?

"I hear the tread of coming thousands from these shadows who will laugh at your flag, who know not the name of your President, or your God, whose heavy hands upon your doors will summon you before the tribunal of the knife, the torch, the bomb to make good your right to live.

"When your population shall number ten millions, and the gulf between the rich and poor shall have become impassable, some gigantic corner shall have doubled the price of bread, starvation spread her black wings, and idle thousands sullen and desperate begin to look with darkening brows on your unprotected wealth, then will come the test of modern society.

"This growth of the city is as resistless and inevitable as the movement of time. Why people continue to turn their backs upon the open fields and crowd into this great foul, rattling, crawling, smoking, stinking, ghastly heap of fermenting brickwork, oozing poison at every pore, is beyond my ken, but they come. They come each year in hundreds, thousands and tens of thousands, crowding the crowded trades, crowding closer the crowded dens in which human beings whelp and stable as beasts. They leave friends and neighbours who love them, leave earth for hell, and still they come. The tenement, huge monster of modern greed, engulfs them, and the word home is stricken from their tongue.

"They tell us that yesterday a man in a fit of insanity murdered his wife and two daughters. Insanity? Love has its hours when death becomes beautiful. Poets sing of old Virginius who slew his daughter to save her from dishonour. May it not be better to die a man than live a beast?

"There are conditions about us where suicide is a luxury and the death of a child a joy. They are gathered to the Potters' Field, but they rest. We pile them one on top of the other in big black trenches, but the dawn does not call them to beastly toil. Their little forms moulder, but they no longer cry for bread and their pinched faces no longer try to smile. They are safe in Death's land-locked harbour.

"Last year the deaths on this island numbered forty thousand. Ten thousand - one in four - were buried from hospitals, jails, almshouses, asylums and workhouses. I have been assailed by a deacon of this church because I no longer preach hell. Why preach hell to people who expect to better their condition in the next world whether they go up or down?

"I am here henceforth to proclaim the acceptable year of the Lord, the healing of the bruised, the release of the captive, and to preach the Gospel to the poor.

"Let snobs and apes hear me. Democracy is the goal of the race, the destiny of the world. American Democracy is but a hundred years old, yet not one crowned head is left on the western hemisphere. Crowns, thrones, scepters, titles, privileges belong to the past; they are doomed. The people already rule the world. Emperors, kings and presidents exist, not by the grace of God, but by the consent of the people, to whom they give account of their stewardship. Empires are the dungheaps out of which democracies grow.

"The historian writes of the common people. Once of kings

and princes were their stories. The eyes of the world are on the masses. Science toils to make Nature their servant. Art portrays their life. Literature, once a clown at the feet of Fortune's fools, now writes of the people. Wealth lays its tribute at their feet. The millionaire, who dies to-day grasping his millions as his own, is hissed while he lives, openly cursed while he lies cold in death, and forgotten in contempt.

"Outside the history of the common people there is nothing worth recording. They are mankind. As a half-million miles make no difference in the vast distance to the sun in figuring an eclipse, so the classes may be disregarded.

"Jesus Christ was the carpenter's son. His home was humble, His birth lowly. He was born poor, lived and died poor. The foxes had holes, the birds of the air nests, but He had not where to lay His head. Our robes and altar cloths, our tin and tinsel, were not His.

"When John Wesley raised his voice for the people the Church of England had the opportunity to become the Church of the Anglo-Saxon race, that is now conquering the world. They called him a liar, a hypocrite, a Jesuit, a devil, cast him out, and the opportunity passed forever.

"I see a man before me who hates this big crowd and yet expects to go to heaven. Heaven is the home of millions - 'a great multitude which no man could number,' says the seer. Hell is the home of swell society."

The words leaped from Gordon's lips a rushing torrent and swept the crowd. Growing each moment more and more conscious of his strength, he attained the heights of eloquence. Intoxicated with the reflex action from the sea of eager listeners, he outdid himself with each succeeding climax of feeling. Never had his voice been so deep, so full, so clear, so penetrating, so thrilling, and never had he been so conscious of its control. Not once did it break. Its loudest trumpet note echoed with sure roundness.

When he turned his eyes from Van Meter after his first assault they rested on the face of Kate Ransom, her magnificent figure tense, rigid, her cheeks scarlet, her blue eyes flashing with tears of excitement. She was stirred to her soul's depths, and no figure in all the throbbing crowd gave to the speaker such inspiring response. Her face flashed back as from a mirror every throb of thought and stroke of his heart.

Van Meter gazed on him hypnotised by the violence of his onrush. When Gordon would suddenly lift his enormous blue-veined hand high over his head in an impassioned gesture the Deacon cowered unconsciously beneath his towering figure.

Pausing a moment, while the crowd held its' breath, watching every movement and every twitch of a muscle of his face, he pointed his long finger at the Deacon and continued:

"And, as if to mock intelligence, Tradition raises the feeble cry of reminiscent senility, 'Back to the old paths!'

"Protestantism is the rebellion of reason against the shackles of authority. Our conscience fettered by tradition stultifies its own life. We must go forward or die.

"Theology is a science, religion a life. The one is a fact, the other an analysis after the fact. The stage-coach yielded to the limited, the sailing craft to the ocean greyhound, but we are told that the only age that ever knew the truth, or had the right to express it, was the age which burned witches, executed dumb animals as criminals, whipped church bells for heresy, held chemistry a black art and electricity a manifestation of the devil or the Shekina of God.

"The men to whom I speak have seen New York grow from a town of three hundred thousand on the lower end of Manhattan Island to be the imperial metropolis of the New World with four millions within her golden gates.

"Within a generation, the Brooklyn Bridge, a dream in the

brain of a man, has spun its spider web of steel across the river, our buildings grown from four stories to towering castles of steel with their flag-staffs in the clouds.

"Our nation has been baptised in blood and a new Constitution established.

"The German Empire has been created, and a new map of the world made.

"Steam and electricity have been applied to travel and speech, and the earth transformed into a whispering gallery. The cylinder press has proclaimed universal education, and the dynamo crowned the brow of humanity with a coronet of light.

"But our churches in New York have merely moved uptown! Their methods are the methods of their fathers - a solecism, stupid, irrational, immoral.

"The superstition that seeks to limit the horizon of the soul to the bounds of ancestral tradition has ever been the deadliest foe of human hope. Doubt is the vestibule of knowledge. They who doubt, rebel and disobey have ever led the shining way of progress and of life.

"Your Traditionalists crucified the Christ. They declared him to be the friend of publicans and harlots.

"Since then they have covered the Church with the infamy of cruelty and blood, flame, sword, thumb-screw, rack and torch. The blackest pages in the story of the martyrdom of man have been written by their hands. They sent Alva into the Netherlands to sweep it with fire. They revoked the edict of Nantes until the soil of France was drunk with the blood of her children. They led the trembling sons and daughters of faith, barefoot and blindfolded, over burning plowshares, stretched them on wheel and rack, tore them limb from limb, sparing not for the groan of age, the lisp of childhood, or the piteous cry of expectant motherhood.

"The Bible they made a bludgeon with which to brain heretics, forged its word into chains, and with its leaves kindled martyr fires.

"They have arraigned the reason, the heart and the knowledge of the race against Jesus Christ and His religion. They stretched Galileo on the rack for inventing a telescope which gave new beauty to the psalm, 'The heavens declare the glory of God and the firmament showeth His handiwork.'

"They are driving manhood from the modern Church. Your New York congregations average four women to one man. Of forty-three Governors of our states, only seventeen are members of any church; yet all profess allegiance to the religion of Jesus. The men have formed secret societies outside the Church.

"The Church triumphant will be a social power. Man to-day is more than an individual. The individual has played his role in the growth of the centuries. This is the age of federation, organisation, society, humanity. Man can no longer live to himself or die to himself.

"I proclaim again the universal priesthood of believers. I call for those mighty forces among the unordained which thrilled the Waldenses, the Franciscans, the Puritan and early Methodists and sent them on their glorious careers. I preach a holy crusade for man as man, in the name of God, whose image he bears. I ask you to join with me as man, not as priest, and build here a 'Temple of Humanity' that shall be for a sign of hope and faith and freedom."

As he closed, a spontaneous burst of applause shook the building, and instead of the usual prayer which ended his sermons he lifted both his big hands high above his head and the audience rose.

"Let us sing the national hymn, 'My Country, 'Tis of Thee, Sweet Land of Liberty,'" he cried, his voice still throbbing with emotion. "And while we sing the ushers will pass the subscription cards that you may join with us in our enterprise."

He dismissed the crowd with the Benediction, and the whole mass lingered, discussing with flushed faces the extraordinary scene they had witnessed and speculating on its outcome. It was evident his action and speech had produced a moral earthquake in the church.

The older and more conservative members slipped out one by one and went home dazed.

The younger and more sensitive crowded about Gordon in hundreds, wrung his hand and pledged their support. For half an hour he could not move, so dense was this struggling mass around him.

He did not see Kate among them. He knew the scene had cut too deeply into her life for such poor expression. The ushers at last handed him a bundle of subscription cards and he hurried to his study to read their verdict.

Thomas Dixon

CHAPTER XI

AN ANSWER TO PRAYER

When Gordon reached his study and locked the door, he turned the bundle of cards over nervously, afraid to look at them.

He untied the package, read the first, and ran rapidly through the pile. The total subscriptions reached only twenty thousand dollars. He had asked for a million.

A sickening sense of failure crushed him. How weak and puerile the eloquence of words or the beat of the human heart against that mysterious force gleaming at him through Van Meter's black eyes!

He sat brooding over the power wielded by a dozen men whose names were linked with the Deacon's in Wall Street. This group of men had personal fortunes of more than eight hundred millions and controlled as much more. He believed that they dictated the policy of railroads, banks, trade, the State, the Nation, and that no king or emperor of the world wielded such despotism over men as these uncrowned monarchs of money. He felt as though he had collided with the stars in their courses and been crushed to dust.

An Answer to Prayer 129

In the middle of the pile of cards he found one signed by Kate

Ransom. She had written across the printed form in her smooth, flowing hand:

"Please call after the service and let me know the result. I will send you my subscription to-morrow."

He knew that she would make a liberal gift, but her fortune could not be more than a million, perhaps not half so large. Her generosity could not save the day even if she gave half of all she possessed, a supposition of course preposterous.

He could not summon courage to go in the bitterness of his defeat. He scrawled a note and sent it by the sexton.

"Feeling too blue to call. Failure complete and pitiful. The subscriptions reach only twenty thousand dollars. GORDON."

There was but one forlorn hope left. He had written personal letters to several millionaires he knew in town. They might respond.

He sat in his study in the afternoon, dull, stupid and sick, feeling an iron band around his brain. He could not think. Ho gave up the work on his evening sermon and determined to repeat an old one.

As he sat in an aching stupor the sexton announced a gentleman who insisted on seeing him on important business.

"I told him you would see no one at this hour, but he says he must see you."

"Show him in," Gordon said, with a frown.

The man entered, gazed at the preacher with curious interest, and stood with his silk hat in hand, smiling.

"This is Doctor Gordon?"

"Leave off the doctor and you have it right."

"I am the bearer of good news. A client of mine has instructed me to call and say that the sum of one million dollars will be placed to your credit in the Garfield National Bank within two years, and that you will be its sole trustee for the building of your projected Temple. One-third of it will be available within three months. I am sorry, I am forbidden to disclose the name."

Gordon sprang to his feet, pale as death, overwhelmed with awe. To have the answer of his prayers, the agonising of his soul for years, answered in the hour of utter defeat thrilled him with a sense of solemnity he had never felt. The man was not a man. He was the messenger swift and beautiful from the courts of heaven, for whose coming his eyes had long strained and his ears listened. Not a doubt of its truth shadowed his mind. He knew it was true. It was the fulfilment of life. It had been ordained from eternity. He had seen it always. Now he saw with his eyes. A paean of exaltation welled within him.

With dimmed eyes he grasped the lawyer's hand and fairly crushed it in his iron grip.

"My friend, your face will always be beautiful to me, and your name a song of joy. You have come to lift me from the gulf of despair and renew my faith."

"With all my heart I congratulate you," he warmly responded.

He left his card, and Gordon locked his door, walked back to his desk and fell on his knees. In transports of childlike gratitude he poured out his soul. All the old faith in prayer was in him again, the breath he breathed. He talked to God as to a loving father, promising in broken accents to cleanse his heart of every selfish thought and consecrate anew every energy to his work.

And then he caught the perfume of flowers, and saw the face of a woman, and she was not the wife of his youth or the mother of his children.

"God forgive me for the drifting of the past," he cried. "I will tear this madness out of my heart and love only Thee. I will be true to the vows taken at Thy altar. I have been wayward and sinned in Thy sight in heart and thought. Wash me in Thy love and I shall be clean, and though my sins be as scarlet they shall be like wool."

He rose from his knees determined to go immediately to Kate Ransom, tell her the news, make a clean breast of his love for her, beg her to put the ocean between them, and for all time end their dangerous relationship.

She greeted him with reserve, and seemed embarrassed.

With impetuous rush he told her the tidings.

"I've been lifted from the depths of Sheol to the highest heaven. Every hope and dream of my struggle is a living reality. An unknown millionaire has given the whole sum needed - a million dollars - and our Temple will rise in grandeur!"

She smiled timidly, and said: "I knew it would be so. You were glorious this morning."

He felt her embarrassment and wondered if she could have divined his grim purpose of separation.

"You do not seem so glad as I thought you would be," he said, with something of reproach in his voice.

"Some joys are too intense for speech. The scene this morning and your burning message went too deep for words."

"I understand," he said softly.

"I wonder if you do?" she asked, dropping her eyes.

"Yes, and I have come to the hardest task of my life, one of the bitterest and one of the sweetest," he said, with deliberation.

She glanced at him quickly and began to tremble.

"Not another hour must pass without a confession to you."

He moved across the room and sat down as if by an effort to put distance between them.

"What is it?" she asked, colouring.

He was silent a moment and then said with low, deliberate tenderness:

"I love you."

She sobbed, and he looked steadily out of the window.

"I dare not sit by your side when I tell you this," he continued passionately. "I have felt it growing in spite of reason or will. I know it's tragedy and sealed my lips with bolts of steel. I have been too weak to keep away from you, strong enough to keep silent. But God has sent his messenger to-day to recall me to duty. There is truth in the old faith. He has heard and answered the prayer of my heart. Somewhere in this Mammon-cursed city there is one beautiful disinterested soul that gives and asks nothing. I have seen, as in a flash of lightning, my danger. I must tear this passion out of my life, though it kill me. I must be true to my vows. I must live without scandal or shame. And you," he paused and his voice sank to a tense whisper - "my beautiful darling, glorious love of my manhood - you must help me!"

He buried his face in his great hands, convulsed with emotion.

"I will, my dearest," she tenderly answered.

"If I had failed to-day," he went on tremblingly, "perhaps in reckless fury I might have forgotten duty, dashed the cup of this martyrdom from my lips, and drowned conscience in the sweetness of your kiss. But God sent success, not failure. And I must be worthy. I have sinned a thousand times as I have gloated over your beauty, heard the music of your voice, touched your soft hand and looked into your soul through those dear blue eyes. It must end. One hour thus face to face we will speak, and never again by word or deed recall that we are aught to one another. I have not asked if you love me. How well I know the tragic truth! But you will tell me once, that my ears may never forget the words on your lips."

"I love you, I love you, I-love-you!" she sobbed in anguish.

"We must never be together alone again," he sighed.

"No."

"We must not see each other any more."

"It is best," she said, with despair.

"I dare not touch your hand - good-by!" he cried, staggering to his feet.

"Good-by, Frank, my hero, my love - my God!"

He took one step toward the door, but his feet carried him to her side.

He trembled, hesitated, and then slowly drew her to his heart. Her arms stole around his neck and her head drooped on his breast, the perfume of her hair was in his nostrils, and their lips met in burning kisses.

"God forgive us! It was more than mortal flesh could bear to go without one moment of love's sweet life!" he cried. "And now we must part."

He took her hands in his and gently kissed them, while she looked away seeing only his face, for it had long since filled the world.

He turned abruptly into the hall, and, moving to the door with swift step, he saw lying on the silver tray the card of the lawyer he had met an hour ago. In a moment it flashed over him that Kate was the unknown messenger. He had not dreamed her fortune of such magnitude.

He seized the card and rushed back into the room.

"Is that your lawyer's name?" he gasped.

She smiled and nodded her head in assent.

"And I never dreamed it possible!"

He looked at her as though in a trance.

"Yes, I will confess now. You have confessed to me. My fortune came direct from my grandmother, who willed me her farm on which the oil was discovered. My father's fortune is worth perhaps five hundred thousand dollars. Mine was worth about two million dollars. I have given one to you. I may give you the other if you ask it. One was all you asked."

Again he took her to his heart.

"I have misread the message. Such love is in itself divine, and its own defense. You are mine by the higher law of life. I will not give you up - you are mine, mine! I will defy the world. I loved my child-wife. I was honest then. I will be honest now. I loved as a boy loves. Now I am a man, with a man's fierce passions, and you are the answer - strength calling to strength, deep answering unto deep! Your eyes, my darling, flash the beauty of every flower that blooms and every star of the sky; in your hair is the rose's breath and the golden glory of the sun! I will not live with one woman and love another."

And the twilight deepened into night while they held each other's hands and smiled into each other's faces.

CHAPTER XII

OUT OF THE SHADOWS

When Gordon announced at the evening service that a million dollars had been subscribed to the new "Temple of Man," and that he had been constituted its sole trustee, the crowd burst into a storm of applause.

In vain he raised his big muscular hand over the tumult.

Troops of young men and women with flushed faces, some laughing, some crying, sprang from their seats, rushed to the platform and seized his hand.

The strains of the national hymn suddenly burst from the crowd, and they rose en masse singing it with triumphant peal. As its last note died away a woman's voice started "Nearer, My God, to Thee," the people caught it instantly and its mighty chorus rolled heavenward. The singing had in it the spontaneous rhythm of hearts transported by resistless feeling. For half an hour they stood and sang the old familiar hymns whose sentences were wet with the tears and winged with the hopes and mysteries of their lives.

Instead of a sermon, Gordon read his resignation as pastor of the Pilgrim Church.

And then, folding his hands behind him, in trumpet tones he cried:

"Next Sunday morning will be the last service I will ever conduct in this church; the Sunday morning following, at eleven o'clock, the first services of the 'Church of the Son of Man' will be held in the old Grand Opera House. It will seat four thousand people. All who wish to join this independent society are cordially invited to be present and bring your friends. The work of building the 'Temple of Man' will begin at once. Within six months we hope to lay its corner-stone."

The meeting was closed at once with the Doxology and Benediction.

The reporters crowded around him for fuller details. He refused to give any further information. They interviewed every officer of the church and congregation from whom any news might be secured, and it was nine o'clock before the excitement had subsided and the crowd left.

The organist and quartet choir lingered to rehearse their music for the following Sunday.

Gordon retired to his study, where he had asked Kate to meet him for an important conference.

The church opened on the cross street and stretched its barn shape through the entire block. The study was beside the pulpit platform, a little beyond the centre of the building. Behind it was the Sunday-school and reading-room, opening on the rear.

Kate had the keys to the reading-room, which was under her direction, and Gordon asked her to come to his study from the rear entrance through the Sunday-school room that she might avoid the suspicion of the reporters. For the same reason he did not wish to be seen at her house. He had left the door of his study unlocked for her, and she entered before the crowd had left the church.

Within a few moments from the time she unlocked the door of

the reading-room, Van Meter's detectives informed him that she was in the pastor's study and that he had left the rear door open for her to secretly enter.

The Deacon despatched one of his men with an anonymous note to Ruth informing her that Gordon was in his study alone by secret appointment with Kate Ransom, and giving to her duplicate keys to every door in the church building.

The detective did not see Ruth, but the maid said she was at home, and he handed her the package.

Gordon had telephoned to her briefly the facts of the excitement of the morning, and told her he was so exhausted that he would not return for dinner, but would take his meals at a hotel and come home after the evening service.

When Ruth received the note and keys she was brooding over his absence and peering in the depths of the widening gulf which separated them in such a crisis of his life.

The note threw her into the wildest excitement. All the old fiery temper and jealousy which she had kept smouldering in restraint now burst its bounds.

Flushed and trembling she rushed from the house and soon reached the church.

She opened the door gently, and with soft feline step was about to enter the Sunday-school room to reach his study, when through the glass sliding partition she heard the voice of Van Meter talking in the dark to a detective and a reporter.

She listened intently.

"I wish you had a flashlight camera," he was saying. "His wife will be here in a few minutes and the scene in that room would be worth ten thousand dollars. I have a good photograph of the woman you can use. You can get his anywhere."

"It will be a great scoop on the other fellows who will write up the Temple without the Priestess!" the reporter whispered.

"I'd give a thousand dollars to see his face in the morning when he picks up your paper and reads its headlines," chuckled the Deacon. "His eloquence, his bullfrog voice, his curling locks, his splendid eyes, will all be needed, and will all of them be inadequate to the occasion."

"It will be tough on that beautiful woman, the scandal - by George, it's a pity," the reporter sighed.

"But it will be a great day for the little black-eyed spitfire wife of his he's been neglecting for the past year. Her revenge will be sweet. I've been sorry enough for her."

"I wonder if she will promptly sue for a divorce?"

"Yes; you can write that down without an interview," the Deacon replied.

Ruth had come raging in anger against her husband. But the cold words of these men, whispering in the dark their joy over his downfall, stopped the beat of her heart.

She could see the big cruel headlines in the morning paper, holding her beloved up to shame in the hour of his triumph. Surely this would be what he deserved. But she loved him - yes, good or bad, she loved him. He was the hero of her girl's soul, the father of her beautiful children, and in spite of all his coldness and neglect he was her heart's desire.

And the feeling came crushing down upon her that perhaps she had failed somehow to do her whole duty. She had been wilful and fretful and had not kept in touch and sympathy with his work. She had demanded a perfect love and loyalty, and in agony she asked herself if she had given as much as she had demanded. Had she not thought too much of her own rights and wrongs and too little of his hopes and burdens? And perhaps because of this he was to be crushed at a blow, and his enemies laugh at his calamity and give to her their maudlin pity.

She could hear the sweet strains of the organ in the church and the soprano singing the Gloria.

She held her hand on her heart for a moment, as though it were breaking, and suddenly her soul was born anew.

Out of the shadows of self and self-seeking she lifted up her head into the sunlight of a perfect love, a love that suffereth long and is kind, vaunteth not itself, is not puffed up, seeketh not its own, believeth all things, endureth all things - love that never faileth.

"Lord, have mercy on me, and help me - I must save him!" she cried in agony.

Rapidly retracing her steps, she passed back into the street and around the block to the front of the church.

To her joy she encountered no one. The Deacon was so sure of his triumph he had withdrawn his detectives from the street and had them massed as witnesses in the Sunday-school room. He was sure they would emerge by that way, for it was Gordon's usual way of exit, and the choir was still singing in the church.

With feverish haste she applied the key to the spring lock of the door for the members' entrance and passed noiselessly down the aisle in the shadows under the gallery, unobserved by the choir. Only the lights about the organ were burning.

When she reached the door of the study she paused.

What if she found him with his arms about her and his lips on hers? Could she control herself? Would she not spring on the woman, with all the tiger of her hot Southern blood from centuries of proud ancestry tingling in her tapering fingers, and tear those blue eyes from her head? She must be sure. No; it was over now. She had conquered self. She would save him.

Slipping the key softly into the lock, she entered and stood a moment, her stormy eyes burning a deep, steady fire.

They were studying a map of the city with eager interest in the location of the Temple and did not see or hear her.

As she saw them thus, a sense of gratitude soothed her excitement and gave perfect control of her voice.

"Frank," she said quietly.

"Ruth!" he exclaimed in amazement, striding toward her, while Kate blushed and, with dilated eyes, stared at her, dumb with fear of a scene of violence.

"Yes," she continued in even, rapid tones, "I have come, in love, not anger, to save you both from shame and disgrace. That room behind you is full of detectives and reporters. They are waiting for the choir to leave to find you here alone. They sent for me to give a fitting climax to the scene. They have your photograph already, Miss Ransom, and the reporter is preparing his article on the hidden Priestess of the new Temple."

"Oh, I thank you!" Kate cried, trembling.

"Keep your thanks. I do this from no regard for you. Frankly, I hate you - hate and envy yoi your terrible beauty that has robbed me of that which I hold dearer than life."

"But I do not hate you, Mrs. Gordon. I have for you only the kindliest feelings," Kate protested.

"I prefer your hatred. But we have no time for talk."

Ruth quickly removed her hat and cloak and handed them to Kate.

"Exchange with me and pass quickly out of the church by the little front door. Keep under the shadows of the gallery and the choir cannot see you."

In a moment it was done, and Gordon faced his wife alone.

"My dear, that was a beautiful deed you have just done."

"Don't say 'my dear' to me again until we have come to an understanding of this meeting," his wife said, closing her lips firmly.

"As you will," he gravely answered.

"When we are at home to-night alone I will hear your explanation."

"What you have told me is of such importance I cannot go home to-night. I must see friends who will reach that newspaper in time to know what Van Meter can have printed. It may keep me the whole night."

"Very well; it will not be the first night I have spent alone," she answered bitterly.

"I will go with you to the elevated station, and will be home certainly early in the morning."

They stepped from the study, and Gordon turned the electric switch, filling the room with a blaze of light.

Van Meter and his men blinked in amazement at the sight of the preacher and his wife quietly walking toward them.

"You contemptible old sneak!" he hissed. "How dare you crawl into this room to spy on me?"

"I thought I had good reasons for being here," he spluttered, nervously clearing his throat.

"Well, you thought a lie as your father, the devil, did before you."

"Apparently a mistake somewhere," stammered the Deacon, looking sheepishly at Mrs. Gordon. "And I'd like to explain to you, sir, that I didn't bring that cat."

"Well, cat or no cat, I give you a parting warning. We will not meet again in this church, and if I ever catch you sneaking around me I'll take a whip and thrash you as I would a cur, you little ferret-eyed imp of hell!"

The Deacon cowered beneath the furious giant figure and beckoned to the detectives.

Gordon and his wife passed by them and out into the night.

CHAPTER XIII

A BROKEN HEART-STRING

The press next morning devoted entire pages to the sensation in the Pilgrim Church. Portraits of Gordon, his life and theories, sketches of the extraordinary scene in his pulpit, a full stenographic report of his address which he had carefully corrected at midnight, portraits of his wife and children, pictures of the old church, its reading-rooms, clubhouses and coffee-house, were exploited.

His letter of resignation and the gift of a millon dollars for building a vast Temple of Humanity, that would be a forum of free thought in the heart of the metropolis, were the subject of separate editorials in every paper.

Speculation as to the identity of this mysterious millionaire, who had apparently deserted the army of entrenched wealth to support this daring young revolutionist, filled columns. But it was all the wildest guessing. Many of the greater magnates hastened to deny with emphasis that they were in any way connected with the scheme. Several of them denounced the preacher as a dangerous man whose wild theories threatened social order. Gordon breathed a sigh of relief when he found not a line hinting at Kate Ransom's part in the drama or linking his name with hers.

After two o'clock, when he finished his last conference with the reporters and his friends, he went to a hotel where he was not known. He spent the rest of the night pacing the floor fighting to a finish the battle between the memory of Ruth and his children and his fierce new passion.

Just before dawn he lay down and fell asleep, dreaming of Kate. The battle between the flesh and the spirit had ended.

He slept until noon, ate a hasty breakfast, called at the Ransom house a moment, and hurried to his home.

His wife had read the morning papers with increasing amazement at the sensation created, and a sense of impending tragedy began to crush her. For hours she had been walking back and forth from her window watching for his approach, until now she dreaded to see him.

At the sound of his footstep she recalled the fact that she was the judge and he the culprit in the scene to be enacted. She had demanded an explanation of the meaning of the meeting with this woman, and she would have it. If his excuse were good she would be generous in her love and beg him to begin once more their old life, even if she threw the last shred of pride to the winds and made herself his veriest slave. And yet her heart misgave her. She felt herself lost and ruined before the battle began, but determined to play her part bravely.

She watched him over the banisters as he stepped into the hall and greeted the children with unusual tenderness.

He took Lucy's little form up and placed her arms around his neck.

"Now hug me long, and hard, and kiss me sweet," he whispered.

The child squeezed his neck and, placing her hands on his cheeks, softly kissed his lips and eyes as she had often seen her mother do. He ran his hand gently through her brown curls that seemed a perfect mixture of her mother's and his own, and Ruth thought his hand trembled as he kissed her again.

"I never saw you quite so beautiful, my baby, as this morning," he said, as he placed her on the floor.

When he entered the room upstairs Ruth had recovered her composure and stood waiting, her petite figure drawn to its full height, her anxious face unusually thin, her eyes, set in the dark rings of a sleepless night, looking blacker and stormier than ever in the shadows of her disheveled hair.

"Sorry I could not come sooner, Ruth," he began, with evident embarrassment. "But I did not get to sleep until just before day, and I was so exhausted I slept until noon."

"Let us waste no words," said the soft, round voice. "I have waited long; I am waiting still for your explanation. Why was that woman in your study alone with you last night at half-past ten o'clock?"

"You wish to know the whole truth?"

"I demand it."

"Very well," he replied deliberately. "The immediate reason is a secret of great importance, I must ask you to guard it sacredly."

"I've kept a dark one in my soul. You have had no cause to complain."

"The morning papers are full of wild speculation as to the millionaire who gave that immense sum to build the Temple. Miss Ransom gave the money."

"Impossible!" she gasped.

"So I thought at first. A lawyer came in the afternoon and told me of the gift without a hint of its author. In answer to a request on a card asking that I inform her of the results of my appeal, I called at her house -"

"Before you called at your own or informed your wife," she interrupted with bitterness.

"Yes; you have ceased to care about rny work. But there was another and more urgent reason why I called,"

"Doubtless!" she cried impatiently.

"When the import of this gift fully dawned on me, the fulfilment of my grandest hopes in the very moment of defeat (for the popular subscription was a failure), I was overwhelmed with gratitude to God. I fell on my knees and thanked Him. And then, Ruth -"

He paused and looked at her wistfully in pity for the little weak figure that would reel beneath the blow of his words.

"And then what?" she asked quickly.

Gordon lowered his chin and rested it on his hand, while a dreamy tone came into his voice, softening it to its lowest notes, and a trance-like look overspread his face.

"And then I recalled that I had been deceiving you and myself and another. I faced for the first time honestly the fact that I was madly in love with a woman not my wife - "

Ruth went white, gave an inarticulate groan, staggered and sank into a chair near him, sobbing in agony.

"Oh! Frank, for the sake of Jesus, the friend of the weak, who loved little children, whose name you have so often spoken, have mercy on me! Do not tell me any more. I am only a woman - I cannot bear it!"

"But the truth is best, Ruth. You must hear it," he went on

rapidly. "I asked God to forgive me for the wrong I had done you and her. I said I would tear that love out of my soul if it killed me, and be true to my marriage vow. I went there to tell her this and ask her to put the ocean between us. I found that she loved me even as I loved her, and she promised. As I started to leave the house, never to enter it again, I saw the card of the lawyer on her table, and the truth flashed over me that she had made this sacrifice of her fortune - greater than I had dreamed - for me and my work, and that because of this I was leaving her forever. It was more than I could bear or ask her to bear. I faced anew the facts. Our love has grown cold. We are no longer congenial. Your ways have ceased to be mine. It is wrong to love one woman and live with another. We must separate."

"No, no, no, no, Frank, dear, my husband, my love, my own. Not this. You do not mean it!" she groaned, as she sank to the floor, buried her face in her arms and stretched out her hand until her tapering fingers rested on his broad foot.

He bent and took her hand as though to lift her.

Suddenly the fever of her hot fingers trembling with overpowering passion, the moisture of her hand, and the tremor of her convulsed body swept his memory with the pain and rapture of his hour with Kate.

Still holding her fingers, he slipped his watch from his pocket with the other hand and glanced quickly at its face to see if it were time for his return to the Ransom house.

"Come, Ruth, this is very painful to me. You must not humiliate yourself so. You have pride and the heritage of noble blood."

She sprang to her feet and stared at him, with infinite yearning in her eyes, gave a faint cry, half anguish, half despair, and threw herself into his arms, holding him with passionate violence while she smothered his lips and eyes with kisses.

He attempted gently to draw her arms from his neck.

"No, you shall not," she cried, holding him convulsively. "I will not let you go. You are my husband - my own, my love, the hero of my girl's dreams, the father of my babies. I have no pride. I will do anything for you if you will only love me."

"But, Ruth, if I have ceased to love you -"

"Don't, don't say it!" she shrieked, placing her hand on his lips. "I will not hear it. You do love me. This woman has lured you with her devil's beauty, and thrown her spell over your baser nature. Ah, Frank, dear, tell me that you love me! Lie to me as meaner men lie to their women. Such a lie I'll hold an honour before the awful shame of desertion. You cannot humiliate me so. See, dear, I am at your feet. Have mercy on me. Do not ask me to bear more than I can endure. Am I not the mother of your children?"

Gordon frowned and withdrew her arms from his neck.

"All this is very painful, Ruth. You cannot mean it. You know I have tried to be honest. I hate a lie. I could not tell one if I tried. You cannot love me and ask this infamy. I could never lift up my head again as a leader and teacher of men and know I was a wilful liar."

The little figure shivered.

"But, Frank, I can't give you up. It was the touch of your hand, the music of your voice that first awoke my woman's soul. You are my mate. You cannot know the young mother-wonder, pain and joy that thrilled my heart as I first bent over Lucy's face, your dear eyes in hers smiling at me. Our very flesh became one in Nature's miracle of love."

"And yet our lives have somehow drifted apart, Ruth."

"But not so far, dear, as this woman has made you believe," she answered tenderly. "I have been selfish and resentful, but I will make it all up. I will lift up my head and be cheerful - live for you, work for you, think only of you, ask nothing for myself but only your presence and your love."

"But if I have given it to another -"

Again she put her hand on his lips.

"But you have not. It is madness. You could not forget our life. Last night I lay alone in silence, with wide-open eyes, dreaming it all over again. This woman I know is more beautiful than I - three years younger; her hair is gold, mine the raven's. She is fair and full and tall, and I am dark and small; but, Frank, dear, love is more than eyes and hair and lips and form. We have been made one in our flesh and blood and inmost soul. There is no other man than you for me. There is no music save your voice."

"Yet, if you feel this for me, and I thus wait in love on another, how can I live the lie?"

"Can you forget the sunlit days of our past?" she pleaded wistfully. "When you lay on the sands of the beach in old Virginia and held my hand while I read to you, idly dreaming through that wonderful summer before our first-born came sailing into port from God's blue sea! You said I was beautiful then. And you were so tender and gracious in your strength. No other woman can ever be to you this first girl-mother."

Her voice melted into a sob. She tried to go on and bit her swollen lips.

Then she rose quietly, and walked to the window and looked down at the city below, whose roar had drowned the music of her life.

He sat silent, waiting for her to regain her strength. He knew that he had the power of hypnotic suggestion over her in his iron will, and that she was beginning to recognise the inevitable.

She turned and faced him again, the hungry fires in her eyes burning with mystic radiance. A tiny stream of blood ran down from her lip and stood in the dimple of her chin. She drew a delicate lace handkerchief from her bosom and wiped the blood away until it ceased to flow. And then in low accents she said:

"You are going to leave me, my love. I feel the cold chill on my heart. It is God's will; I bow to it. One look into your dear eyes, one last embrace, one farewell kiss, and you will be gone. A little gift I will make you in this, the saddest, lowliest hour my soul has ever known. This handkerchief, stained with blood from lips you have kissed so tenderly in the past - that bled to-day because I tried to keep back the cries of a broken heart. I ask that you keep this as a token of my love."

She handed it to him and Gordon placed it in his pocket with a sigh, brushing a tear from his own eyes.

CHAPTER XIV

THE VOICE OF THE SIREN

Gordon left the house with a lingering look at Ruth's window and turned his face toward Gramercy Park, where another woman was waiting for his footstep.

He had suffered intensely in the scene with his wife. He did not believe it possible that she retained such power over him. He drew a deep breath of relief that it was over. Her pride would come to the rescue; for he knew that with her tenderness she combined strength, and with her delicacy, supreme energy.

The exaltation of his great victory of yesterday welled within him and drowned the sense of pain. It had been the most momentous day of his life. Visions of his Temple with gorgeous dome of gold - rising in the sky from its pile of gleaming marble rose before his fancy. He could hear the peal of the grand organ, the swell of the chorus choir, and the response from five thousand eager faces before him. He was speaking with inspiration as never before. He was leading not a forlorn hope against overwhelming odds, but a triumphant host of free, godlike men and women to certain victory.

He thought of the love that filled the heart of the woman to whom he was hurrying, that she should do this unheard of thing while yet breathing the breath of the capital of Mammon.

And then there stole over him, as oil on slumbering fires, the memory of her kisses, the melting languor of her eyes, the odour of her hair, the fever of her creamy flesh, until his senses reeled as drunk with wine. A smile played about his lips; he quickened his pace, lifted his head high, his nostrils dilated wide; he looked dreamily over the housetops into the sky and saw only the face of a woman.

He was in the grip of superhuman impulses. In the quickened throb of his heart and the rush of his blood was the sweep of subconscious forces of nature playing their role in the cosmic drama of all sentient life, laughing at man's laws, making and unmaking the history of races and worlds.

He was justifying his desires now in his new-found Social philosophy, which he had studied closely since Overman's suggestion of its scope.

He knew instinctively that between these elemental impulses and the Moral Law there was war. He would reconcile them by leading a revolution that should decree a new basis for the Moral Law itself. He would make these very subconscious forces the expression of the highest Moral Law. It suddenly flashed over him that this was the key to the paradox of life. He would be the prophet of the new era, and this beautiful woman his comrade in leadership in the Social Revolution it must bring.

His face flushed with the new enthusiasm, and the glorious autumn day about him seemed one with his spirit. The sky was cloudless with fresh breezes sweeping over the seas from the south.

When he stepped to the downtown platform his eye wandered up and down Twenty-third Street and Sixth Avenue and lingered on rivers of women, below.

His own drama, his million-dollar gift, the enormous sensation it had made in the morning press, had not produced a ripple on this swirling tide of flesh. They crowded the windows filled with feathers and hats, elbowed and jostled one another on the pavements, pushed and squeezed and trampled each other's feet and skirts fighting for standing room around the Monday bargain counters, oblivious of the existence of the spiritual world, church, God, or devil.

Again the ceaseless roar of the city, calm and fierce as the sea, one with its eternity of life, stunned him with its immensity and its indifference. He felt himself once more but an atom lost in the surging tides that beat on these stone pavements, worn by the surge of myriads dead and waiting for the throb of hosts unborn. What did they care? If he were to drop dead that moment, in the morning of his manhood, with the shout of victory on his lips, they would not lift an eye from their gaze on hat or ribbon to watch his funeral cortege trot to the cemetery. A brief obituary and he would be forgotten.

"After all," he mused, "Nature will have her way about this old world and its destiny. Self-development is the first law of life, not self-effacement."

His brow clouded for a moment as he recalled Kate's strange reserve and shrinking at his morning visit. Would she, womanlike, at the last moment contradict herself and withhold the full surrender of life? It was impossible, and yet he felt a vague fear. At any rate, he had burned the bridges behind. His way was clear. He would bring to bear every power he possessed to win her, and in the vanity of his powerful manhood he laughed with the certainty of victory.

When he greeted Kate and bent to kiss her she drew back, blushed and firmly said:

"No; we have had our moments of madness."

And the man smiled.

"I mean it," she said, shaking her head.

"You will change your mind. It's a woman's way. Those moments of bliss, so intense it was pain, when our souls and bodies met in a kiss, have made a new world for you and me."

"But we will keep ourselves pure and unspotted," she answered slowly. "All night I fought this battle alone. Our love is a hopeless tragedy."

"It shall not be so for you, my shining one."

"There are others," she said, nervously clasping her hands, "whose lives are linked with ours. The face of your wife I saw last night will forever haunt me with its pathos. I've seen your children once - so like you, and yet so like her."

"Even so. Life has no meaning now except that you are mine and I am yours."

"But may you not be mine in a nobler way than the cheap surrender to our senses? We can love and suffer and wait. You love me. It is enough."

"But, Kate, my dear, there can be no middle course between right and wrong, a lie and the truth."

She fixed on him an intense look.

"Have you told her?"

"Yes, and we have separated as man and wife. She leaves for Florida for the winter. She has agreed at my request to secure a divorce, and you and I will marry under the new forms of Social freedom. Our union will be a prophecy of the revolution that shall redeem society."

"You are doing a great wrong," she protested, her full red lips drawn with pain. "When I think of your wife and children, of her tears and reproaches, I am sick with fear."

"Perfect love will cast out fear. The world is large. The soul is large. Lift up your head and be yourself. You said to me in this room once you were not afraid."

"Yes; I had not kissed you then, or felt the bliss and agony of your strong arms about me. Now, I am afraid of you" - her voice sank to a tense whisper - "and I am afraid of myself!"

He seized her hand.

"You will take the risk. You are cast in such a mould," he said, with ringing assurance. "You are the chosen one, my dauntless comrade in a holy crusade. We will call womanhood from enslavement to form, ceremony and tradition, in which the brute nature of man has bound her, out and up into her larger self, the mate and equal of man."

She shook her head, and her hair began to fall in waving ringlets about her forehead, temples and neck.

"I am afraid. I cannot permit this sacrifice on your part. You must break with society, your friends, your father, your past, your wife and children. I must brave the sneers of gossip and the tongue of slander. It will destroy your work and end your career."

"It will give it grander scope. Back of the dead forms of the age, the living heart of a new life is beating. It will burst its bounds as surely as the dead limbs in that park will in spring put on their shimmering satin which Nature is now weaving in her mills beneath the sod. You and I will open the doors of the soul and body to a new and wider life. And, after all, the body is the soul. I know it as I drink the madness of your beauty."

"I do not fear the world so much, I shrink from striking a woman a mortal blow. I know what it is to love now," she insisted sadly.

"Ruth and I have grown out of each other's life. Besides, you do not know her. Beneath her little form are caged powers you have not guessed," he replied, with a curious smile. "I groan and bellow in pain until you can hear me a mile. It is my way. She can take her place on the cold slab of a surgeon's table, feel the crash of steel through nerve and muscle and artery without a groan. I might rave, commit suicide or murder in a tempest of passion, but mark my word, she will lift her lithe figure erect and, with soft, even footstep, go her way."

He said this with a ring of tender pride, as though she were his child about whom he was boasting.

"I believe you love her still," Kate said, flushing with a look of surprise.

"You know her love could not live in the fires with which my eyes are consuming you," he said with intensity.

She lowered her gaze and glanced uneasily about as though afraid of him.

"Must the strength of manhood be forever throttled by the impulses and mistakes of youth? Great changes in society are impending. You have felt it. The whole world is trembling at their coming. Changes in the forms of marriage must come that shall give scope for our highest development. I ask you to enter with me into this new world as a comrade pioneer and priestess. We will enter into a marriage so free, so spontaneous no chains shall gall it; and yet in the breadth of its freedom so sweet, so strong, so harmonious it will be a sublime revelation to the world."

"And you think me fit for such priesthood?" she asked. "There are hidden fires beneath this form you deem so fair. I have never known restraint except in the willing slavery of your love. You do not know me - I warn you. I did not know myself until I felt the mad rush of blood from my heart in your arms yesterday. I am afraid of this woman I met for the first time in the wild joy of your kiss."

"I'm not afraid of you," he laughed, springing to his feet and striding toward her.

She trembled at his approach, but did not protest except with a helpless look in her violet eyes.

He stood for a moment towering over her, his feet braced apart, his big hands fiercely locked, his wide chest heaving with the exultant joy of the mastery of her life, his steel-gray eyes sparkling with the insolence of strength.

"We were born for one another," he said, in low, burning tones. "It was for me you were waiting. Lo! I am here, and you are mine. In you I have seen the ideal that haunts every full-grown man's soul, of comradeship in every work, sympathy with every hope, the glory of a perfect body, and perfect faith with perfect freedom."

"And you see all this in me?" she asked earnestly.

"Yes. You are my affinity, nerve answering nerve, thought echoing thought. In our union I see a love so strong, of such utter surrender, of such devotion of intellect, such mystic enthusiasm and physical joy, its waves must break in ecstasy on our souls forever."

She arose with a sigh, looked appealingly at him, and her lips mechanically said:

"It is wrong."

But the man saw the flash of unutterable love in her eyes and the tender smile about her full lips; and laughing aloud, he took her deliberately in his arms.

He kissed a tear from her lashes. A tremor shook her splendid form, she closed her eyes, breathing deeply, slipped her arms around his neck and sighed:

"My darling!"

Thomas Dixon

CHAPTER XV

GOEST THOU TO SEE A WOMAN?

Again Gordon was seated in Overman's library and his single eye was asking some uncomfortable questions.

"I sent for you, Frank, because I discovered by accident, in the office of a newspaper of which I am a stockholder, that some curious things are going on between you and a young woman of your congregation. I put two and two together, and I've guessed the secret of your Temple. There's more behind all this than religious enthusiasm. That gift was not laid on God's altar, but on the altar of one of his little images here below. Out with it. You can't fool me."

"Well, your guess is correct. She gave the money. I love her and she loves me. Ruth will go South for the winter, and we have separated. A divorce will be obtained in due time, and I will marry Miss Ransom under the new forms of Social Freedom, and you will be my best man."

"Not on your life," Overman slowly growled, bringing his enormous jaws together and twisting the muscles of his mouth upward as though he smelled something.

"Can't stand the rustle of a woman's dress?"

"Oh, I might survive. You know they say the only really happy people at a wedding are the old bachelors."

"Then why not?"

"I draw the line at the progressive harem idea."

"And a bachelor?" Gordon sneered.

Overman nodded. "Many things may be forgiven sinners, but a bishop must be the husband of one wife."

"I'm not a bishop. I'm a man. I ask no quarter of my enemies."

"You have but one enemy. You can see him in the mirror any time."

"It's funny to hear you preach!"

The banker bent forward.

"Frank, you're joking. You don't mean to tell me that your Socialist poppy plant has borne its opium fruit so soon? That you are going to desert that charming little woman, shy, timid and tremulous, with her great soulful eyes, the bride of your youth, the mother of your babes, and take up with another woman, just as any ordinary cur has done now and then for the past four thousand years?"

Gordon winced.

"No. I am going to form a union with this beautiful woman which shall be a prophecy and a propaganda of the freedom of the race, when comrade life shall forget the ancient fears, each shall be free to find and love his own, love be loosed from tragedy, doubt or moan, each life be its own, original and masterful, each man a god, arrayed and beautiful!"

Overman laughed softly.

"So fine as that? You're great on the frills. You have dressed it up nicely. But when two of your man-gods, arrayed and beautiful, get their eyes, set on the same woman-god, still more beautiful, arrayed or unarrayed, you'll hear the rattle of the police wagon in the streets of Heaven, with the ambulance close behind."

The banker grinned and fixed his eye on his friend with a quizzical look.

"Don't be a monkey," Gordon scowled.

"Why not? You propose to go back to forest life."

"I propose to make human society a vast brotherhood," the preacher cried, with a wave of his arm.

"Well, don't forget that Cain killed his brother Abel for less than a woman's smile."

"Society is lost unless some great upheaval shall clear the rubbish and we build new foundations on truth and fellowship and freedom."

Overman put his hand on Gordon's knee.

"Frank, I'm a godless, crusty bachelor, but I read history. Destroy the integrity of the family and the salt of the earth is lost. The whole thing will rot."

"But I propose to purify and glorify the home its life by building it on love."

"Your dream's a fake and its world peopled with fools."

"Love must conquer all," the dreamer insisted.

"And to do it, Frank, it must begin at home. You are blinded by a woman's beauty."

"No; I love her with the one master passion of manhood. Such love is itself the highest expression of life."

"Confound you," snapped Overman, "love as many women as you please, but don't desert your wife and children. It's too vulgar. I'm ashamed of you."

"I will not live a lie," Gordon said, with emphasis.

"Strange madness. I urge you to tell a tiny little polite lie and save your wife and children. You're too good to lie, so you kill your wife, proclaim an insane crusade of lust, and call it a religion!"

"We can't control the beat of our hearts," was the dreamy reply.

"No, you can't; but you can control the stroke of your big, blue-veined fist! You have struck the mother of your children with your brute claws. It's a mean, low thing to do, call it by as many high names as you please. Love as many women as you like, but for decency's sake - can't you honour your wife with a polite lie?"

"It's not in me to lie, or to love but one woman."

The banker's massive shoulders went up and his bushy brows lifted.

"You'll end with a dozen, and it's such a stupid old story. You think the performance an original drama in which you are playing a star role. It's as old as the brute beneath the skin of your big hairy hand. Alexander could conquer the world, but he died in drunken revelry with a worthless woman. Caesar and Mark Antony forgot the Roman Empire for the smile of Cleopatra. Frederick the Great became a puppet in the hands of a ballet dancer. She spoke and he obeyed. Conde, in the meridian of his splendid manhood, the pride and glory of France, sacrificed his family, his fortune and his friends for an adventuress, who murdered him. Charles Stewart Parnell, the uncrowned king of Ireland, forgot his people and stumbled into death and oblivion over the form of a woman. The hills and valleys of the centuries are white with the bones of these fools."

"There was never a case just like mine."

"So every fool thought."

"But you have not seen this woman. You do not know her," Gordon protested, hotly.

"No; and I don't want to know her. 'Goest thou to see a woman? Take thy whip!' Women, savages and children are inferior and immature forms of evolution. But they are going to prove more than a match for you, my boy."

"Yes; I've heard you talk such rubbish before," Gordon replied, dreamily. "Mark, I'm sorry for the poverty of your life. The man who has not loved is not a man. He is a monstrosity out of touch of sympathy with the race. You cannot understand me when I tell you that our love is so pure, so wonderful, so perfect, it is its own defense."

"Indeed! Which love? For Ruth or Kate? Frank, I marvel at the childlike simplicity of your folly and your mental antics to justify it. It's enough to make that cat laugh that broke up your sermon."

"We are going to bear in our union and life the flaming standard of a revolution that will yet redeem society."

"I admire your ingenuity. Just a plain rooster-fighting sinner like me would never have thought of making his sin a holy religion. You haven't studied theology for nothing. I'll bet you could argue the devil or the Archangel Michael to a standstill on any proposition you'd set your heart on."

The preacher smiled.

"I never saw my course with greater clearness."

"Yes; but a nail in the pilot-house will draw the needle and drive the mightiest ocean greyhound on the rocks with the captain at the wheel dead sure of his course."

"Mark, it's utterly useless to talk. You and I are miles apart at our starting-point and we get farther with every step. You look at it from the vulgar point of view of the world. What I am doing is a great act of the soul, a breaking of bonds and chains. You see only the body. I am going to lead a crusade that shall so purify and exalt the body that it shall become one with the soul. The freedom of man can only be attained in unfettered fellowship, and this beautiful woman will be with me a comrade priestess to teach the world this sublime truth."

"And will you be the only priest with her in the Temple of Humanity?" asked the banker, quizzically.

Gordon laughed with insolent assurance.

"In her eyes, yes."

"But other men have eyes."

"Their gaze will not disturb the serenity of our love, because it will be built on oneness of ideal, hope, faith, taste and work."

"And yet dark hair loves the blond, and blue eyes hunger for the brown. It's an old trick Nature has played before, Frank."

"Well, we are going to show you a miracle, and you are coming with us by and by and be a deacon in this Church of the Son of Man."

Overman drew his straight bushy brow down over his one eye until it looked like the gleam of a lighthouse through the woods, turned his head sideways, peered at his friend and growled:

Thomas Dixon

"Well, you are a fool!"

"I have faith that will remove mountains."

"You'll need it. I've been waiting for a church in New York broad enough to invite the devil to join. I'll come when it's ready."

"Good. We'll give you a welcome."

Overman grunted, and gazed into the fire with his single eye, frowning and twisting the muscles of his mouth into a sneer.

CHAPTER XVI

THE PARTING

The night before the day Gordon had fixed for their final parting Ruth slept but little. The task of gathering his things scattered about the house was harder than she had hoped.

Over each little trinket that spoke its message of the tender intimacy of married life she had lingered and cried. She wished to keep everything.

At last she placed the clothes in his trunk, his collars, cuffs, cravats and such odds and ends as he would need at once, and the rest she packed away carefully in bureau drawers and locked them up.

His slippers and dressing-gowns she knew he would want, but she made up her mind she would keep them. The slippers were an old-fashioned pattern with quaint Spanish embroidery worked around the edges. She had made the first pair before they were married, with her girl's heart fluttering with new-found happiness. She had allowed him no other kind since their marriage. This bit of sentiment she had guarded even in the darkest days of the past year's estrangement. She had worked each pair with her own hand.

His dressing-gowns, in which he often studied at home in her room late on Saturday nights, she had always made for him, changing their designs from time to time as her fancy had led her.

Around these two articles of his wardrobe her very heart-strings seemed woven.

She placed them in his trunk once, telling herself through her tears:

"He may think of me when he sees them."

Then the lightning flashed across the clouds in her eyes.

"She might touch them! Let her make them for him after her own devil's fancy!"

She took them out, kissed them and packed them away. His picture she took down carefully from the walls, his photographs from her mantel and bureau and dresser. The life-sized one she locked in a closet and packed the others with his belongings she meant to keep.

On a wedding certificate, set in a quaint old gold frame, she looked long and tenderly. She took it down from its place over her bureau, where it had hung for years, and brushed the dust from the back. On its broad white margins he had written a poem to her on the birth of their first baby. He had sent her yards of rhymes during their courtship, but this was a poem. Every line was wet with his tears, and every thought throbbed with the sweetest music of his soul wrought to its highest tension of feeling.

She read it over and over again and cried as though her heart would break as a thousand tender memories came stealing back from their early married life.

"Oh, dear God!" she sobbed. "How could he have felt that - and he did feel it - and now desert me!"

She sat for an hour with this framed emblem of her happiness and her sorrow in her hands, dreaming of their past.

She was a girl again in old Hampton, Virginia, her heart all a-quiver over a ball at the Hygeia, where she was to meet a guest, a distinguished young preacher resting for the summer just from his divinity course. He had seen her in the crowd at the hotel and begged a friend to introduce him. She was going to meet him in the parlours, dressed in the splendour of her ballroom dress that night, and conquer this handsome young giant. And from the moment they met, she was the conquered, and he the conqueror.

The incense of their honeymoon in a village of southern Indiana during his first pastorate, when the wonder of love made storm days bright with splendour and clothed in beauty the meanest clod of earth, stole over her soul - each memory added to her pain, and yet they were sweet. She hugged them to her heart.

"They are all mine at least!" she sighed. "And I am glad I have lived them."

At two o'clock she went into the nursery and looked at the sleeping children. She bent over the cradle of the boy. He was dreaming, and a smile was playing about the corners of his lips.

He was so like Gordon, with his little mouth twitching in dreamy laughter, she fell on her knees, and buried her face in her delicate tapering hands, crying:

"How can I bear it!"

She placed her arms on the rail of the cradle and gazed at him tenderly.

"Lord, keep him clean and pure, and whatever he may do in life, may he never break a woman's heart!" she softly prayed.

Into her first-born's face she looked long and in silence. How like her, and how like him, and how marvelous the miracle of this union of flesh and blood and spirit in a living soul! Lucy was growing more like her every day. She could see and hear herself in her ways and voice, until she would laugh aloud sometimes at the memory of her own childhood. And yet to see her very self growing into the startling image of her lover who was deserting her cut anew with stinging power.

Again she was softly praying: "Dear Lord, whatever shall come to her, poverty or riches, joy or pain, honour or shame, sunshine or shadow, save her from this. My feet will climb this Calvary, and my lips drink its gall, but may the cup pass from her!"

After a few hours of fitful sleep, she rose and looked out her window on another radiant November morning. So clear was the sky she could see the flag-staffs of the great downtown buildings and back of them in the distant bay the pennant masts of ships at anchor. The trees in Central Park seemed to glow with the splendour of the dying autumn's sun. The glory of the day mocked her sorrow.

"What does Nature care?" she sighed. "And yet who knows, it may be a token! I must bravely play my part and leave the rest with God."

Watching at the window she saw Gordon coming, his broad feet measuring a giant's stride, his wide shoulders and magnificent head high with unconscious strength.

She wondered if he would stop in the parlour as a visitor or come to her room as was his custom, and a sharp pain cut her with the thought of their changed relationship.

He stopped in the hall, asked the maid to send the children down at once, and stepped into the parlour.

He felt a strange embarrassment in his own home. This house he had bought for Ruth soon after their arrival in New York. It had just been built in the wide-open space of the cliffs on Washington Heights. The Pilgrim Church's members were long since scattered over every quarter of the city, and, by arranging his study in the church, he was able to have his home so far removed from the noise of the downtown district. He had thus fulfilled Ruth's passionate desire for a home of her own within their moderate means. He recalled now with tender melancholy how happy they had been decorating this little nest, and how far from his wildest dream had been such an ending of it all.

But he had come with important news, and he hoped her pain would be softened by its announcement.

The children entered with shouts of delight. First one would hug him, and then the other, and then both would try at the same time.

Lucy put her hands on his smooth ruddy cheeks and kissed his lips and eyes with the quaintest imitation of her mother's trick of gesture.

"Where have you been, Papa? We thought you were never coming? Mama said you were gone for a trip and would come to-day, but" - her voice sank - "she's been crying, and crying, and we don't know what's the matter. I'm so glad you've come."

"Well, you and brother run upstairs to play and tell her Papa wishes to see her."

The children left and Ruth came down at once.

As she entered the room, he was struck by the change in her face and manner. She seemed transfigured by a strange, spiritual elation. She was gracious, natural and friendly. The anxiety had passed from her face, and the storm in her dark eyes seemed stilled by a steady radiance from the soul.

"I'm glad to see you looking better, Ruth," he said, with feeling.

"Yes, I have a new standard now of measuring life, its pain and its joy. The soul can only pass once through such a moment as that I lived, prostrate on the floor at your feet last Monday. I have looked Death in the face. I am no longer afraid."

"I am very, very sorry to give you such pain. I did not think you cared so deeply," he said, gently.

"Yes, I know I have seemed indifferent and resentful for the past year. I thought you would come back to your old self by and by. In my poor proud soul I thought I was punishing you. How little, dear, I dreamed of this! The thought of really losing you never once entered my heart. It was unthinkable. I do not believe it yet. Such love as ours, such tenderness and devotion as you gave to me once, the delirium of love's joy that found itself in my motherhood and wrought itself in the forms of our babies - no, Frank, it cannot die, unless God dies! And I shall not lose you at last, unless God forgets me, and He will not."

Her face, even through her tears, was illumined by an assurance so strong, so prophetic, the man was startled.

"I need not tell you, Ruth, that I desire your happiness. And, strange as it may seem to you, Miss Ransom regards you with tenderness."

The dark eyes flashed a gleam of lightning from their depths.

"Thanks. I can live without her maudlin pity."

"You misjudge her," he cried, raising his hand.

"Perhaps; but I'll ask you, Frank, not to dishonour me, or this little home you were once good enough to give to me, by mentioning that woman's name within its doors again."

The sensitive mouth closed with an emphasis he could not mistake.

"But I am the bearer from her to-day of a token of her regard. She has determined to turn over to you as quickly as possible a half-million dollars of her remaining fortune."

Ruth sprang to her feet, her face scarlet, her breast heaving, her lithe figure erect and trembling.

"And you dare bring this message to me? This offer to sell my husband and my love!"

"Come, come, Ruth, a woman has no need to sacrifice a great fortune in New York for a husband. They are cheaper than that."

"They do seem cheap," she answered, bitterly.

"You should have common sense. The spirit of sacrifice in this great gift to you and the children is too deep and honest to be met with a sneer. It is my desire and hers that you shall be forever beyond want."

Ruth's face softened and a tender smile lit it once more.

"Frank, my darling, you cannot think me so base? You know there is not a drop of mean blood in me. Can gold pay for my heart's desire? The price for my beloved? Pile the earth with diamonds to the stars, I'd hold it trash for the touch of your hand!"

The man moved nervously.

"You must have some sense, Ruth. Surely, I'm not worth all this if I leave you so. You must take this money."

She moved closer to him and held up her delicate hands, with the sunlight gleaming through the red blood of her tapering fingers.

"You see these hands? They have only known the gentle tasks of love. Well, I'll scrub, sew and wash the clothes of working-men before one dollar of her gold shall stain them!"

"You cannot be so foolish," he protested, impatiently. "Besides, she has given me this money to give to you."

"Ah, my love," she went on, as though she had not heard his last words, "if you were frankly evil as other men, I might bear this shame with better grace. Others before me, as good as I, have borne its burden. But when I think that you are making your sin a religion, and that you are going to preach with the zeal of a prophet this gospel of the brute and call it freedom, how can I bear it?"

They were both silent for a moment.

"Let us change this disgusting subject, Frank," she said at length. "I wish you to leave with something kindlier to remember in my face than this shadow. You see, I have taken your pictures all down and locked them up. I have placed your clothes, all I could spare, in your trunk - for even these little things to me are heart treasures now. I could not let you take the slippers I have made for you with my own hands, or your dressing-gowns. That woman shall never touch them. The marriage certificate, with the little poem written to me on the birth of Lucy, I've packed up, too, with your pictures. I've put them away, because, just now, it would break my heart to look at them after this parting with you. When I come back from the South I will be stronger, and I will bring them out again. Your ring is mine until God's hand shall take it. I'll teach our babies always to love you."

Her voice broke, and he looked away.

"I will tell them that you have gone on a long journey into a strange country, and that you will come back again because you love them."

He stirred uneasily in his chair, crossed his legs and frowned.

"And I wish you to leave me to-day with the certainty - you can read it in my eyes, if you doubt my lips - that I will love you to the end, though you kill me. You can go on no journey so long, in no world so strange, that I shall not follow. My soul will envelop you. For better, for worse, through evil report and good report, I am yours."

Again a convulsive sob shook her, and she was silent.

Gordon felt an almost resistless impulse to take her in his arms and kiss and soothe her.

Through her tears she smiled at him.

"How beautiful you are, my dear! You will not forget that I love you? The spring, the summer, the autumn, the winter will only bring to me messages from our past. The way will be lonely, but the memory of the touch of your hand, our hours of perfect peace and trustfulness, the sweetness of your kisses on my lips, the living pictures of your face in our children, I will cherish."

He stooped to kiss her as he left, but she drew back trembling.

"No, Frank, not while your lips are warm with the touch of another and your flesh on fire with desire for her. It will be sweet to remember that you wished it - for I know, what you do not, that deep down in your soul of souls you love me. I will abide God's time."

He left her with a smile playing around her sensitive mouth and lighting the shadows of her great dark eyes.

CHAPTER XVII

THE THOUGHT THAT SWEEPS THE CENTURY

On the Saturday following Gordon's drama with Kate and his wife, his dream of secrecy was rudely shattered. Van Meter's ferret eyes, by the aid of his detectives, had fathomed the mystery of Kate Ransom's appearance in the study and her more mysterious disappearance.

They found that Gordon had separated from his wife, after a terrific scene; that he was a daily visitor to the Ransom house; and that his great patron was none other than the young mistress of the Gramercy Park mansion.

All day long he was beseiged by reporters. Ruth was compelled to hire a man to stand on the doorstep to keep them out. The Ransom house was barred, but Gordon could not escape.

He saw at once that they knew so much it was useless to make denials, and he prepared a statement for the press, giving the facts and his plans for the future in a ringing address. He submitted it to Kate for her approval, and at three o'clock gave it out for publication.

Their love secret had not been fathomed, but it had been guessed. He feared the reports would be so written that it would be read between the lines and a great deal more implied.

His revolutionary views on marriage and divorce and the fact that he was from Indiana, a state that had granted the year before nearly five thousand divorces, one for every five marriages celebrated, - were made the subject of special treatment by one paper. They submitted to him proofs of a six-column article on the subject, and asked for his comments. He was compelled to either deny or repeat his utterances advocating freedom of divorce, and finally was badgered into admitting that this feature was one of the fundamental tenets of Socialism.

He was not ready for the full public avowal of this principle, but he was driven to the wall and was forced to own it or lie. He boldly gave his position, and declared that marriage was a fetish, and that its basis on a union for life without regard to the feelings of the parties was a fountain of corruption, and was the source of the monopolistic instincts that now cursed the human race.

"Yes, and you can say," he cried, "that I propose to lead a crusade for the emancipation of women from the degradation of its slavery. Love bound by chains is not love. Love can only be a reality in Freedom and Fellowship."

This single sentence had changed the colouring of the whole story as it appeared in the press on Sunday morning, and was the key to the tremendous sensation it produced.

The next day long before the hour of service the street in front of the Pilgrim Church was packed with a dense crowd.

The police could scarcely clear the way for the members' entrance. Within ten minutes from the time the large doors were opened every seat was filled and hundreds stood on the pavements outside, waiting developments, unable to gain admission.

So many statements had been made, and so many vicious insinuations hinted, Gordon was compelled to lay aside his sermon and devote the entire hour to a defense of his position.

The crowd listened in breathless stillness, but he knew from the first he had lost their sympathies and that he was on trial. Unable to tell the whole truth, his address was as lame and ineffective as his outburst the Sunday before had been resistless. When he dismissed the crowd he noticed that some of his warmest friends were crying.

As he came down from the pulpit, Ludlow took him by the hand and, with trembling voice, said:

"Pastor, you know how I love you?"

What he did not say was more eloquent than a thousand words, and it cut Gordon to his inmost soul. He knew his failure had been pathetic, and that his enemies were laughing over the certainty of his ruin.

It angered him for a moment as he looked over the silent crowd filing out of his presence and out of his life.

He cursed their stolid conservatism.

"The average man does not aspire to liberty of thought," he mused with bitterness, "but slavery of thought. The mob must have its fixed formulas easy to read, requiring no thought. Well, let them go."

Suddenly a confused murmur, with loud voices mingled, came through the doors of the vestibules. The exits were blocked, and the moving crowd halted and recoiled on itself as if hurled back by the charge of an opposing army, and a cheer echoed over their heads.

The people inside, who had been halted, stretched their necks to see over the heads of those in front, crying:

"What is it?"

"What's the matter?"

"It sounds like a riot," some one answered near doors.

Gordon wedged himself through the mass that had been thrown back on the advancing stream and reached the door-way. He was astonished to find packed in the street more than five thousand men, evidently working-men and Socialists. They had been quick to recognise his position in the vigorous statement he had given to the press.

When Gordon's giant figure appeared between the two opposing forces a wild cheer rent the air.

A Socialist leaped on the steps beside him and, lifting his hat above his head, cried:

"Now again, men, three times three for a dauntless leader, a free man in the image of God, who dares to think and speak the truth!"

Three times the storm rolled over the sea of faces, and every hat was in the air.

Gordon lifted his big hand and the tumult hushed.

"My friends, I thank you for this mark of your fellowship. At the old Grand Opera House, next Sunday morning, the seats will be yours. You will get a comrade's welcome. I will have something to say to you that may be worth your while to hear."

The crowd, who had never seen or heard him, were impressed by his magnificent presence and his trumpet voice. They liked its clear ringing tones and its consciousness of power.

The unexpected demonstration restored his self-respect and blotted out the aching sense of failure.

His few words were greeted with tumultuous applause, renewed again and again. The air was charged with the electric thrill of their enthusiasm.

Gordon looked over the seething mass of excited men with exultant response.

He flushed and his big fists involuntarily closed. He had felt in his face the breath of the spirit that is driving the century before it.

CHAPTER XVIII

A VOICE FROM THE PAST

From a college town in Indiana the aged father, William Gordon, Professor Emeritus of History and Belles Lettres, hurried to New York to see his son.

When he read the Sunday morning papers, which reached him about three o'clock, he pooh-poohed the wild reports the Associated Press had sent out from New York announcing the separation from Ruth and linking his son's name in vulgar insinuations with another woman.

He hastened to find the telegraph operator, and got him to open the office. He sent a long telegram to Frank, urging on him the importance of correcting these slanderous reports immediately.

He walked about the town to see his friends and explain to them.

"It's all a base slander," he said, drawing himself up proudly. "My son's success has been so phenomenal, he has made bitter enemies. The press has published these lies out of malice. His popularity is the cause of it. I have wired him. He will correct it immediately."

But when he failed to receive a denial, and the Monday's press confirmed the facts with embellishments, he quietly left home

Thomas Dixon

and hastened to New York.

He was a man of striking personality, a little taller than his distinguished son, six feet four and a half inches in height. Now, in his eighty-fifth year, he still walked with quick, nervous step, and held himself erect with military bearing. His face was smooth and ruddy, and his voice, in contrast with his enormous body, was keen and penetrating. When he rose in a church assembly his commanding figure, with its high nervous voice, caught every eye and ear and held them to the last word.

He was the most popular man that had ever occupied a chair in the faculty of Wabash College. He taught his classes regularly until he was eighty years old, and when he quit his active work he was still the youngest man in spirit in the institution. He read with avidity every new book on serious themes, and he was not only the best read man in the college town - he was the best informed man on history and philosophy in the state, if not in the entire West. He had the gift of sympathy with the mind of youth that fascinated every boy who came in contact with him. His genial and beautiful manners, his high sense of honour, the knightly deference he paid his students, his enthusiasm in the pursuit of knowledge, his quenchless thirst for truth, were to them a source of boundless admiration and loyalty.

The one supreme passion of his age was love for his handsome son and pride in his achievements. He had married late in life, and Frank's mother had died in giving him birth. The tragedy had crushed him for a year and he went abroad, leaving the child with a nurse. But on his return he gave to the laughing baby, with the blond curling hair of his mother, all the tenderness of his love for the dead, and his sorrow tinged his whole after life with sweetness and romance.

The only evidence of advancing age was his absentmindedness from boylike brooding over the days of his courtship and marriage and his day dreams about his long-lost love. He recognised it at once and laid down his class work.

Gordon met him at the Grand Central Depot with keenest dread and embarrassment. Hurrying out of the crowd, they boarded a downtown car on Fourth Avenue.

The old man glanced uneasily about and said:

"Son, isn't this car going down the avenue?"

"Yes, father. We are going to my hotel."

"Hotel? I don't want to go to a hotel. I want to go to your house. I want to see Ruth and the children at once."

"We'll go to my study at the church first, then, and I'll explain to you."

The old man's brow wrinkled, and he pressed his lips tightly together to keep them from trembling.

Gordon was glad he had not yet given orders for the removal of his study, and when they entered he drew the lid of his roll-top desk down quickly, that his father might not see Kate's picture where he had once seen Ruth's.

"Of course, my boy," the old man began, "I know there is some terrible mistake about this. I told my friends so at the College. But I couldn't wait for a letter, and I couldn't somehow understand your telegram. I'm getting a little old now, so I hurried on to see you. I'm sure if you and Ruth have quarreled you can make up and begin over again. Lovers' quarrels are not so serious."

"No, father, our separation is final."

The old man raised his hand in protest.

"Nonsense, boy, you have an iron will and Ruth a fiery temper, but a more lovable and beautiful spirit was never born than your wife. I was so proud of her when you brought her home! Of all the women in the world, I felt she was The One Woman God had meant for the mother of your children. In every way, mentally and physically, she is your complement and mate. Your differences only make the needed contrast for perfect happiness."

"But we have drifted hopelessly apart, father,"

"My son, the man and woman whom God hath made one in the beat of a child's heart cannot get hopelessly apart. It's a physical and moral impossibility. Do you mean to tell me that if your mother had lived after your birth, and we had bowed together over your cradle, height or depth, things past, present or to come, or any other creature, could have torn us asunder? You must make up this foolish quarrel. You must be patient with her little jealousies. It's natural she should feel them when you are the centre of so many flattering eyes."

Gordon saw it was useless to avoid the heart of the difficulty. So with all the earnestness and eloquence he could command he told his father the history of Kate Ransom's work in the church, the growth of their love, the drifting apart from Ruth, and the final dramatic climax of the day that she gave the money to build the Temple.

The old man with fine courtesy listened attentively, now and then brushing away a tear, and sighing.

"And so, father," he concluded, "a divorce is the only possible end of it all."

"And what has Ruth to say?" he asked, pathetically.

"She has accepted the situation, and at my request will bring the suit."

"And you will marry this other woman while Ruth lives?"

"Yes, father, and our union will be a prophecy of a redeemed society in which love, fellowship, Comradeship and brother-hood shall become the laws of life."

The old man's brow wrinkled in pain.

"But the family at which you aim this blow, my son, is the basis of all law, state, national, and international. It is the unit of society, the basis of civilisation itself. To destroy it is to return to the beast of the field."

"It must be modified in the evolution of human freedom, father."

"But, my son, it is the law of the Lord, and the law of the Lord is perfect!" the old man cried, with his voice quivering with anguish and yet in it the triumphant ring of the prophet and seer.

"Yes, father, your view of the law," the younger man quietly answered.

"My boy, since man has written the story of his life, saint and seer, statesman and chieftain, philosopher and poet have all agreed on this. There can be nothing more certain than that my view is true."

"Just as men have agreed on delusions and traditions in theology, but you now see as clearly as I how foolish many of these things are."

"But, my son, new theology or old theology, Bible or no Bible, Heaven or no Heaven, Hell or no Hell, God or no God, it is right to do right!" Again his high nervous voice rang like a silver trumpet.

"I am trying to do right."

"Yet greater wrong than this can no man do on earth - lead, captivate the soul and body of a gracious and innocent girl, teach her the miracle of love in motherhood, and then desert her for a fairer and younger face."

"But, father, I cannot live a lie."

"Then you will cherish, honour, love and protect your wife until death; and the old marriage ceremony read, 'until death us depart.' Your vow is eternal and goes beyond the physical incident of death itself."

"Yet how can I control the beat of my heart? We must go back to the reality of Nature and her eternal laws, in spite of illusions and theories," maintained the younger man.

"Ah, my boy, these things you call illusions I call the great faiths of our fathers, the revelation of God. Call them what you will, even if we say they are illusions, they are blessed illusions. They are the steel bars behind which we have caged the crouching, blind and silent forces of nature, fierce, savage and cruel as death."

His voice sank to a whisper, he leaned over and placed his trembling hand on Gordon's arm and added:

"I once felt the impulse to kill a man. It was natural, elemental and all but overpowering. Remember that civilisation itself is impossible without tradition. I know that progress is made only by its modification in growth. But growth is not destruction, and progress is never backward to beast or savage. Marriage is not a mere convention between a man and a woman, subject to the whim of either party. It is a divine social ordinance on which the structure of human civilisation has been reared. It cannot be broken without two people's consent and the consent of society, and then only for great causes which have destroyed its meaning."

"But I have begun to question, father, whether our civilisation is civilised and worth preserving?"

"And would you civilise it by giving free rein to impulses of nature that are subconscious, that lead direct to the reign of lust and murder? Is not man more than brute? Has he not a soul? Is the spirit a delusion? Ah, my boy, do you doubt my love?"

"I know that you love me."

"Yes, with a love you cannot understand. You can touch no depths to which I will not follow with that love. But I'd rather a thousand times see you cold in death than hear from your lips the awful words you have spoken in this room here this morning with the face of Jesus looking down upon us from your walls."

He seemed to sink into a stupor for several moments, and was silent as he gazed into the glowing grate.

At length he said:

"You must take me to your house. I will spend a few days with Ruth and the children."

Gordon could not face the meeting between his father and Ruth. He accompanied him to the door and gently bade him good-by, promising to call the next day.

A singularly beautiful love the old man had bestowed on Ruth, and she on him; for he was resistless to all the young. When he kissed her as Frank's bride he seemed to have first fully recovered his spirits from the shadows of his own tragedy. In her great soft eyes with the lashes mirrored in their depths, her dimpled chin and sensitive mouth, her refined and timid nature, the grace and delicacy of her footsteps, he saw come back into life his own lost love. Above all, he was fascinated by her spiritual charm, haunting and vivid. He had never tired of boasting of his son's charming little wife, and he loved her with a devotion as deep as that he gave his own flesh and blood.

When she entered the room, in spite of his efforts at control, he burst into tears as he kissed her tenderly and slipped his arm softly around her.

"Ruth, my sweet daughter!" he sobbed.

"Father, dear!"

"You must cheer up, my little one; I've come to help you."

"You must not take it so hard, father. It will all come out for the best. God is not dead; He will not forget me. I'm a tiny mite in body, but you know I've a valiant soul. You must cheer up."

She led him gently to a seat.

"I'll bring the children now; they'll be wild with joy when I tell them grandfather is here."

But at the sight of the children the old man broke completely down and sat with his great head sunk on his breast.

He drew Ruth down and whispered:

"Take them away, dear. It's too much. I - can't see them now."

When she returned from the nursery, he said:

"Come, Ruth, sit beside me and tell me about it, and I'll see my way clearer how to help you."

She drew a stool beside his chair, leaned her head against his knee, took one of his hands in hers, and, while his other stroked her raven hair, she gently and without reproach told him all.

When she had finished, his eyes were heavy with grief beyond the power of tears.

"And my boy told you to - take - this - money, Ruth?" he slowly and sorrowfully asked.

"Yes, father."

"Do you know an honest lawyer, dear?"

"Yes; an old friend of mine, Morris King."

"Call him over your telephone immediately, and take me to your desk. My fortune is not large, as the world reckons wealth - perhaps fifty thousand dollars carefully saved during the past thirty years of frugal living. It shall be yours, my dear."

"But, father, you must not take it from yourself in your age!"

"Are you not my beloved daughter? And do not your babies call me grandfather? It's such a poor little thing I can do. I've enough in bank to last me to the journey's end, and I'll stay near to watch over you. I can have no other home now."

The lawyer came within an hour, and the will was duly witnessed.

He handed it to Ruth and she kissed and thanked him.

He wandered about the house in a helpless sort of way for half an hour, sighing. His great shoulders for the first time in his long life lost their military bearing and drooped heavily.

Ruth watched him pace slowly back and forth with his hands folded behind him, his head sunk in a stupor of dull pain, wondering what she could do or say to cheer him, when he suddenly stopped and sank into a heap on the floor.

The doctor came and shook his head.

"He may regain consciousness, Mrs. Gordon, but he cannot live."

Ruth called the hotel and summoned Frank. He was out and did not get the message until five o'clock. When he reached the house, she was by the bedside. The old man was holding her hand and talking in a half-delirious way to his friends, explaining to them how impossible that these wild reports could be true about his son.

Soon after Gordon came he regained consciousness. Taking him by the hand he said:

"Well, my boy, my work is done. I have fought a good fight. I have kept the faith. I love you always. You will not forget - right or wrong, you are my heart's blood and your mother's, dearer to me than life. When I go from this lump of clay, if you will open my breast you will find an old man's broken heart, and across the rent your name will be written in the ragged edges. How handsome you are to-night! How fair a lad you were! Such face and form and high-strung soul, the heart of an ancient knight come back to earth, I used to boast! God's grace is wonderful, His ways past finding out. When we seem forsaken, He is but preparing larger blessings on some grander plan whose end we do not see. He is my shepherd; I shall not want. He leadeth me - I rest in Him."

As the twilight wrapped the great city in its gray shadows, slowly deepening into night, he fell asleep.

CHAPTER XIX

THE WEDDING OF THE ANNUNCIATION

At the end of a year from the death of Gordon's father the divorce was granted, and Ruth elected to retain her married name.

The Temple of Man was rapidly rising. The building fronted three hundred feet on each cross street. Its great steel-ribbed dome, modeled on the capitol at Washington, was slowly climbing into the sky from the centre to dominate the architecture of the Metropolitan district.

The success of Gordon's meetings in the old Grand Opera House had been enormous. Its four thousand seats were filled and every inch of standing-room the police would allow. The religious element in Socialism had found in him its high priest. His eloquence, his magnetism, his daring, his aggressive and radical instinct for leadership made him at once their idol.

The prestige given him by the rapid building of his magnificent Temple in the heart of the wealth and splendour of the Metropolis, and the crush for admission by strangers who had read of him and his work, were adding daily to his power.

His bold avowal of love for Kate Ransom, and his determination to win and marry her by a new ceremony of "announcement," which should challenge the forms of civilisation, had stilled the tongue of gossip and made him the hero of the sentimental.

At the same time it had made him the object of bitter attack by the conservative forces of society, and the violence of these attacks daily added importance to his every act.

His triumphant appeal to the masses against the classes was making him a master spirit of the modern mob that has humbled king, emperor and pope, at whose breath statesmen tremble, and at whose feet coward and sycophant of every cult cringe and fawn.

With fierce enthusiasm he proclaimed, "Now is Eternity. To reach Heaven we must build a new earth, and lo! we are in Heaven."

The response from sullen working-men who had hitherto held aloof from Socialism and its leaders was remarkable. With the fiery zeal of the pioneer of a religious movement he preached in season and out of season his new faith, and proselyted with success even among those who scoffed.

He gave a new emphasis to the dogma of the Immanence of God, the charming Pantheism of which appealed to the childlike minds of the people. With mystic fervour he proclaimed the unity of life, and in all and over all and working through all - God! In bud and flower, in sun and storm, in dewdrop and star, in man and beast, in soul and body, the divine everywhere. As never before he glorified the body and its beauty as the incarnation of God, His veritable image. The advent of every child he hailed as great a miracle as the birth of the Babe of Bethlehem.

Life itself became an ever-growing wonder, and existence an infinite joy. Gradually he began to ridicule the theology of "Sin." "Sin" he declared a figment of the human mind. The sin which is the wilful and persistent violation of known law he ignored.

He proclaimed the advent of the Kingdom of Love universal, all embracing, all conquering.

His marriage to Kate Ransom by the new ceremony he had devised commanded the attention of the world. Its romance, and the tragedy of a broken heart behind it, at once interested the average mind; and its social and religious challenge appealed to the thoughtful.

It was announced to be a marriage without form or ceremony. It was celebrated on a Saturday evening, that his friends among the working-men might attend.

It was early in May. The grass was green behind the high iron bars of Gramercy Park, and the trees were putting on their new satin robes. The air was warm with the sensuous languor of spring. The rain poured in torrents, but the Ransom mansion was a blaze of light, and a canopy with rubber roof stretched down the high brownstone steps across the sidewalk to the curbing.

It was past the appointed time, the last carriage had long since snapped its silver lock beside the awning, and still the bride and groom tarried. The guests were assembled in the great parlours, and a band in the conservatory, from which floated the perfume of flowers in full bloom, was softly playing primitive love melodies, simple, tender and full of. mysterious beauty.

Besides the personal friends of the bride, the. guests assembled were a remarkable group.

A churchless clergyman who had become a Socialist, and whose church building was for sale, was on hand to make the "Announcement." A handsome poet, a disciple of William Morris and a man of international fame, was there. Socialists, Anarchists, Theosophists, Spiritualists, Buddhists, Communists, Single-Taxers, Walking Delegates, Presidents of Labour-Unions, editors of Radical papers, Ethical gymnasts, and lecturers mingled in the throng.

Kate refused to allow Gordon to see or speak to her before her entrance. They had agreed to make no elaborate preparations. She was to prepare no traditional wedding trousseau. They were simply to stand by each other's side before their friends, greet them with the announcement of their love and unity of life, and receive their congratulations.

When she at length summoned Gordon, he was amazed to see her arrayed in the most magnificent conventional bridal dress he had ever seen.

A frown clouded his brow for an instant, and then melted into a smile as his eyes feasted on the barbaric splendour of her beauty.

She stood silent and thoughtful, with her arms folded in front across the lines of her voluptuous form, her head poised high, erect as an arrow. Her mass of dark red hair rolled upward in a great curling wave from her face. From its crest a bunch of orange blossoms gleamed, clasping the filmy veil which fell, a white cascade, over the wilderness of delicate lace forming her train. She had turned half around, and this great train of shimmering stuff enveloped her feet and swept out in graceful curve into the room. The collar, which completely covered her rounded neck, was made of rows of linked opals, and a necklace of pearls rested on her beautiful breast, spreading out in heart shape, with a single strand encircling the neck.

Her face was tragic in its seriousness. A new and charming melancholy shadowed her violet eyes, causing the heavy lashes to droop till their shadows showed on the creamy velvet of her cheek. Her mouth, with scarlet lips drawn close, was earnest and solemn as he had never seen it.

With the regal bearing of a queen she looked at him thoughtfully without a word. She was giving him his first lesson in perfect freedom and perfect equality of will. She had changed her mind at the last moment and determined to be the bride her girlhood dreams had pictured.

But the man saw only the ripened, luscious woman in the hour of supreme surrender, and gazed in rapture. So superb was her health, so rich and vital the splendid figure, no conventional art of bridal costumer could confine or conceal the glory of its beauty.

"You see, my beloved," she said. "I am not going to promise to obey, so I have chosen with this old conceit to disobey your first expressed wish. Do you like me thus?"

"You are glorious!" he answered, smiling.

"And my father will give me away, and you will place a ring on my hand when you make your little speech, before I respond."

He bowed gracefully. "As you will, my dear."

He would have promised anything.

As they entered the hall leading to the crowded parlours, the organ in the music-room suddenly burst into the strains of the Wedding March, and again she looked seriously into his face, and he laughed.

"My beautiful rebel, I'll tame you in due time, never fear!"

"And you're not angry?"

"Angry? I am more madly in love than ever."

And she flushed in triumph.

When they had entered the room, the invalid father rose, pale and trembling, and, in accordance with Kate's wishes, declared:

"My friends, I announce to you that I have given my daughter to be married unto this man."

Gordon took her hot hand in his massive grasp and said:

"We believe, friends, in fellowship. We have asked you to-night to share with us the sacrament of the unity of our lives which we thus announce. For years this unity has made us one. We thus make it manifest unto the world. In the woman I have chosen as my comrade, behold the living soul of serene-browed Grecian goddess and German seeress of old, whose untamed eyes of primeval womanhood, the equal and the mate of man, proclaim the end of slave-marriage and the dawn of perfect love."

He placed the ring on her hand, and Kate responded:

"This is the day and the hour that we have chosen to announce to you our union."

The Socialist preacher said:

"We are here to-day, called by a sacrament, not in the conventional sense, but in the elemental meaning of the word which reflects the mind and the being of the Eternal. Human life incarnates God. We are not met here to inaugurate a marriage. Words can add nothing to the sublime fact of the union of two souls. This is the supreme sacrament of human experience. It proclaims its inherent divinity. This oneness no more begins to-day than God does. Time loses its meaning, but there is no yesterday or to-morrow in the harmony and rhythm of two such souls. Love holds all the years that have been and are to be.

"This is a day of joy - overflowing, unsullied, serene, a day of hope, a day of faith. It is a day of courage and of cheer, and to the world it speaks a gospel of freedom and fellowship. It proclaims the dawn of a higher life for all, the sanctity and omnipotence of love. It asserts the elemental rights of man.

These friends of ours announce to-day their marriage.

"Inasmuch as Frank Gordon and Kate Ransom are thus united in love, I announce that they are husband and wife by every law of right and truth, and pray for them the abiding gladness that dwells in the heart of God forever."

Kate's mother kissed her and cried in the old-fashioned way, and they sailed next day for a bridal tour abroad.

CHAPTER XX

AN OLD SWEETHEART

Ruth had fulfilled Gordon's prediction. She had lifted up her head and serenely entered her new and trying life.

The year had brought many bitter days, but she had bravely met each crisis. She had hoped to maintain her membership in the Pilgrim Church, and with humility and earnestness returned to her duties. The new pastor had given her a hearty greeting, but the task was beyond her strength. She found that she no longer held her former social position - in fact, that she had no social status. The best people of the church were coolly polite and clumsily sympathetic. She preferred their coolness. The poorer people were frankly afraid of her. The innocent victim of a tragedy, the world held that she was somehow to blame - perhaps was equally guilty with the man. She suddenly found herself outside the pale of polite society.

She was stunned at first by this brutal attitude of the world. To women of weaker character such a blow had often proved fatal in this defenseless hour. To her it was a stimulus to higher things. She fled to the solitude of her home and found refuge in the laughter of her children. She cried an hour or two over it, and then swept the thought from her heart, lifted up her proud little head and moved on the even tenor of her way.

But greater troubles awaited. She had no business training and met with misfortune in the management of her property.

Morris King had been her attorney, since she first came to New York, in the management of a small trust estate. He had always refused any fee, and she had accepted this mark of his faithfulness to their youthful romance simply and graciously. Secure in Gordon's love, she had long since ceased to consider the existence of any other man as a being capable of love. Marriage had engulfed her whole being and life, past, present, future.

But the tender light in King's eyes when he called to see her on her arrival from the South was unmistakable.

She was startled and annoyed, curtly dismissed him as her attorney and undertook the management of her own business affairs.

Within six months she had invested her estate in stocks that had ceased to pay an income and were daily depreciating.

When her support failed, she advertised for pupils to teach in her home, obtained two scholars, and they were from parents whose ability to pay was a matter of doubt. But she had bravely begun and hoped to succeed.

When King saw her pathetic little advertisement he threw aside his pride and called promptly to see her.

He was a muscular young bachelor of thirty-seven. A heavy shock of black hair covered his head, and his upper lip was adorned by a handsome black moustache.

He was a leader of the Tammany Democracy, a member of a firm of lawyers, and had served one term in Congress.

He had made himself famous in a speech in the National Convention in which he had attacked the reform element of his own party seeking admission with such violence, such insolent and fierce invective, he had captured the imagination of his party in New York. He was slated as the machine candidate for Governor of the Empire State and was almost certain of election. Visions of the White House, ghosts which ever haunt the Executive Mansion at Albany, were already keeping him awake at night.

He was a man of strong will, of boundless personal ambitions, and in politics he was regarded as the most astute, powerful and unscrupulous leader in the state. His personal habits were simple and clean to the point of aceticism. His political enemies declared in disgust that he had no redeeming vices. He was a teetotaler, and yet the champion of the saloon and the idol of the saloon-keepers' association. He did not smoke or gamble, and was never known to call on a woman except as a business duty.

In his profession he was honest, dignified, purposeful and successful. He had landed in New York fourteen years before with ten cents in his pocket, and his income now was never less than twenty thousand dollars a year. He had received a single fee of fifty thousand dollars in a celebrated case.

Before coming to New York he was a poor young lawyer in the village of Hampton, Virginia, just admitted to the bar. But the law did not seriously disturb his mind. His real occupation was making love to Ruth Spottswood, who lived across the street in a quaint old Colonial cottage. If any client ever attempted to get into his office, it was more than he knew. He was too busy with Ruth to allow other people's troubles to interfere with the work of his life.

He had taken her to the ball at the Hygeia the night she met Gordon, little dreaming that this long-legged Yankee parson from the West, who did not even know how to dance, would hang around the edges of the ballroom and take her from him. They were engaged after the child fashion of Southern girls and boys - always with the tacit understanding that if they saw anybody they liked better it could be broken at an hour's notice.

The next day when he called Ruth said with a laugh:

"Well, Morris, our engagement ends at three o'clock this afternoon. A handsomer man is going to call. You must clear out and attend to your business."

"Oh, hang the law, Ruth. I'll sit out under the trees and write you a poem till this Yankee goes."

"No, I don't propose to be handicapped. We are not engaged any more, and you can't come till I tell you."

He put up a brave fight, selling his law books to buy candy and pay the livery bill for buggy rides, but it was all in vain.

At last, when she told him she was going to marry Gordon and the day had been fixed, he turned pale, looked at her long and tenderly and stammered:

"I hope you will be very happy, Ruth. But you've killed me."

"Don't be silly," she cried. "Go to work and be a great man."

He closed his law office and went over to Norfolk, debating the question of suicide or murder. He walked along the river-front to pick out a place to jump overboard, but the water looked too black and filthy and cold. He saw a steamer loading, boarded her, and landed in New York with ten cents in his pocket and not a friend on earth that he knew.

He had never spoken a word of love to a woman since. Ambition was his god, and yet, mingled with its fierce cult, its conflicts and turmoil, he had cherished a boyish loyalty to Ruth's last words as she dismissed him.

"Be a great man," she had said. He would - and he had dreamed that some day, perhaps, he might say to her: "Behold, I am your knight of youthful chivalry. Your command has been my law. It is all yours."

The day she had curtly dismissed him as her attorney he was elated with the first assurance his associates had given him that he would be the next Governor of New York. Her unexpected rebuff had cut his pride to the quick. The old hurt was bruised again, and by a woman who had been deserted by a cavalier husband. He had sworn in the wrath of a strong man he would go this time and never return. And now he was hurrying back to her side and cursing himself for being a fool.

She greeted him cordially.

"I'm glad to see you, Morris," she frankly said - she had always called him by his first name. "I've gotten into deep waters since I sent you away so foolishly. I would have sent for you, but I was afraid you were angry and would not come. I've had about as many humiliations as I can bear for awhile."

He looked at her reproachfully.

"You did treat me shamefully, Ruth, after years of faithful service. I don't know why. I might guess if I tried. When I saw that pitiful card this morning, I knew what it meant. So I've come back to take charge of your business. And you can't run me away with a stick. I am going to look after your property and make it earn you a living."

"It is very good of you, and I am grateful," she replied, gently.

"How much are your stocks worth?"

"About forty thousand dollars, I'm told. But I can't sell them. They are not listed on the Exchange."

"I'll sell them for you, and by the end of the week have your money paying you an income of two hundred dollars a month. Send those two children home. You were not made for a school-teacher."

He looked at her with intensity, and she lowered her eyes

in embarrassment.

He sprang to his feet and walked swiftly to the window, and then came back and sat down beside her.

"Ruth," he said, impulsively, "it's no use in my trying to lie to you. We might as well understand one another at once. Of course, I know why you sent me away."

"Please, Morris, don't say any more," she pleaded.

"Yes, I will," he cried. "I love you. How could I keep you from seeing it in my eyes, when you were free at last, and I knew you might be mine?"

"You must not say this to me!" she protested.

He scowled and pursed his lips.

"I will. I am coming to this house when I please. I am going to give you the protection of my life. Every dollar I have, every moment of my time shall be yours if you need it. Ah, Ruth, how I have loved you through the desolate years since you sent me away! Men have called me cold and selfish and ambitious, when I was lying awake at night eating my heart out dreaming of you. Every hour of work, every step I've climbed in the struggle of life, was with your face smiling on me from the past. All my hopes and ambitions I owe to you. The last message you spoke to me has been my guiding star. And when this man threw you from him as a cast-off garment - you, the beautiful queen of my soul - I would have killed him but for the fierce joy that now I could win you!"

She shook her head and a look of pain overspread her face.

"I know what you will say," he went on rapidly. "You need not protest. I will be patient. I will wait, but I will win you. I've sworn it by every oath that can bind the soul. I have no other purpose in life. I'm going to be the Governor of New York simply because I'm going to lift you from the shame this man has heaped upon you and make you the mistress of the Governor's mansion of this mighty state. Washington is but one step from Albany. My dream is for you. I will be to you the soul of deference and of tender honour. Your slightest wish will be my law, I will be silent if you command. But you cannot keep me away. If you leave me, I will follow you to the ends of the earth."

Ruth was softly crying.

"You must not cry, my love. I will make your life glorious, and light every shadow with the tenderness of a strong man's worship."

"And you love me like this when another has robbed my soul and body of their treasures and cast me aside?" she asked, wistfully.

His mouth suddenly tightened and his eyes flashed.

"Yes, and I'd love you so if you were broken and every trace of beauty gone. My love would be so warm and tender and true it would bring back the light into your eyes, the roses to your cheeks, and life even to your dead soul."

"How strange the ways of God!" she exclaimed, through her tears.

He looked at her with yearning tenderness.

"But you are not old or broken, Ruth. You have grown more beautiful. This great sorrow has smoothed from your face every line of fretfulness and worry, and lighted it with the mystery and pathos of an unearthly beauty. It shines from your heroic soul until your whole being has come into harmony with it. I loved you in the past; I worship you now."

She turned on him a look of gratitude.

"Worry and jealousy did exhaust me. I am glad you see in my face and form the change reflected from within. It is very sweet to me, this flattery you pour on my broken heart. I thank you, Morris. You have restored my self-respect and given me strength. It is an honour to receive such love from an honest man. You must not think ill of me if I tell you I cannot love you."

"I'll make you!" he cried, fiercely. "You cannot cling to the memory of a man so base and false."

"He is my husband. I love him."

King flushed with anger.

"He is not your husband. He has deserted you, lured by the beauty of another woman."

A gleam of fire flashed from her eyes, melting into a soft light.

"Yes, I know, marriage is an ideal, the noblest, most beautiful. We have not yet attained its purity in life. Man is only struggling toward its perfection. We will not attain it by lowering the ideal, but by lifting up those who are struggling toward it. Another marriage while Frank lives would be possible for me only when I ceased to feel the meaning of sin and shame. I will never regret my life. I have cast all bitterness out of my heart. Better the happiness and pain of a glorious love than never to have known its joy. I have lived."

"And I will yet teach you to live more deeply," he firmly said.

She shook her head and looked at him sadly out of her dark eyes from which the storm had cleared at last. They beamed now with the steady light of a deep spiritual tenderness.

CHAPTER XXI

FREEDOM AND FELLOWSHIP

The six months abroad which Gordon and Kate had spent in love's dreaming and drifting had been the fulfilment to the man of the long-felt yearnings of his fierce subconscious nature.

To the woman it had been the revelation of a new heaven and a new earth. She had found herself, the real self, at whose first meeting in the kiss of a man she had trembled. She was no longer afraid. The elemental clear-eyed goddess had taken possession. She had claimed her own, the throne of a queen, and the man who had dreamed of kingship was her courtier.

She was smiling at him in conscious power, her violet eyes flashing with mystery and magic, the sunlight of Italy gleaming through her dark red hair, her full lips half parted with dreamy tenderness, and her sinuous body moving with indolent grace.

"To be your slave is crown enough for man," he cried.

"And I am in heaven," she answered, proudly.

"Only, thus, in perfect freedom," he said, in rapture, "is the fulness of life. Beauty and harmony and love are of God. Surely this is communion with Him - the joy of embraces, the touch of sunlight, the glory of form and colour, the magic of music, the poetry of love, the ecstacy of passion, the kiss of the senses - He is in all and over all."

"Can such happiness be eternal?" she asked, under her breath.

He kissed her softly.

"If God be infinite."

They reached New York the first week in November, and Gordon returned to his work with renewed zeal.

The success of his movement was a source of continued surprise and fear to the more thoughtful students of social and religious life.

But Gordon had found on his return an increasing amount of friction between opposing groups in his church which was a source of intense surprise and annoyance. Two factions had broken into an open quarrel in his absence. He found it necessary to devote a large part of his time to smoothing out these quarrels between men who had come together with the principles of unity and fellowship as the foundation of their association. He saw with disgust that he was gathering a crowd of cranks, conceited and stupid, vain and ambitious for fame and leadership. It was all he could do to prevent a battle of Kilkenny cats.

He discovered that many things glittered at a banquet to celebrate universal brotherhood which did not pan out pure gold in the experiment of life. He had heard at such a love feast an aristocratic poet extoll in harangue the unwashed Democracy, a Walking Delegate read a poem, a Jew quote the Koran with unction, a Mohammedan eulogise Monogamy, a Single-Taxer declare himself a Democrat, a Socialist glorify Individualism, and an Anarchist express his love for Order.

But he found next day that as a rule the Egyptian resumed the use of garlic and the hog went back to his wallow.

He found to his chagrin that mental freedom could be made a cloak for the basest mental slavery, and that the most hidebound dogmatist on earth is the modern crank who boasts his freedom from all dogmas. He found the Liberal to be the most illiberal and narrow man he had ever met.

The absurdity of allowing this mob of Kilkenny cats any authority in his church he saw at once. His dream of triumphant Democracy faded.

He seized the helm at once.

Without a moment's hesitation he threw out twenty ringleaders of as many factions and restored order. Under such conditions he dared not even incorporate his society under the laws of the state as a religious body lest these incongruous elements control its property and wreck its work. He continued to expend the vast funds needed for his Temple in his wife's name, leaving its legal ownership vested in her as before.

Within a few months the extraordinary beauty and vivacity of his wife made their house on Gramercy Park the rendezvous of a brilliant group of free-lances and Bohemians. Her mother and father had moved to a house on the opposite side of the park. Men and women of genius in the world of Art and Letters who cared nought for conventions had crowded her receptions. She was nattered with the pleasant fiction that she had restored the ancient Salon of France on a nobler basis.

The increase of her social duties required more and more of her time at the dressmaker's, and left less and less for work in Gordon's congregation.

At first he had watched this social success with surprise and pride, and then with an increasing sense of uneasiness for its significance in the development of her character.

The sight of half a dozen handsome men bending over her,

enchanted by her beauty, and the ring of her laughter at their wit, irritated him. He had not been actor enough to conceal from her the gleam of, worry in his eyes and the accent of fret in his voice at these functions. She observed, too, that he attended them with regularity, however important might be the work which called him outside.

He was anxious for her to cultivate a few of his intimate friends, but this crowd of strange men and women bored him.

He was especially anxious that she should meet Overman, and by her magnetism and beauty crush him into the acknowledgment of the sanity and right of his course.

But Overman had promised without coming.

Gordon was at his bank on Wall Street again urging him to call.

"It's no use to talk, Frank," he said, testily. "All I ask of women is to be let alone."

"But, you fool, I want you to meet my wife. She's not a woman merely. She's the wife of an old college chum, the better half by far."

Overman pulled his moustache, a humorous twinkle in his eye.

"Well, how many halves are there to you? I've met the other half once before. This makes one and a half," he said, peering at his friend with his single eye.

Gordon laughed.

"Yes, I am large."

"I've my doubts whether you're quite large enough for the job you've undertaken."

"You're a pessimist."

Overman's face brightened and his mouth twisted.

"Yes, the more I see of men, the more stock I take in chickens. I've a rooster at home now that can whip anything that ever wore feathers, and he's so ugly I love him like a brother."

"Shut up about roosters," Gordon growled. "Will you come to see me and meet my wife?"

Overman turned his eye on his friend, frowning.

"Frank, I'm afraid of the atmosphere. There's enough dynamite in 'Freedom and Fellowship' to blow up several houses. I don't like to get mixed up with women in any sort of fellowship - to say nothing about freedom and fellowship."

"Well, I've asked my wife to call by the bank here for me to-day and I'm going to introduce you."

Overman did not hear this statement, for his head was turned to one side and he was peering out of his window on Broad Street with excited interest.

He sprang to his feet, suddenly exclaiming:

"Well, what the devil is the matter?"

"What is it?" Gordon asked, stepping to the window.

It had begun to snow on an inch of ice which was still clinging to the stone pavements. At the corner of Broad and Wall Streets the ground dips sharply, forming a difficult crossing.

Gordon saw his wife approaching the bank, laughing. She was dressed in a sealskin cloak which reached to the ground. Its great rolling collar of ermine covered her full breast and stretched upward almost to her hat, rearing its snowy background about her heavy auburn hair, which seemed about to fall and envelop her form. She wore an enormous hat of white fur bent in graceful curves.

She was close to the building now, and her blue eyes were dancing and her cheeks flushed with laughter. The perfect grace and rhythm of movement could be seen even through the heavy seal cloak, whose sheen changed with each touch of her figure.

"Look at the idiots!" cried Overman, excitedly. "So busy stretching their necks to see a woman, there's five piled up on the ice. They're ringing for the ambulance. She's fractured one man's skull, broken another's leg, and, by the pale-faced moon, I believe she's killed one. And you're after me to meet another woman - great Scott, look, she's coming in here!"

"Well, she won't hurt you."

"I don't know!"

Overman made a break to reach his inner office when Gordon seized his arm.

"Stop, you fool," he thundered; "it's my wife. She's calling by for me, and you're going to meet her, if I have to knock you down and sit on you."

There was no help for it. He heard the rustle of the silk lining of her cloak and she was at the door.

She shook Overman's hand heartily, her violet eyes smiling in such a friendly candid way he was at once put at ease.

"I am so glad to see you," she said, earnestly. "I've heard Frank speak of you so often and laugh over your college ups and downs. I feel I've known you all my life. And then he says you're such a woman-hater -"

"He's a grand liar, Mrs. Gordon," he interrupted, suddenly colouring. "I never said anything of the kind in my life. I'm a great admirer of the fair sex!"

"Then you must prove it by coming to dinner with us to-night and admiring me the whole evening."

"Nothing could give me greater pleasure," he answered, bowing his big neck with an ease and grace Gordon noted with amazement.

When they left, Overman walked to the window and watched them thread their way through the crowd.

"Holy Moses and the angels - what a woman!" he said, softly whistling. "By the beard of the prophet, no wonder!"

Long after they disappeared he stood, looking without seeing, as if in a dream.

CHAPTER XXII

A SCARLET FLAME IN THE SKY

From the night Overman had taken dinner at the Gramercy Park house he became a constant visitor.

For six months he had usually spent two or three evenings each week in his friend's library, rehearsing their boyhood days, discussing new books, art and politics, Socialism and religion.

Overman's cynicism had piqued Kate's curiosity and opened new views of things she had accepted as moral finalities.

At these battles of wit she was always a charmed listener. She seemed never to tire watching the sparks fly in the rapier thrust of mind in these two men of steel and listening with a shiver to the deep growl of the animal behind their words. The one, so homely he was fascinating, with massive neck, and enormous mouth pursing and twisting under excitement into a sneer that pushed his big nose upward, the incarnation of a battle-scarred bulldog; the other, with his giant figure, hands and feet, his leonine face and locks, his deep voice, handsome and insolent in his conscious strength, the picture of a thoroughbred mastiff.

With the grace of a goddess she would sit and watch this battle to the death in the arena of thought.

Overman had keenly interested her from the first, and she

Thomas Dixon

stimulated him to unusual brilliancy. His remorseless logic, his thorough scholarship, his grasp of history, his savage common sense presented so sharp a contrast to the idealism of Gordon, she was shocked and startled.

He fell into the habit of calling on Sunday mornings and walking with them to the Opera House. They would leave Gordon at the stage entrance and sit together during the services.

He would comment softly to her on many of the little absurdities of the preacher's flights of sentiment, and often convulsed her with laughter by a single word or phrase which made ridiculous his mysticism. He did this with his single eye fixed on Gordon without the quiver of a nerve or the movement of a muscle to indicate ought but profound rapture in the speaker and his message.

Overman's business ability had been of great service in the Temple enterprise, which had involved difficulties with contractors, and Gordon had opened an account in Kate's name with his banking house. Her signature to legal documents had made her a frequent visitor to the bank, and she often took lunch with him.

Alone with her at these impromptu lunches, without the restraint of Gordon's presence, he had revealed to her a new phase of his character which had interested her still more deeply. It was here that she discovered the secret of his real attitude toward women, his deep hunger for love, tenderness and sympathy, and his terror lest his ugliness and the loss of his eye might entrap him into hopeless suffering.

She laughed at his fears.

"Ridiculous," she cried, closing her red lips. "You ought to have sense enough to know that a woman of character past the schoolgirl age is often fascinated by the ruggedness of such a man. Savage strength is sometimes resistless to women of rare beauty."

"You think so?" he asked, pathetically.

"Certainly; I know it," she answered, her lips twitching playfully.

Overman looked at her steadily.

"Sort of beauty-and-beast idea, I suppose. There may be something in it. It never struck me before."

"I'll put you in training for a handsome woman I know," she said, with a curious smile playing about her eyes.

"No, thank you," he quickly replied. "I'm just beginning to feel at home with you. I am content."

The opening of the Temple was an event which commanded the attention of the world. Leaders of Socialism from every quarter of the globe poured into New York.

The building was one of imposing grandeur. The auditorium filled the entire space of the first-four stories. It seated five thousand people within easy reach of the speaker's voice. The line of its ceiling was marked outside by the serried capitals of Greek columns springing from their massive bases on the ground. The grand stairway was of polished marble, its wainscoting and walls of onyx.

Resting on the capitals of the columns, the outer walls of rough marble rose twenty stories to the first offset. Dropping back fifty feet, another structure, crowned by Greek facades, sprang ten stories higher, forming the base of the central dome. From each corner rose a tower of bronze supporting the figures of Faith, Hope, Love and Truth, while scores of minarets flamed upward, flying the flags of every nation.

From the centre of this pile of marble, the huge dome, finished in gold, solemnly loomed among the clouds, higher than its model in Washington, dominating the city from every point of the compass. The magnificent sweep of Jefferson Avenue, stretching through miles of palatial homes, terminating at its base, seemed a tiny pathway leading through its grand arched and pillared entrance.

The dome was crowned by a statue of Liberty holding aloft a steel staff, from which flew the solid red battle-flag of Socialism, flinging into the heavens its challenge to civilisation, rising, falling, waving, fluttering, quivering, rippling in the wind, a scarlet blaze sweeping a hundred feet across the sky far above the cross on the Cathedral spire.

The cost of the building had exceeded the estimate, and it had been finished by a loan of two million dollars secured by a mortgage held by the banking house of Overman & Company. It could have commanded a larger loan, as the entire structure, except the two stories below ground and the auditorium, was devoted to business offices occupied by the best class of tenants. The auditorium was for rent at a nominal sum during the week, and was designed to be the forum of free thought for the nation.

The dedication programme began on Monday, lasting through an entire week, day and night, and culminated on Sunday with Gordon's address at eleven o'clock. The elaborate ceremonials and speeches had worn out Kate's body by Saturday, and the praise of pygmies had long before worn out her soul.

Ruth had read with interest the accounts of these meetings, and Morris King tried in vain to dissuade her from attending the Sunday exercises at which Gordon was to speak.

"It's useless to talk, Morris," she said, firmly. "I am going. I'd as well tell you I've been slipping into the gallery of the Opera House the past six months. I've tried to keep away, but I had to go. I am going to-day. I've heard him talk and dream and plan so much of this, it seems my own."

"Well, I'm going with you. You shall not enter that den of Anarchists alone again."

She hesitated.

"You may go if you'll agree to sit behind a pillar in the gallery where we will not be seen."

When they were seated he whispered to Ruth: "But for you, I wouldn't be caught dead in this place. I'll soon be the Governor, and it will be my duty to see that some of these gentlemen are carefully packed in quicklime at Sing Sing."

She started suddenly, her brow clouded, and she placed a trembling hand on his arm.

"Hush, Morris."

"It'll be so, mark my word."

"Hush!" she repeated, with such a shudder of pain he hastened to whisper.

"I beg your pardon, Ruth. You know I was joking."

Gordon rose and gazed for a moment over the sea of faces. His quick sympathies and brilliant imagination were stirred to their depths.

When the beautifully modulated voice first filled the room, Ruth felt with quick sympathy, beneath the tremor of his tones, the storm of suppressed feeling. Her eyes filled, and she bent forward, following him breathlessly.

He held the crowd spellbound.

Even the foreign Socialists, unable to understand a word of English, hung on every gesture, held by the magnetism of his powerful personality.

As he reached an impassioned climax, Ruth was startled to hear a note of suppressed laughter from a woman sitting in the same row behind the next pillar.

She looked quickly, and saw Overman's massive head cocked to one side, his face an immovable mask, and his single gleaming eye fixed on Gordon, with Kate beside him.

Overman stayed to dinner and congratulated his friend on his effort.

"Frank, you surpassed yourself," he said. "You made the grandest defense of an indefensible absurdity I ever heard."

"H'm, that's saying a good deal for you."

Overman pulled his moustache thoughtfully.

"But I couldn't help wishing I were an orator to jaw back at you. A preacher has such an easy thing, with no back talk except the sonorous echo of his own voice."

"Think you could have talked back to-day?"

There was a moment's silence. Overman leaned back and locked his hands behind his massive neck.

"If you hit a man with a brick, he may hurt you. Drop a millstone on him, he'll not even reply. If I could have gotten at you to-day, your wife would have lost her insurance policy, because there wouldn't have been anything to identify."

"Nothing like a good opinion of oneself," Gordon replied, good-naturedly.

Overman nodded.

"I never heard you explain so beautifully that 'Back to Nature' idea. I went West once and lived a year with some red folks who have been so fortunate as to never get away from Nature. They have been doing business at the same stand for several thousand years. Their women are old hags at your wife's age, and their men die at mine - forty-five. Their social institutions are an exact reflection of their personal attainments."

"But we propose," Gordon flashed, "to make institutions an advance on man's attainments and so lead him onward and upward."

"Exactly," he answered, dryly. "Make human nature divine by writing it on paper that it is so, pile water into a pyramid upside down, and repeal the law of gravitation by the vote of a mob. I don't like the law of gravitation myself, but I haven't time to repeal it."

"You are a hopeless materialist."

"Yet you, who preach the Spirit, propose to build a heaven here out of mud."

"Socialism may be the great delusion, but it's coming. It sweeps the imagination of the world," Gordon cried, with enthusiasm.

"There you go! Every time I pin you down, you sail off into space with prophecy or poetry. If it does conquer the world, the world will not be worth conquering. The one thing worth while is character, and your Socialistic pig-pen cannot produce it. In this herd of swine to which you hope to reduce society an Edison or a Darwin is rewarded with the pay of a hod-carrier. The hod-carrier gets all he's worth now. This instinct for the herd, which you call Solidarity and Brotherhood, is not a prophecy of progress; it is a memory - a memory of the dirt out of which humanity has slowly grown."

Gordon grunted contemptuously.

"Yet only a brute can be content with the cruelty and infamy of our present society."

"All our ills can be met by careful legislation. You propose to pull the tree up by the roots because you see bugs crawling on a limb."

Kate rose and left the room, saying she would return in a moment, and Overman leaned back in his chair again, gazing at the ceiling.

Suddenly straightening himself, he drew his brow down close over his eye, half closing its lid, bent toward Gordon, and in a low tone slowly asked:

"But I would like to know, Frank, what in the devil you really meant by that 'Freedom and Fellowship' in marriage?"

"Just what I said."

"Bah! You don't mean to apply such tommyrot to your own wife now that she's yours?"

"Certainly."

"It's beyond belief that you're such a fool. You say to your wife and to the world, 'This peerless woman is my comrade, but she is free; take her if you can.'"

Gordon laughed.

"Yes; but, Mark, old boy, God has not yet made the man who can take her from me."

The one eye dreamily closed, the banker whistled softly, and said:

"I see."

CHAPTER XXIII

THE NEW HEAVEN

Overman had appeared on the scene of Kate's life in a peculiar crisis. Married two years, she had passed through the period of love's ecstacy which woman finds first in self-surrender. She had just reached the point of sex growth when a revolt against man's dominion became inevitable.

This mood of revolt was made stronger by Gordon's fret over her social gatherings. In the dim light of the pulpit, preaching with mystic elation, he had seemed to her a god. Now, in the full blaze of physical possession, the divine glow had paled about his brow. She had found him only a man, self-conscious, egotistic and domineering. He had many personal habits she did not like. He was overfastidious in his dress, and critical and fussy about her lack of order in housekeeping. He was finicky about his food. He hated tea, declaring the odour made him sick. She felt this a covert thrust at her five-o'clocks.

To his criticisms she at last coolly replied:

"I claim the perfect freedom you preach. I will do as I please. You can do the same."

He laughed in a weak sort of way and declared he liked her independence.

At this moment of reaction, satiety, and the beginning of

Thomas Dixon

friction he had introduced her to Overman. His candour, his brutal realism, his defiance and scorn for poetic theories, presented to her the sharp contrast which made him doubly fascinating. Just at the moment Gordon was growing peevishly dogmatic in the reiteration of his ideals, she had suffered a physical disillusioning and begun to tire of poetry.

The sheer brute power of the other man, the incarnation of the thing that is, with a cynic's contempt for dreams and dreamers, had given voice to her own rebellion and drawn her resistlessly.

The boyish tenderness underlying Overman's nature, which she discovered later, had made his ugliness and brute strength added charms.

He had a pathetic way of looking at her with a doglike worship, as though conscious of his defects, which pleased and nattered her own sense of the perfection of beauty.

They were seated in his box at the Metropolitan Opera House while Gordon was at the farewell banquet to his foreign delegates.

"I feel," he said, bitterly, "every time I see this play of 'Faust,' and hear Edouard De Reszke's deep bass speak for His Majesty the Devil, that His Majesty really made this world. I'd know it but for the paradox of such divine perfection before my eyes in the living reality of a woman like you."

His voice throbbed with earnestness.

"I'm growing to love the world. It's a beautiful old place," she answered, with a lazy smile.

"Well, it's the only one I'm likely to travel in, so I'm going to make the best of it, work with its mighty forces, dare and defy the fools who cross my purposes. If the future has for me only pain, I'll not complain. I'll grin and bear it, but I'll confess to you I get a little lonely sometimes."

Her eyes lifted with surprise.

"I never heard you admit that before."

"No; and what's more, no one else ever did or ever will."

He looked at her pathetically, and a deeper colour flooded her cheeks.

When they reached home Gordon had just returned from the banquet and was bubbling over with enthusiasm.

"Mark, we have had a grand time to-night - organised a movement that will put out a sign 'To Let' on every den of thieves in Wall Street."

"What? Founded another church already?"

"A new Brotherhood within the Church Universal."

Overman shrugged his shoulders.

"Talk plain English. What will be its name at Police Headquarters?"

Gordon smilingly and proudly replied, "The Federated Democracy of the World."

"H'm; what are you going to do? Federate the hobos of all tongues and demand better straw in empty freight cars and shorter stops at sidings for express trains to pass?"

"Our purpose will be to inaugurate the Cooperative Commonwealth of Man. The movement will bring into harmonious action the insurgent forces of the world. Within ten years an earthquake will shake the social fabric. Within twenty years profound political and social revolutions will lift the human race over centuries of plodding into a new world of real liberty, equality, and fraternity."

Overman growled cynically.

"That has a French accent. I hear there are fifty thousand active Socialists in France divided into exactly fifty thousand factions. Which division of this grand army will lead the movement in Gaul?"

Gordon ignored his interruption, and his voice thrilled with passionate eloquence.

"We have abolished crowns and scepters. It is a moral and physical absurdity that, in a democracy, a whiskered babe, whose labour value to society is just ten dollars a week, should inherit millions of dollars that give him the power over men more terrible, absolute and irresponsible than a Caesar ever wielded over the empire of the world. No wonder our papers shiver when these babes sneeze, and report their daily life with servile pride."

"And would the oil of anointment of your new king, the walking delegate, be strong enough to temper the onion in his breath? I'd like to know that before drawing too near the throne." The banker's mouth twisted into a sneer with the last word.

"This new Democracy will itself be the highest nobility, an ethical aristocracy, and when it comes the Kingdom of Heaven will be at hand."

The one eye glanced quickly at the speaker and blinked.

"Let me know before it gets here," said Overman, a reminiscent look overspreading his rugged face, while Kate leaned closer with eager interest.

"Why?"

"Because I'm going somewhere. When I was a boy I had to go to church. Our old preacher faithfully urged us for hours at a time to get ready for heaven, a glorious place away up in space where all wore crowns and there wasn't a Democrat in town, everybody played psalms on big gold harps, and every day was Sunday. I early learned to hate heaven and look on hell as my only home. Now you come along, rub hell off the map, and threaten me with a heaven here on earth worse than the old one. Hell would be a summer resort to this thing you've conjured up. If it comes, I'll get off the earth."

"Get your flying machine ready."

"Oh, ten cents' worth of 'rough on rats' will do me."

Gordon shook his head thoughtfully.

"It's a strange thing to me you conservatives are blind to the coming of this revolution. It will be the grimmest joke Fate ever played on the pride of man. Within the generation now living a Cooperative Commonwealth will supplant the whole system of slave wages."

The banker suddenly straightened his massive neck and his eye flashed.

"You mean establish a system of universal slavery. Suppose under your maudlin cry of brotherhood you set up your fool's paradise, where would reside the authority of your Commonwealth?"

"In the State, of course."

"And who would be the State? You talk about the State as though it were some mysterious Ark of the Covenant of God, let down out of heaven and enshrined in capitals of marble. The State is simply made out of common dirt called Tom, Dick and Harry, whom a lot of other plain Toms, Dicks and Harrys set up in power. Will not your pig-pen you call the Cooperative Commonwealth have men in charge with authority to call the pigs to dinner and drive them to the fields to root?"

"Certainly, there must be authority," Gordon snapped.

Overman mused a moment.

"Yet your patron saint, William Morris, proclaims a heaven here below without law, where man kills his fellow man and answers only to his own conscience; where we will tear up the railroads and walk, blow up our steamships and use rowboats, in our harvest fields the whetstone on the old hand-scythe will still the music of the McCormick reaper. With his delicate tastes he fears the hoof-beat of your herd. But you all agree that to go backward means to go forward, and that the way to save civilisation is to lapse into barbarism. Whether you call yourselves Socialist or Anarchist - that is, whether you long for the herd or the solitude of the forest, you mean the same thing and don't know it, that your mind has not been able to adjust itself to the speed of modern progress, and has broken down under the strain. You preach 'Fellowship,' herd-life, as the cure. You believe in law and authority."

"Yes," Gordon cried, with pride. "Our ideal is constructive in the largest and noblest sense."

"And if a man can work and will not work?"

"He will be made to work."

"Very well. Suppose your pig heaven established and the herd duly penned. The Labour Master of your local pen would naturally be a man after the heart of the herd. He would be a greasy Labour agitator. No other man could be elected. Suppose he should become interested in the extraordinary beauty of your wife. Suppose you were presumptuous enough to resent this, and, in revenge for your insolence, your Master transferred you, the scholar, idealist and orator, to the task of cleaning the spittoons in the City Hall, and ordered your wife to scrub the floor of his office. You both refuse, you who walk with your head among the stars, What then? The dirty-fingered one, your Labour Master, sends you to prison for the first offense. For the second, you would be stripped, placed in the public stocks and flogged, man and woman alike in this kingdom of equality. For, mark you, enforced labour is the only possible foundation of such a society."

Gordon listened with dreamy disgust.

"You've set up a man of straw. In this new world each would choose his work and labour would be a joy," he answered, with lofty scorn.

The banker chuckled.

"No doubt they would all choose joyous jobs. But there would be a surplus of joyous labourers hunting for joyful tasks, and a dearth of fools looking for disagreeable work. In your pig paradise everything must be fixed. There could be no uncertainty about the future - no worry, or fret, or anxiety - hence no hopes or fears. Man would be guaranteed food, clothes, shelter and children, just as the chattel slave. There could be no inducement to work unless compelled to, and no man except an idiot would do a disagreeable task unless forced to do it. You must remember there could be no lawyers or bankers, preachers or orators. The chief occupation of your Labour Master would be the assignment of people he didn't like to the hard, dirty jobs, and the granting of favourite tasks to such people as made themselves agreeable to His Majesty. Witness the master of the Russian Commune, who is notoriously the lord of all the wives of the village."

Overman was still a moment, and then growled from the depths of his being:

"I call this the lowest, the most degrading, the most bestial nightmare the human mind ever dreamed!"

Gordon waved him off with an eloquent gesture.

"You have assumed that a free commonwealth of godlike men and women would choose their worst units for their leaders."

"Nothing of the sort," he snapped. "I've supposed they would do the inevitable - choose the strongest man who looks like the majority and smells like the majority."

"A bad man would be removed," the dreamer quickly replied.

"What difference if your master be changed by an election now and then? All the worse. If I am to be a slave, I prefer the old chattel system with a master whose favour I could win and hold for life by faithful service. The old slaves often loved their masters. Could you love the Executive Officer of a Bureau for the Enforcement of Labour? Do convicts become infatuated with their keepers? To assassinate such a man would become a positive joy. How many years of such life would it take to crush out of the human soul the last spark of hope and aspiration and reduce man to a beast?"

"But we affirm the inherent divinity of man. You assume him to be a child of the devil."

There was another silence, and then the banker's brow wrinkled.

"Affirm. Yes, you fellows are all orators. You must affirm else the crowd will leave you. You never have doubts and fears. You always know. Only affirm a thing enough and never try to prove it, and thousands of fools will accept it at last as the word of God. That is the secret of the power of all demagogues and emotional orators. The slickest horse-thief that ever operated in the West was a revivalist who migrated there with a tent. While he held the crowd spellbound with his eloquence, his confederates loosed the horses in the woods and got them to a safe place. Oratory is one of the cheapest tricks ever played on man, but an everlastingly effective one, because it is based on affirmation. Any man who is too hard-headed and honest to affirm a thing he don't know and can't know never leads a mob. They will only follow a man who speaks with the sublime authority of knowledge he does not possess."

While Overman was talking Gordon's brow clouded as he watched Kate's face flash with interest and a smile now and then play between her eyes and lips.

"We seem to be developing another orator," he slowly answered.

Overman pursed his lips.

"I haven't wasted so much breath in a long time. Your French programme stirred me. I wonder if you recalled the decline of the French nation in modern times, and its causes, in arranging for your conquest of France? A little while ago the Anglo-Saxon race numbered but a few millions, and the Latin ruled the world. Now the flag of the Anglo-Saxon flies over one-fourth the inhabitants of the globe, his army can withstand the combined armies of the world, his navy rules the sea, and his wealth is so great he could buy the entire possessions of the rest of mankind. Why? Because he developed the most powerful individual man in history, while other races have sought refuge in the herd idea of communal interests. I noticed you never preach now from the old text, 'What shall it profit a man if he gain the whole world and forfeit his life?' Why save the world if you destroy man?"

But Gordon had ceased to listen to Overman. With his great blue-veined fist clenched on his chin and a new gleam of light in his steel-gray eyes he was watching his wife's face.

CHAPTER XXIV

COURTIER AND QUEEN

Overman was quick to detect the hostility of his friend's unusual silence, and hastily rose.

"Excuse me, old boy," he said, apologetically, "if I've hit too hard. I think the world of you in spite of your fool theories. You know that."

"Don't worry, Mark," he answered, carelessly. "I haven't been listening to you at all. I've been thinking of something else. Life's too short to pay any attention to your big Philistine jaw."

The banker smiled.

"Well, you have the instrument handy with which Samson slew the Philistine."

"Yes, if you would only loan it to me. Goodnight."

When he had gone, Kate leaned back on the lounge and said with evident amusement:

"You forgot something in parting with your old schoolmate."

"Yes, I thought it quite unnecessary to tell him to drop in any time, unless you wish to let the front room."

A tremor of catlike fun slyly played about her mouth.

"And yet women have been called fickle. Mr. Overman was no college chum of mine."

"No; but he is evidently trying to make up for it now."

A low musical laugh seemed to come from the depth of Kate's spirit.

"And I thought I was pleasing you by neglecting my Bohemians and cultivating your powerful friend."

"Still it is not necessary to hang on his words with such melting interest," he said, with quiet emphasis.

She looked up sharply and a gleam of cruelty flashed from her blue eyes and struck the steel-gray in his. Beneath the quiet words of the man and woman there was raging the mortal struggle of will and personality, the woman in fierce rebellion, his iron egotism demanding submission.

"'Oh, I see," she purred, softly. "There is to be but one man-god, arrayed and beautiful, if I may quote your formula. There may be many women-gods in paradise. I saw Ruth in the Temple the first Sunday you spoke, hanging on your words as the voice of the Lord."

Gordon flushed and turned uneasily in his chair.

"I'd as well be frank with you, Kate. Overman is coming to this house too often. I was shocked beyond measure when I failed to find you in your accastomed seat on the Sunday of the dedication of the Temple. I was told you were in the gallery with him."

She straightened herself up suddenly.

"You took the pains to find that out?"

"Yes."

She fixed on him a look of scorn.

"And stooped to ask an usher instead of asking me? You, who boldly say to the world that I am your free comrade, the mate and equal of man?"

"An odd way you took to show comradeship in such an hour," he answered, doggedly.

"Am I a slave, to sit in solemn rapture at your feet and await your nod?"

"You seemed to eagerly await the nod of another man to-night."

She laughed.

"Am I not your serene-browed Grecian goddess whose untamed eyes of primeval womanhood proclaim the end of slave marriage?"

Gorden winced, scowled and was silent.

"I like the beautiful ceremony you invented. I've memorised every word of it," she said, teasingly.

He sat for several minutes sullenly looking at her with a strange fire in his eyes, now and then moistening his lips as though they burned.

At length he said: "It will be necessary for you to go to his office to-morrow to sign papers in the transfer of the deed of the Temple to me. The lawyers informed me to-day that everything was in readiness for your signature. After this event there will be no business requiring your further attendance at his bank."

She closed her eyes lazily.

"I am not going to sign any such deed," came the firm answer.

Gordon turned pale, nervously fumbled at his watch-chain and stammered:

"Kate, you don't mean this?"

"I do."

The man hesitated, as though stunned.

"After your announcement to the world, and all that has passed between us, would you humiliate me by the withdrawal of your gift?"

She lifted her beautiful brows.

"Humiliate you? Surely I have honoured you with the richest gift woman can bestow on man: myself. The ownership of property can have no meaning after this. I claim my rights as your equal. Your eloquence and genius give you power. This money is scarcely its equivalent. You have your Temple, and I still have my fortune. Its investment in this building has enhanced its value. What more can you ask?"

"The fulfilment of your word of honour to the cause of truth," he firmly answered.

She smiled.

"Nonsense! You were my cause, my truth - the god I worshiped. I desired you. Now at closer range the aureole has slightly faded, though you are as handsome as ever, Frank, dear. What is money between us? We are equals. I will take the worry of financial details off your shoulders and leave you free for your inspiring work."

Gordon's eyes grew soft; he went over to the lounge on which she was resting, sat down and slipped his arm about her.

The full lips smiled with conscious cruelty.

He bent and kissed her passionately.

"You are my priceless treasure, my dear. I am honoured in your beauty and love. Money is nothing to me, so long as you are mine."

She drew his head down and kissed him in a sudden burst of intensity.

"You know I love you, Frank!"

"And we must not quarrel," he said, wistfully, slipping to his knees with one arm still encircling her waist. "You and I have gone through too much for harsh words or thoughts to ever shadow our life. But you must give me more of your time, and other men less. A growing uneasiness and the loss of the sense of finality in life are robbing me of my capacity for thought and work."

"Not so bad as that surely," she cried, with teasing laughter. "You're not afraid of losing me?"

"No; but you will promise?" he asked, tenderly.

She placed one of her arms about his neck, a soft warm hand under his chin, and, still laughing, slowly kissed him and murmured:

"I'll do just what I please, and you may do the same."

CHAPTER XXV

THE IRONY OF FATE

Morris King had ended a brilliant campaign for the Governorship of New York with victory. The entire ticket was elected by large pluralities.

The campaign had given scope to his ability, and he more than fulfilled the hopes of his friends. From the moment of his election, he became the leader of the party in the nation, and began at once the work of strengthening his position as a Presidential possibility.

Yet in the din and clash of this battle in which his personal fortunes, his future career, and perhaps the destiny of a great national party hung, he had not forgotten Ruth.

He made it a point every day, wherever he was, or whatever the task or excitement of the hour, to write her a love letter. Sometimes it was only a few lines hastily scrawled while on the train between stations where he addressed the crowds at each stop. Sometimes he sent a dainty box of flowers.

She never replied to his letters or little gifts. But it made no difference. He kept steadily on the course he had mapped out, dogged, purposeful, persistent.

The night of the election, when he received the first assurance of his success, before he spoke to any of his lieutenants or received a single congratulation, he closed his door, locked it, and called Ruth over his telephone, which he had connected with her house by special secret arrangement that afternoon.

He recognised her soft contralto voice, and his hand trembled with the joy of the triumph which he felt brought him nearer to his heart's desire.

He was so excited he could not speak for a moment, and again the low soft voice called,

"What is it? Who is it?"

"This is Morris, Ruth. My door is locked, and this is a private wire connected with your house; I am alone with you and God. I am the Governor-elect of New York. I have spoken to no one until I tell you. One word from you I will prize more than all the shouts of the world with which the streets will ring in a moment."

There was a movement of the phone at the other end.

"With all my heart I congratulate you, Morris. You are a great man. I can never tell you how deeply I feel the delicate honour you pay me."

The man sighed and his voice was husky with emotion.

"Ah! Ruth, if you only meant that conventional phrase, 'with all my heart,' I'd be the happiest man in the world to-night. But I must go; the boys are trying to beat the door down. My success I lay at your feet, my love. When you hear the shouts of hosts and see the sky red to-night with illuminations, remember that it is all for you. I am yours. - Good-by."

She sat at her window long past the hour of midnight and watched the blaze of rockets from end to end of Manhattan, over Brooklyn, and from the farthest sand-beaches of Coney Island, dreaming with open eyes, soft with tears, of the mystery of love and life.

The unterrified Democracy of the great city had gone mad with joy over their daring young leader's success. She could hear the distant murmur of the tumult of thousands of shouting, screaming men packed around Tammany Hall, filling Fourteenth Street in solid mass, jamming Union Square and Madison Square and surging round the Madison Square Garden, where a jollification meeting of twenty thousand cheering, excited men was in progress. It sounded like the boom and roar of some far-off sea breaking on the rocks and echoing among the cliffs. All Harlem was ablaze with bonfires now, and the tumult of horns and shouting boys filled the streets on Washington Heights.

She sighed and rested her dimpled chin in her hand.

"Surely, I must be a foolish woman to cling to Frank and reject the glory and strength of this old sweetheart's chivalrous love! I cannot help it. He is my husband. I love him. Perhaps he may need me some dark night in life. Who knows? If he calls, I will be ready."

The year had proved a trying one to Ruth. The sensation of the completion of the Temple and the stir made by its dedication had increased Gordon's fame, and the story of her sorrow had been repeated again and again. A hundred petty details, utterly false, had been added as the story had passed from paper to paper, until she was afraid to look in a public print lest she find her own name staring her in the face. From the Socialist point of view, she was attacked as a blatant scold who had made her husband's life intolerable, until he had been rescued by the beautiful woman who was now his wife. By the conservative press, she was timidly defended, damned by faint praise and humiliated by pity.

The children, growing rapidly, were beginning to feel the mother's position. In the public schools, the story of her life and desertion by her husband had tipped the tongues of the spiteful with poison, and Lucy had come home more than once trying to conceal from her mother the hurt of her sensitive child's soul.

Morris King, now the distinguished Governor-elect, hastened to press his suit.

Her faithful knight, he was now laying lovingly at her feet the tribute of a powerful man's life.

To every worldly view of her position and future his suit was a temptation well nigh resistless. His love had stood the test of years. He would worship her as his wife as he had worshiped her as his ideal. She knew this by an intuition as unerring as that by which she knew she could never love him as she loved Gordon. And yet she felt a singular dependence on him, and a tender gratitude for the protection he had given her life.

He knew his position was strong, and pressed it with quiet intensity. He was careful that his attentions should not become the subject of public comment, and the tongue of gossip cause her pain. Not for one moment did he doubt that he would win.

The Sunday before his inauguration he spent with her, and, much to his disgust, she insisted on going to the Pilgrim Church.

"Of all churches, Ruth, for heaven's sake don't go there," he pleaded, with impatience.

"Yes," she quietly answered. "I've tried the others. I don't seem at home. I've ceased to mind what any one there thinks. The congregation has changed completely in the past two years, Deacon Van Meter tells me. He called to see us the other day to ask after the children and my financial welfare, offering to help me in any way his experience could serve me. He has aged very much lately, and the death of his wife seems to have completely broken the old man's heart. He has withdrawn from business entirely. My sorrow seems to have touched him in a very tender spot. He begged me in such an earnest way to come back to the church and join in its work, I've made up my mind to go."

King rubbed his hand over his head hopelessly.

"Well, if you've made up your mind, you will go. Ruth, you are the hardest-headed woman to have such a beautiful spirit I ever knew."

The dark eyes smiled into his face.

"You may go with me, Morris."

He took up his cane and coat.

"I'll grudge the minutes I can't talk, but I'll sit and look at you. You are growing more beautiful every day, Ruth. I am grateful for the honour you are going to do me in attending the inauguration. I'll agree to anything you say to-day."

They slipped into a seat under the gallery unobserved. The new usher did not recognise either Ruth or her distinguished escort.

The services moved her with a strange power. In every hymn she heard the deep rich voice of Gordon as she had seen him so often stand in that pulpit. The swell of the organ's full notes throbbed with his memory. The man she heard was no longer the new pastor, but her beloved, and she was living over again the sweet days of the past when he was her own and she had filled his life.

The preacher was reading the most beautiful psalm in the language of man: "The Lord is my shepherd; I shall not want. He maketh me to lie down in green pastures: He leadeth me beside the still waters. He restoreth my soul."

A strange peace came over her as the music of these grand old sentences, throbbing with the passionate faith of centuries, swept her heart.

He was reading from the old Bible that rested on the same golden lectern pulpit Gordon had hurled behind him that awful day in their history. The same crimson cloth he had twisted into a shapeless mass and thrown aside once more hung from its front. She could see a ragged break in the gold of the cross where his enormous hand had crushed it that day.

The thought of God's eternal life and unchanging purpose, binding all time within His mighty plan, soothed her spirit. Men might come and go behind that pulpit and from its pews, but the Church of God, symbol of the eternal, would go on forever. In the deep rhythm of the psalm to which she listened she felt the heart-beat of its continuous unbroken life stretching back to creation's dawn and on until Time shall roll into the ocean of Eternity.

Suddenly the red blood leaped from her heart with a thought, "What God hath joined together man cannot put asunder!"

King's face grew somber as he saw her elation.

He knew that some mysterious spirit had suddenly dropped a veil between them.

When they returned home she was very quiet and her dark eyes shone with unusual brilliance.

"Ruth, you are thinking of that man," he said, with a scowl.

She nodded gently.

King trembled and his fists clenched.

"I could kill him, the great egotistical brute! How strange the madness that binds a woman to the man to whom she first surrenders! I sometimes think it is the most blind, pathetic and tragic instinct that ever shadowed the soul of a human being. It is degrading. You are a woman of character and intelligence. You must shake off this peasant's mania."

She shook her head with a yearning, mystic look.

"I believe God had a great purpose when He made a woman's heart like that. I love him. My very soul and body have become in some mysterious way one with him."

King's eyes blazed.

"Yet he flaunts his love for another woman in your face."

She flinched as from a blow, but answered tenderly.

"Yes; he is mad now. The flesh has mastered the spirit in its struggle for the moment. She holds his body" - a pause and a smile - "but his soul is mine. He may not know it now. He will some day. I know it, and I abide God's time."

"How long can you hold such a delusion, I wonder?" he asked, with angry amazement.

"Forever." she softly whispered.

He drew himself up with grim force.

"I am going to win you, Ruth," he said, slowly lingering with his lips over her name as though he could taste its sweetness.

He looked at her beautiful face and figure tenderly and with an intensity that gave to his eyes a strange glitter.

She turned from him with a sigh and gazed on Gordon's portrait hanging over the mantel.

"No, Morris. I have made up my mind to play my part in

harmony with Love's eternal law. If the world is full of discord, I will still make the sweetest music my soul can sing. I will not try to drown the din, but in my own way sing in perfect time with the beat of God's heart. Perhaps some soul beside me on life's way will catch the note, and it will not be in vain. This may be a blind instinct, but it is not degrading. He who counts the beat of a sparrow's wing, teaches the stork her appointed time, and whispers his call to the swallow in the autumn wind, will not lead me astray."

The man shaded his eyes with his hand as though to hide their misery.

"You are throwing your sweet life away," he said, reproachfully.

"But I shall find it again. When I see the fury of murder in your eyes, and gaze into the gulf of fierce passions into which Frank has descended, I cannot seek my own happiness. The sense of motherhood, the feeling of kinship to all women, brings to me again the certainty that I am right, that one great love unto death can alone give the soul peace and strength, and give to man and the world happiness."

He bent forward quickly.

"But if he were dead you might love me?"

"Not as I love him."

"He is dead a thousand times to you and your life," he cried, bitterly. "He is your wilful murderer. You will see this by and by, and I will win you. I will be content with such love as you can give me. Mine will be so full, so tender, so warm it will be resistless."

She shook his hand kindly and bade him good-by.

"I will send a carriage for you and the children to-morrow.

You will go to the capital with me in my private car."

"I'd rather not, Morris, but I have promised you, and it shall be so."

The ceremony of the inauguration was the most elaborate seen at Albany in years.

Tammany came to the capital thirty thousand strong, and thirty thousand strong they marched through the streets, with their shining silk hats glistening in the sun and their lusty throats shouting for their leader. They had voted the ticket faithfully, and sometimes too often the same day, unkind critics had said, in the years of the past, but for the first time in generations they had placed a full-fledged Grand Sachem of their own Great Wigwam in the Governor's chair, and they made the welkin ring. In the joy of their faces, the steady hoof-beat of their big feet on the pavement and the stalwart pride with which they marched, one saw the secret of their victory. They were in dead earnest. Politics was the breath they breathed and the blood that fed their hearts.

King felt the contagion of their loyalty and enthusiasm, and his inaugural address was inspired and inspiring.

He placed Ruth and the children in choice seats near the speaker's stand, and in every movement of his body, every word and accent, from the moment he appeared till the last shout of his victorious henchmen died away, he was conscious of her presence.

She could feel the intensity of his powerful will pressing upon her in this triumph he was deliberately laying at her feet.

When the ceremonies were over, and his address was being flashed over a thousand wires, he sent the children for a drive, and showed Ruth over the stately executive mansion. He knew the hour was propitious, and he had planned to make a desperate attempt to win some sort of promise from her for their future.

"Now, Ruth," he said, softly, "sit here on this sofa by the open fire. We will be alone for awhile. I've something to show you."

His face was still aglow from the excitement of his triumph. He drew from his inner pocket an official envelope tied with a piece of ribbon.

She leaned over with interest, thinking he was going to read to her some scheme of legislation on which he had been at work.

Instead he drew out a package of her old letters and a lot of faded flowers - every scrap of paper and trinket she had ever given him in her life. He showed her each one, and gave the history of every flower, when she had given it to him, and what she had said.

Ruth buried her face in her hands, and he silently watched her.

"This one," he cried, with a tremor in his voice and a tightening about his eyes, "you gave me the night I took you to that ball at the Hygeia. How soft and delicate your hand felt as you placed it in the lapel of my coat! I could see myself, as in a mirror, in your great dark laughing eyes. I never saw that picture again, Ruth, and the laughter went out of them forever. They were always full of storm and shadows for me after that night."

Her lips were trembling as she turned these leaves from the story of the sunlit days of her girlhood.

The man went on steadily and passionately. "I could show you messages to-day from scores of national leaders offering me their support for the Presidency. This token I am going to show you now has no value to the world or at a bank, but there is not money enough on this earth to buy it."

He drew from his pocketbook a little pink-covered tintype of a boy and girl.

The tapering fingers shook as she held it.

"This is the one priceless treasure I own - this little old tintype we had taken together in fun one day in the tent of the strolling photograph man. You remember he guessed we were sweethearts, and grouped us by the old rules he knew so well. You see, he placed me solemnly in his single chair, with my legs crossed, and made you stand close beside and put your beautiful hand with its slender fingers on my shoulder. You laughed and took it down. He scowled, and put it back, and told you to behave. It was your birthday. You were just seventeen. I was not half as proud to-day, when those thousands who love me shouted and hailed me as their chief, as I was that moment with your dear soft hand on my shoulder. I have felt it there every hour since. You see, I have kissed it until I've worn your face almost away, but the smile is still there."

He took her hand gently.

"Ruth, dear, let me bring the smile back to your living face. These great rooms will be empty and lonely. I wish to hear the patter of your children's feet in them, and the echo of your soft footsteps behind them. You are just thirty-five, in the full glory of perfect womanhood, far more beautiful than this girl of seventeen. Promise me that at the end of a year you will be mine, and let me make your life as glorious to the world as the beauty of your soul and body is to me - you, the forsaken, whom fools pity or blame."

Looking away through her tears, she gently withdrew her hand, bent low and burst into sobs.

"No, no, no! I love him. He is my husband!"

CHAPTER XXVI

AT CLOSE QUARTERS

Ruth had been deeply shaken by the events of the inauguration. She returned to New York in the Governor's private car in a dazed stupor, from which she did not recover for several days.

Morris King's appeal had stirred elements of her character she had long ignored or suppressed. The old pride of blood from races who had been the conquerors and rulers of the world began to beat its wings against the bars of love.

The special swept along the banks of the majestic Hudson, roaring through cities where she saw crowded express trains held on the side tracks for her to pass.

She drew herself up proudly, and a wave of fierce resentment against the man who had deserted her came like a blast of icy wind from the snow-tipped mountains beyond the western shore of the river.

The splendour of the stately mansion on the hill, the enthusiasm of the people for her old lover, his tenderness and deathless loyalty, and the memories that linked him to her in a cloudless girlhood, began to draw her with terrible fascination.

There was something so old-fashioned and chival-rous about King and his love, she felt a strange melting within her heart.

This element of romance she knew he had inherited from her own medieval, home-loving South which she loved. It appealed to her now with a peculiar force - this old-fashioned people and their ways, and a sense of alienation and hostility to Gordon and his radicalism swept once more the storm-clouds across her dark eyes.

She began to question her position and the sanity of her course. She felt the stirrings of social instincts from the high-bred women of old Virginia, the Mother of Presidents and the home of the great constructive minds which had created the Republic. She knew instinctively that she could preside over the White House at Washington with the ease and distinction of the proudest woman who had ever graced it.

Her old lover seemed certain to be the nominee of his party, and his chance of election was one in two. Whatever the outcome, he was young and already a figure of national importance. He was sure to play a greater role in the future than he had ever played in the past.

The idea that she ruled his life and made him what he was, and might be, brought a smile to her lips and the red blood to her cheeks. His fame as a man of cold and selfish ambitions made her knowledge of the secret of his inner life the more sacred and charming.

For two months this battle of pride and blood with the one great passion silently raged in her soul, until she became afraid to hear the ring of her doorbell lest it should be the Governor.

She determined to go to Florida for two weeks on a visit to an old schoolmate in Tampa. There, amid the sunshine and the soft breezes from the gulf, she hoped to see her life and duty in clearer outline.

It was the first week in March which found her seated in the centre of a Pullman car of the Florida Limited of the Atlantic Coast Line.

The train had passed Richmond and was sweeping through the desolate broom-sedge fields still furrowed by those mortal trenches around Petersburg.

Her father had been killed in one of those trenches, a gallant colonel cheering a ragged handful of half-starved men in gray, unmindful of the order of retreat until engulfed by the grand army that swept over them like a tidal wave.

She took the children into the dining-car and found every table full except one, and two seats at that one already reserved. Lucy was placed next to the window, Frank next to the aisle, and the mother crowded between them with an arm encircling each.

She had given the order to the waiter, and was pointing out to Lucy the lines of the battle-field on which her father had died.

"There, dear, it is," she said, with a tremor in her voice, pointing to an angle in the trench on the crest of a ridge. "There is where grandfather was killed."

While Lucy looked and Frank climbed into her lap and was peering out the window, the conductor placed a beautiful woman and tall, distinguished-looking man in the reserved seats at the same table, opposite.

The boy turned, still on his knees, in his mother's lap, and faced the newcomers, whom Ruth had not been able to see for the child's movements.

He stared for a moment at the man with wide-dilated eyes, his body suddenly stiffened, and with a half sob, half cry, he sprang to the floor.

"Look! Mama, dear - look! It's Papa!"

He threw himself on Gordon, and his little arms held his neck convulsively.

The man blushed like a girl as his great trembling fingers smoothed the boy's hair.

Kate's face was scarlet, Ruth turned pink and white, and Lucy, trembling and sobbing, began to scramble across her mother's lap.

The boy's hands tenderly framed his father's crimson cheeks, he kissed him, and again and again his arms clung in passionate clasp about his neck.

"Oh, Papa, we've got you at last! Why didn't you come? We've been praying, Lucy and me, every night for you, and we thought you'd never come back. Mama said you'd gone a long, long way -"

Ruth was choking with emotion, and yet she smiled through her tears. She knew those tiny hands were deep down in the man's soul sweeping his heart-strings with wild, sweet music.

The brunette looked across the table into the trembling face of the fair one. The dark eyes were now tranquil, whatever the storm within. A faint sinile suffused her face with mantling blushes.

Lucy pulled the boy's arms from around her father's neck and slipped her own softer, slender ones there. She kissed him, and laid her brown curls on his breast. Her little hands patted his broad shoulder, and she murmured:

"Papa, dear, I love you!"

Kate attempted to rise, bit her lip, and fairly hissed in Gordon's ear:

"End this scene! Find another table!"

Gordon drew Lucy's arm from his neck and whispered:

"They are all filled, my dear."

The blue eyes blazed with fury as she cried under her breath:

"Get up and let me out!"

Gordon gently drew the children's arms away, placed them back in their seats, rose, still blushing, and accompanied Kate back into their car.

At first the boy was too astonished to speak or protest. When he found his voice he whispered in wonder:

"Mama, who is she?"

Ruth placed a finger on her trembling lips and shook her head.

"Will she let him come back?" he asked, anxiously.

"Hush, dear," the mother said, softly.

The boy put his arms on the table and burst into tears.

Lucy sat very quiet, glancing into her mother's face wistfully. And then she felt under the table, found one of her hands and began to stroke it gently.

When Gordon returned to his car, immediately behind the one in which Ruth was riding, Kate sat for half an hour in furious silence, refusing to speak or answer a question. He had never seen her so beside herself with anger.

She turned on him in a sudden flash and asked with frowning emphasis:

"I wonder why you dragged me off on this idiotic trip?"

"I was worn out and needed the rest," he answered, quietly.

She looked at him with defiance.

"I don't believe a word of it," she said, indignantly. "You wish to get me out of New York. You were too much of a coward to tell Overman your suspicions that he was trying to win your wife."

Gordon looked out of the window in silence.

"We will stop at the next station and go back. I don't care for any more free vaudeville shows in the dining-car."

"Don't be absurd, my dear; you need not meet again."

Gordon smiled in spite of himself.

Tears of vexation filled the violet eyes. "For all of your loud talk of freedom, I believe you still love that first wife of yours! And I am beginning to despise you."

"Come, Kate, this is too absurd. How could I help the accident of such a meeting? I had not seen the children since our separation. She has always taught them to love me. How could I prevent it if I wished?"

"Yes; and you love her, too," she insisted stubbornly, and the full red lips trembled and parted, and then softened into a - smile.

"But don't flatter yourself I care, or am jealous, because this scene has humiliated and angered me. You're not worth a moment's jealousy, you great hulking baby!"

Gordon pressed the button and ordered a lunch served in their seat, and smilingly refused to continue the quarrel.

When the train crossed the North Carolina line it ran into the belt of the advancing spring rains from the South. At Wilson, it was pouring in torrents and had been raining steadily for two days. At Fayetteville, the train was an hour late, delayed by a washout.

Lucy had gone to sleep with her arm around her mother's neck and one hand resting softly on her cheek. Ruth's heart had been deeply touched by this gentle and silent sympathy of the dawning sex consciousness of her daughter's soul. The quick little eyes had seen the tragedy, and a voice within whispered its soft words of new, mysterious kinship.

Soon after the train pulled out of Fayetteville it struck the long, straight run of the South Carolina low country. For thirty miles the track is as straight as an arrow, and before the gleaming headlight of the engine shows on the track the watchers at the stations can see the trembling light in the distant sky beyond the sixteen-mile line of the horizon.

The dark eyes were dozing in fitful sleep with the old spell of love once more enveloping the soul. She was dreaming of him, laughing at some boyish prank.

Over the straight track, down grade, the Limited was sweeping at full speed through the black storm.

Suddenly Ruth was awakened by a sickening crash as though the earth had collided with a star and been crushed as an egg-shell. The car seemed to leap a hundred feet into the air, plunge through space, and strike the ground with a dull smash that sent dust and splinters flying through every inch of space.

She instinctively seized the children, trembling and dazed, and hugged them close. Merciful God, would it never stop! Now the car was plowing through the earth - now falling end over end, straining, grinding, roaring, smashing into death and eternity!

At last - it had seemed an hour - it stopped with a shivering crash.

And then the blackness of night, the swash of gusts of rain overhead, and the moan of the wind. Not another sound. Not a groan or a cry or a human voice.

Was she dead or alive? Ruth felt she must scream this awful question or faint. The children began to sob and she gasped in gratitude:

"Thank God, they are not dead!"

She attempted to get out of her berth and found she must climb. The car was lying on its side. She looked out into the aisle through her curtains and everything was dark. The air choked her with dust, and she caught the odour of burning wool. Deep down below somewhere she could hear, in the lull of the wind, the roar of waters, and feel the car sway as though it were hanging on the edge of an embankment or trestle and about to topple into a torrent.

She pulled the children out into the aisle and tried to crawl toward the end of the car, only to find it crushed into a shapeless mass and the way piled with debris.

A light suddenly flashed up and the steady crackle of flames began. From the debris below came the scream of a woman for help.

She drew back her slender fist and tried to smash the double plate glass windows and only bruised her tapering fingers.

She found a step-ladder and broke the windows out.

Lifting herself on the seat, and peering through, she saw by the glare of the buring wreck the swirling waters of the river twenty feet below.

She rushed back to her berth, on the lower side, smashed the windows, and found the car resting on another sleeper. The blow had broken through both sets of windows.

She lightly sprang through and drew the children after her. A stifled groan, as from one straining the last muscle in some desperate effort, came from a berth. Rushing forward, still dragging the children, she found Kate pinned on her back, with the flames leaping closer each moment.

The violet eyes turned pitifully on Ruth, staring wide with the set agony of speechless fear and searched her face for the verdict of life.

A faint cry came from the full lips, white at the thought of death:

"Help me, for God's sake; I'll be burning in a moment!"

Did the dark eyes waver with an instant's hesitation as she thought of her children imperiled by the delay and of the shame this woman's life meant to her? If so, she who cried did not see it. Swiftly the lithe form sprang to the rescue. She ran her hands over Kate's magnificent figure and tore her robe loose where it was pinioned between the timbers, loosed the wealth of auburn hair caught in the snap of the folding rack of the berth, and she was free.

She took Ruth's hand and kissed it impulsively.

"Thank you. You are an angel."

"Come, we will be burned to death if we don't get out of here in a minute," Ruth cried, excitedly.

She found the berth ladder she had thrown through the window and broke the windows out on the lower side of the car, and called:

"Is any one down there?"

Only the roar of the water and crackling flames answered.

She looked and saw a strip of ground on the bank of the river some eight feet below. They might slide down the trestle if no one could help.

The black eyes flashed into the blue for a moment and the little brunette face went white.

"Where is Frank?" she gasped.

Kate shivered and glanced at the flames.

"I don't know. He was in the berth in front of mine. I hope he is gone for help."

Ruth handed her the children and leaped back to the berth. It was smashed upward and a great hole torn through the roof.

She hurried back and again peered down through the broken window at the narrow strip of ground on the river's brink lit by the rising flames.

And then she gave a cry of joy at the sound of a voice somewhere amid the mass beneath,

"Ruth! Ruth! Is that you and the children in that car?"

"Yes, Frank," came back the steady answer.

"Are you hurt?" he cried, with breathless intensity.

"I think not," she replied, cheerfully.

"Thank God!" she heard his deep voice burst out with trembling fervour.

"Have you seen Kate?" he called.

"Yes; she is here."

"Come, get out of there quick. You will be burned to death!" he shouted. "Hand the children to me and then swing down - I can catch you, one at a time."

She held the boy's hands and dropped him in his father's arms, then swung Lucy through and saw her clasp his neck and kiss him. She helped Kate hold and swing down into his arms. And when she felt him tremble at the touch of her own petite figure her arms tightened about his neck, she kissed him and whispered:

"My own dear love!"

They climbed up the river bank and walked around in the pouring rain, barefoot and treading on broken glass at every step.

Neither the conductor of the train or Pullman cars were anywhere to be seen. Only one porter appeared to have survived, and he sat moaning on a piece of debris.

The great engine, like a huge living monster that had seen with its single eye the abyss of the broken bridge in time, had leaped the chasm and gone plunging and faring over the ties and rails a half mile beyond the wreck, with the engineer and fireman clinging to it.

The lighter portion of the train had struck the embankment of the narrow river. The day cars were piled across the track beyond; the threes Pullmans, smashed and heaped on top of one another, hung on the edge of the broken bridge.

Gordon, with the two women and children, finally found a man who had some sense - a fat drummer seated on his sample-cases calmly putting on his shoes by the light of the burning cars.

He was talking to a younger drummer sitting near, who fidgeted and kept looking about nervously.

"Take it easy, sonny. Put on your shoes," he said, soothingly.

"This is awful!" the young one sighed.

"Well, we're all right, top side up, marked 'with care.' Don't worry. Put on your shoes. You can't walk in this glass barefoot."

When he saw Gordon and his party he stopped tying his shoes and laughed.

"Well, partner, you look like a patriarch who's lost his way. Ain't none of your family got shoes?"

He looked at Gordon's bleeding feet and at Kate and Ruth shivering behind him in the rain.

Gordon smiled and shook his head.

The fat man hastily pulled off his own shoes, snatched off those of the younger man beside him and offered them to the ladies.

"They won't be what you might call a stylish fit, madam," he said gallantly to Ruth, "but they'll beat broken glass for comfort."

Paying no attention to their protests, he made them sit down on the sample-cases and put them on.

Turning to Gordon and his companion, he called cheerfully:

"Come, men, that Pullman's full of blankets; we must get them out for the women and children before it's too late. It's too dark to find our umbrellas. I believe that fool conductor's got mine anyhow and gone home with it. I haven't seen him anywhere."

In a few minutes, he had blankets for all the passengers who had lost their clothes. By daybreak he had found the conductor, counted his tickets, and discovered that out of fifty passengers on the train twenty had been wounded, none fatally, and that thirty had escaped without a scratch. The train had dropped most of its passengers during the day and had only an average of ten people to a coach, and they were seated and sleeping near the centres of each car. By what seemed a miracle, none were killed.

Just as the sun rose, the drummer formed the passengers in line, with the conductor bringing up the rear, and marched them to a cabin where he saw smoke curling up from the edge of a field.

The relief train from Florence, four miles away, arrived at eight, just four hours from the time the accident occurred, bringing the surgeons and new officers to take charge, and the drummer resigned his command.

The new conductor took the name and address of each passenger as they sat in grim array swathed in blankets in the cabin.

Gordon gave the name of "Mr. and Mrs. Frank Gordon, New York," for himself and Kate, who sat beside him. Ruth, not hearing him, with an absent look gave the address, "Mrs. Frank Gordon, New York."

The conductor looked from one to the other, puzzled, and the drummer grinned.

"A Mormon Elder, by the Lord - and he lives in Gotham!" he whispered to the youngster he had in tow.

Lucy lay in her mother's lap suffering from an ugly gash across her forehead. Gordon had bathed her forehead as soon as he had discovered it, and carried her to the cabin, with her soft arms clinging around his neck.

He was watching her lips twitch.

She had grown in the three years out of all resemblance to the child he had left. Her eyes now looked at him with the timid light of a maiden.

As she had clung to him while he carried her to the house, he had felt her lips soft and warm with the dawn of sex when she kissed him and murmured:

"Papa, dear, it's so good to have you carry me. I love you."

For the first time there came into his soul the sweet and terrible realisation that his own flesh and blood had become one with Ruth's in the greatest miracle of earth, the heart of a woman - a woman who could live and suffer and whose heart could break even as her mother's! Her eyes were all his, her hair a perfect mixture of the pigments with which theirs had been coloured. The strength of the man trembled with tender pride and wonder as he looked at her - his living marriage vow, written out before his eyes in a beautiful poem of flesh and blood. In the gentle beauty of her face he saw reflected himself blended with the young vision of Ruth as he had first met her a laughing girl - the little stranger a growing woman, himself and his first love dream in one. Her face held him fascinated.

Kate watched him furtively.

The doctor examined and dressed Lucy's wound, and told Ruth it must be sewed up at once if the child were saved from an ugly scar that would disfigure her for life. He pronounced the heart action too weak from the shock to use an anesthetic.

"It can only be done, madam," he gravely said to her, "if you can get her consent to endure the pain."

"Will you bear it, dear?" the mother asked.

She raised herself up and beckoned to her father.

Gordon had heard the doctor's remark, came at once and bent over her.

"I can if Papa will hold me in his arms and you take one hand and he the other," she said, eagerly.

Gordon took her and told the surgeon to take the stitches without delay.

The first one she bore bravely. But when the steel needle cut the flesh the second time, and the sharp pain sent its chill to her heart, the little face went white and she gasped:

"Kiss me, Papa - Mama, quick -"

They both bent at once, and the blond locks of the man mingled with the dark hair of the woman as their lips touched her face.

The doctor paused, and Lucy smiled faintly.

"I'm better now. I can stand it."

Gordon felt a strange thrill to the last depths of his soul as he sat there holding one of his daughter's hands while Ruth held the other. A sense of mysterious unity with their life came over him.

The little woman saw his emotion and knew its meaning.

She bent close and, while a smile played around her eyes, whispered softly and triumphantly:

"Frank, I'd go through another wreck for this."

And the man was silent.

At Florence, clothes were brought to the train, and those who had none were rigged out after a fashion for the return home.

Not a passenger on the train wished to continue his journey except the fat drummer. He went on to the next station where he had intended to stop, as though nothing worth talking about had happened, and sold a bill of goods before dinner.

Ruth and the children returned to New York on the first train, and Gordon and Kate followed on the next.

Kate had scarcely spoken a word since he had lifted her from the wreck. She was in a deep reverie, but from the occasional gleam of her eyes Gordon knew she was passing through some great crisis. He wondered what the effects of this hour face to face with death would be on her character.

He was amazed at the changes in Ruth since he had last seen her. She had blossomed into the perfect beauty of woman-hood. Not a trace of anxiety was left on her face. Her great dark eyes were calm and soft. Her lips were fuller, and her complexion white and pink, wreathed in its raven hair. Her figure was now the perfection of the petite Spanish type, in full, voluptuous lines, yet erect, lithe, with small hands and feet and tiny wrists, her whole being breathing a spiritual charm. Grace, delicacy, and distinction were in every movement of her body, and over it all, an unconscious and winning dignity.

After several hours of silence, as they sped back toward New York, Kate looked at him curiously and laughed.

"You're not quite so handsome, Frank, in those trousers that stop at the top of your shoes and that coat that pauses just below your elbow."

He held up his long, powerful arms and said, meditatively:

"No. Gestures arrayed like that could hardly move an audience."

The shadows fell across the blue eyes again and they swept him with a critical expression.

"I didn't tell you that Ruth saved my life."

Gordon turned suddenly.

"Yes, and it was a shock to me I'll never get over. I don't know whether I could have done as much for her under similar circumstances, with two children clinging to me and life depending on a moment's time perhaps. But she did it, swiftly and beautifully. To tell you the truth, I've quite fallen in love with her. She is a wonderful little woman. I've been sitting here for hours wondering at the meanness of a man who could desert her. Those great soulful eyes of hers! When I looked up into them, crying like a poor coward for life - I, who had robbed her of what she held dearer than life - I saw only a tender mother's soul looking down at me. Frank, I fear your spell over me is broken. You're a poor piece of clay. The blaze in that car lit up some corners of my soul I never saw before. I think I'll despise all men and love all women after to-day. What fools and puppets we are!"

The man made no reply. He only looked out the window at the flying landscape and saw the sweet face of a little girl.

CHAPTER XXVII

VENUS VICTRIX

The flames of those burning cars, leaping into the skies above the tops of the storm-tossed trees, had lighted some dark places in Gordon's soul, and he was sobered by the revelation.

The clasp of Ruth's arms about his neck, the warm touch of her plump figure, the pressure of her lips on his, and the passionate murmur of the low contralto voice in his ears, "My own dear love!" thrilled him with tenderest memories.

He sat by Kate's side brooding over the days and nights of their married life. Baffled and puzzled, his mind would come back with everlasting persistence to the strange feeling that held him to Ruth - a subtle and sweet mystery, the most intimate relation the soul and body can ever bear on earth, the union in love in the morning of life and its tender blossoming into a living babe.

He began to ask himself had not their being mingled somehow in essence? Had they not been really united by that vital process which sometimes makes married people grow to look alike, and often to die on the same day?

Intimately he knew this little woman, to her deepest soul secrets, and yet she had still eluded him, and now revealed subtle spiritual and physical charms he had never seen nor felt before.

Thomas Dixon

He was conscious at the same time of a new feeling of repulsion on Kate's part, and the thought filled him with nervous foreboding. Whatever change her disillusion had brought, his own physical infatuation for her was, if possible, deeper and more unreasonable.

She could not make him quarrel, but he would sit doggedly gloating over her beauty, his gray eyes flashing and gleaming with the fever for possession that is the soul of murder.

He was not long left in doubt as to the turn her thoughts had taken from the crisis through which she had passed. Her drawing-room was crowded. These receptions were protracted until long past midnight, and he had never seen her so gay or reckless in manner.

She dressed with a splendour never affected before, and received the attentions of Overman with a favour so marked it could not escape the eye of the most casual observer. She made not the slightest effort to conceal it, and her manner was so plain a challenge to Gordon he was stunned by its audacity.

Overman felt this challenge in her mood, and, alarmed, withdrew from the scene. He did not return to the house during the week, and on Saturday he received a dainty perfumed note from her by messenger. It was the first missive he had ever received from a woman.

He turned it over in his broad hand, touched it nervously, and opened it with his fingers trembling as he recognised her handwriting.

"My Dear Mr. Overman: I have been sorely disappointed in not seeing you again this week. I write to command your presence Sunday morning at ten o'clock to accompany me to the Temple, if I choose to go, and to dine with me. Sincerely, KATE RANSOM GORDON."

He wrote an answer accepting and then sat holding this note

in his hand as though it were something alive. For an hour he paced back and forth in his office alone, screening his eye behind his bushy brows, wrinkling his forehead, twisting his mouth, and now and then thrusting his hand into his collar and tugging at it, as though he were choking.

Gordon's new study was in the dome of the Temple commanding a wonderful view of the great city, its rivers and bays, and the long dim line of the open sea beyond the towers of Coney Island. It was his habit to take an early breakfast on Sunday mornings and spend the three hours before his services there.

When Overman reached the house at ten o'clock, clouds had obscured the sun, The air was wet and penetrating, and charged with the premonition of storm. He felt nervous, excited and irritable.

The maid showed him into the spacious library, where a cheerful fire of red-hot coals glowed, and his spirits rose.

He stood before the fire without removing his top coat, and the maid said:

"Mrs. Gordon says to make yourself comfortable. The day is so raw she will not go out. She will be down in a moment."

He removed his coat, sank into an easy chair, and began to wonder what could be the meaning of that note. He knew intuitively that he was approaching a crisis in his life.

He felt a sense of anxiety and discomfort at the idea of spending the morning alone with his friend's wife. Yet he told himself he had no choice - it was fate. A woman had arranged it.

When Kate entered the room, he sprang to his feet with a cry of amazement at the vision of radiant beauty sweeping with sinuous step to meet him. He had never seen her so conscious of power or with better reason for it.

She was dressed in a gown of pink-and-white filmy stuff, which clung to her form, revealing its beautiful lines from the rounded shoulders to the tips of her dainty slippers. The sleeves were open to the elbow, showing the magnificent bare arms. From the shoulders, soft diaphanous draperies hung straight down the length of her figure, revealing by contrast more sharply the graceful curves of the body. The throat was bare, and her smooth ivory neck glowed in round fulness against the background of her hair falling in waves of fiery splendour.

Around her shapely waist hung a double cord of silver, knotted low in front and drawn below the knee by heavy tassels.

The effect of the dress was simplicity itself. There was not a superfluous ruffle or ribbon. Its sole design was not to attract attention to itself, but to reveal the superb charms of the woman who wore it, with every breath she breathed, every step, and every gesture.

The rhythmic music of her walk - quick, strong, luxurious - breathed an excess of vitality. The full lips were smiling and her cheeks aflame with pleasure at his admiration.

Her eyes spoke straight into his with a candour that was unmistakable. They knew what they desired and said so aloud. They had thrown scruples to the winds, and in untamed, primeval strength gazed on life with daring freedom.

Overman stammered and cleared his throat, bowed, and blushed.

She took both his hands cordially and smiled into his face.

"Why didn't you come back to see me this week?"

He hesitated, disconcerted.

"I know," she went on rapidly, leading him to a lounge by the fire.

"You saw the jealousy in Frank's big baby face and you stayed away - now, honestly!"

He pulled nervously at his moustache and his eye twinkled.

"That's about the size of it."

"Well, I'm not a child and you are not. We are both full grown. I am thirty-one years old. I am not Frank Gordon's slave, nor his property. I am a free woman by his own words. And I am going to be free."

Overman glanced at the door.

"Oh! You needn't try to run," she laughed. "I've got you to-day. You can't get away, and I'm going to tell you something. Can you guess what it is?"

The banker began to tremble.

Kate paused, leaned back in the easy chair she had drawn close in front of him, placed both of her dazzling arms behind her head, burying them in the mass of auburn hair, a picture of lazy tenderness and dreamy languor.

"Can't you guess?" she repeated.

"I'm not so bold as to dare," he answered, gravely.

"I will dare," she said, eagerly leaning forward and bending so close he caught the perfume of her hair.

The blood rushed in surging tumult to his face.

"When I found myself caught in that wreck," she began in slow, mellow tones, "it flashed over me that I had been leading a sham life. I, who profess freedom, had been living a slave to form. One desire, the most intense, the most passionate, the most wilful I had ever known was ungratified. Do you know the one thing I asked when the past and present and future flashed before me in a moment?"

She paused, caught her breath, and gave him a look of passionate intensity.

"I only asked for one hour face to face with a great masterful man I know, that I might say the unsaid things, dare, and live the utmost reach of my heart's desire."

Her voice wavered and hesitated. Then, with calm, laughing audacity, she said in sweet, sensuous tones:

"I love you, and you love me - loved me from the first moment you looked into my eyes! Is it not so?"

Overman rose awkwardly, pale as death, his great breast heaving with emotion, and looked again helplessly toward the door.

Kate leaped forward with a laugh, seized his hand, and felt it tremble in her grasp.

"Is it not so?" she repeated, beneath her breath.

He looked down into her shining eyes, sighed, and suddenly swept her to his heart. Her arms circled his massive neck and their lips met.

"Kiss me again," she whispered. "Again! Crush me - kill me if you like! I could die in your arms! Tell me that you love me!"

"I've loved you always," he said slowly. "But why did you do this thing? Frank is my best friend. I would have died sooner than betray him."

"Yes, I know," she cried, impetuously; "that's why I told you. I have no scruples. I am free. It is our compact. I'm done with his maudlin sentiment. I have chosen you. You are my master, my king. I am yours."

"Tragedy to me as it is," he said, with a smile, "it seems too sweet and wonderful to be true, that the most beautiful woman on this earth should love a gnarled brute like me. How is it possible?"

She smoothed his rugged face with her soft hand, drew his head down and kissed tenderly the sightless eye that had caused him so many bitter hours of anguish in life.

The strong man's body for the first time shook with sobs. And the woman soothed him as a child.

"You are my soul's mate," she cried, in a transport of tenderness. "Frank Gordon is no longer my husband. You are my beloved, my chosen one. I will never recognise him again. We will separate from this hour. I am yours and you are mine."

Overman took her hand and, still trembling, said:

"Do you know what that means?"

"Yes," she answered, eagerly. "I know you will be my lord and master, and I desire it. I am sick of sentimentalism."

"It means exactly that," he said, with emphasis. "Out of this bog of fool's dreams I will lift you forever, my own, the one priceless treasure around which I will draw the circle of life and death."

"Yes, yes, I know," she cried, in a glow of ecstatic feeling. "I desire it so. I wish you to be my master. Your service will be sweet; your savage strength will be my joy."

And while they sat planning their future life, Gordon's footstep echoed in the hall.

CHAPTER XXVIII

THE GROWL OF THE ANIMAL

When Gordon entered the library he glanced uneasily at his wife and she smiled in insolent composure.

Overman rose hastily.

"Sorry the weather was so threatening I couldn't persuade your wife to go to the Temple, Frank."

"Yes, the rain is pouring in torrents and it's getting colder," he answered, rubbing his hands before the fire.

"I'll not stay to dinner; I've an engagement at my club," the banker said, briskly.

The one eye ran from the man to the woman in embarrassment at the threatening silence. Kate walked with him to the door.

"You will return at seven o'clock," she said, in even tones.

"If you command it," he coolly answered.

"I do. We will have our parting this afternoon. He can remove to his old quarters at the hotel. I will receive you alone, and we will arrange for the divorce and our marriage."

"Promptly at seven," he said, crushing her hand in his parting grasp.

Gordon ate his dinner in obstinate quiet, now and then looking at his wife's dazzling beauty with fevered yearning in his eyes.

When she rose from the table he said:

"I wish to speak with you in the library, my dear."

"Very well, I'll be down directly," she carelessly replied.

He paced the floor for half an hour, and rang for the maid.

"Tell your mistress I am waiting," he said, abruptly.

The maid did not return, and his anger grew with each lengthening minute.

At the end of an hour, Kate appeared.

He fixed her with a look of angry amazement.

"Well, what is it?" she asked, impatiently.

"Why did you keep your maid and send no answer to me?"

"I was writing a letter. Are you a king? What is it?" she repeated, coldly.

"I wish to say something of the utmost importance both to you and to me, and to another man," he said slowly, in a voice pulsing with a storm of emotion.

The violet eyes danced and laughed in his face.

"So tragic?" she asked, mockingly.

He locked his big hands nervously behind him, stood before the fire, and a scowl settled over his face.

"Yes," he said, with quiet force. "More than you understand, I fear. I have had enough of Mark Overman in this house."

The fair face flushed with excitement. She walked quickly up to him, paused, and slowly pointed to the door.

"Very well. This is my house. You know the way to the hotel, or shall I ring for my maid to show you?"

He stared at her in a stupor, and a sense of sickening terror choked him.

"Kate, are you crazy?" he stammered.

"Never was more myself than in this moment of perfect freedom," she replied, defiantly.

His great jaws snapped in silent ferocity, and his hairy hands closed slowly like the claws of a bear. He planted his big feet apart, and the sparks flew from the gray eyes that seemed to crouch now behind his brows.

"What do you mean?" he sullenly asked.

The woman drew back with uncertainty, chilled by the tone of his voice.

"Just what I said," she answered, with returning courage. "This is my house. I am a free woman. I mean to do what I please. Permit me to repeat your own words from the ceremony of Emancipation, and lest I shock you later, announce that I love Mr. Overman -"

"Kate!" he cried, in bitter reproach.

"Yes, and he loves me. I announce to you this unity of our

Eves. For months it has made us one. May I repeat your ceremony? I have memorised it perfectly. 'Human life incarnates God. Words can add nothing to the sublime fact of the union of two souls. This is the supreme sacrament of human experience. It proclaims its inherent divinity. There is no yesterday or to-day in the harmony and rhythm of two such souls. Love holds all the years that have been and are to be.'"

She paused, smiled, and went on:

"'This is a day of joy - overflowing, unsullied, serene; a day of hope, a day of faith. It is a day of courage and of cheer, and to the world it speaks a gospel of freedom and fellowship. It proclaims the dawn of a higher life for all, the sanctity and omnipotence of love. It asserts the elemental rights of man,' With joy I announce to you my approaching marriage to your friend and schoolmate, Mark Overman, a man in whose strength I glory, whom I shall delight to call my lord and master."

Trembling from head to foot, the veins on his neck and hands standing out like steel cords, Gordon said in a hoarse whisper:

"Kate, darling, this is a cruel joke! You are teasing me."

Again she laughed, sat down lazily, and threw her arms behind her head.

"I never was more serious in my life," she quietly replied.

He hesitated a moment, his eyes devouring her beauty, stepped quickly to her side, knelt and took her hand.

She snatched it roughly, pushed him from her, and cried angrily:

"Don't touch me!"

He attempted to take her hand and place his arm about her.

She sprang up, repulsing him with rage.

"It is all over between us. You are not my husband. I love another."

He arose, walked back to the fireplace and leaned his elbow on the mantel. A wave of agony and blind rage swept him. And then the memory of the hour he spent in such a scene with Ruth caught him by the throat. He could feel the soft touch of her tapering fingers on his big foot as she lay prostrate on the floor before him.

He turned with a shiver toward Kate, who was still gazing at him with insolent languor.

Again his eyes swept the lines of her superb form with the wild thirst for possession that means murder. Two bright red spots appeared on his cheeks.

With slow vehemence he said:

"And do you think the man lives who will dare to take you from me?"

"Dare? I will dare to turn you out of this house. I have chosen the man, and made love to him as his equal. His scruples as your friend bound him. They do not bind me. Thank yourself if this means a tragedy. You challenged the world in your strength. You proclaimed freedom in comradeship. Under the old laws of life, this man would have cut his right arm off rather than betray you. You invited him here. Has he no rights - have I no rights you must respect under such conditions?"

He ignored her question and continued to look at her in stubborn, curious silence.

"Do you know what you are saying?" he asked, brusquely.

"Certainly. Repeating to you the secrets you have taught me."

"Well, I'll teach you something more before this drama has ended, young woman," he said, with a touch of ice in his tones.

She gave an angry toss of her head and cried with sneering emphasis:

"Indeed!"

"Yes. I'll show you, if you push me to it, what a return to the freedom of nature really means. I, too, have had some illuminations in the past months."

She laughed again.

"Ah, Frank, you are a born preacher, and your threats are scarcely melodramatic; they are merely idiotic."

The gray eyes grew somber. He drew his right arm up until its muscles stood a huge twisted knot, fairly bursting through his sleeve, seized her hand roughly and held it with iron violence on his arm.

"It's worth your while to take note of that," he said, steadily disregarding her angry effort to withdraw her hand. "It's made out of threads of steel - that muscle. Few men are my equal. I am talking to you in the insolence of physical strength that proclaims me a king - a savage viking, if you like, but none the less a king."

She attempted again to free her arm from his brutal grip.

"Be still," he growled. "I feel throbbing in my veins to-day the blood of a thousand savage ancestors who made love to their women with a club and dragged them to their caves by the hair - yes, and more, the beat of impulses that surged there with wild power before man became a man."

With a sob of rage, she tore herself from his grasp.

"Oh, you brute!" she cried, stiffening her figure to its full height, her dark-red hair falling in ruffling ringlets about her ears and neck, as she rubbed her arm where his hand had left the blue finger-prints.

"I warn you," he said, his voice sinking lower and lower into a mere growl. "I am your husband. You are my wife. Whatever may have been my dreams, I'm awake now. Man once aroused is an animal with teeth and claws and Titanic impulses, huge and fateful forces that crush and kill all that comes between him and his two fierce elemental desires, hunger and love."

The splendid form of the woman shook with anger. Her eyes ablaze, her cheeks scarlet, her voice sobbing and breaking with wrath, she said:

"And did you call it that when you threw your little wife into the street for me? Is this your boasted freedom - freedom for man's desires alone?"

"I warn you," he repeated, ignoring her question. "You will bring that man into this house again at the peril of his life and yours."

"Yes, you are talking to a woman now," she hissed. "Babbler, preacher, parson, coward! Why did you not say this to him?"

"I'll say it in due time," he answered, deliberately folding his arms. "In the meantime, I will inform you, as you are in search of a master, that I am your master and the master of this house."

With a stamp of her foot, she swept from the room, throwing over her shoulder the challenge:

"We shall see!"

CHAPTER XXIX

BULLDOG AND MASTIFF

Gordon remained in the house during the entire afternoon.

Kate called a boy and sent two messages. One of them summoned her lawyer, the same polite gentleman who had brought the wonderful message from that house a few years before.

At 6:30 Gordon went to his study. The wind had risen steadily and was blowing now a gale from the northwest, and he could feel the cut of hail mixed with the raindrops. It was fearful under foot, and he knew his crowd would be small.

His mind was in a whirl of nervous rage.

"Bah! It's this infernal storm in the air," he cried, in disgust.

A feeling of suffocation at last mastered him. He turned the service over to an assistant, left the Temple, and returned to Gramercy Park with feverish step.

Overman was in the library in earnest consultation with Kate.

They both sprang to their feet as he hurriedly entered, and he could see that Kate was trembling with excitement and dread.

The banker was cool and insolent.

Gordon walked quickly to Kate's side and spoke in icy tones of command.

"Go to your room. I have something to say to this gentleman it will not be necessary for you to hear."

She hesitated and glanced inquiringly at Overman.

"Certainly; it's best," came his low, quick answer.

The hesitation and appeal to the new master were not lost on Gordon. He squared his gigantic shoulders, and wet his lips as if to cool them.

"Very well," she said, facing Gordon. "Before I go I wish to announce to you that it will not be convenient for you to spend another night in this house. If you do not go, I will."

He bowed politely and waved her away with a graceful gesture.

"That will do. I do not care to hear any more."

Kate turned and quickly left the room.

"Won't you sit down?" Gordon said, offering Overman a chair with excessive courtesy.

"Thanks; I prefer to stand," he answered, gruffly.

The single eye was fixed on the man opposite in a steady blaze, following every step and every movement in silence.

Gordon took his place by Overman's side, thrust his big thumbs into his vest at the armpits, and looked off into space.

"It's no use, Mark, for us to mince words," he began, in even, clear tones. "I understand the situation perfectly."

"Then the solution should be easy under your code," the

banker dryly remarked.

"All I ask of you now," Gordon continued, quietly, "as my best friend, is to let my wife alone. Is that a reasonable request?"

"No," was the emphatic answer. "Did I seek your wife? Yet nothing could have wrung from me the secret of my love had you not flung the challenge in my face again and again; and even then my love for you sealed my lips until she broke the spell to-day with words that cannot be unsaid."

Gordon's face and voice softened.

"Granted, Mark, I've been a fool. I know better now. I appeal to your sense of honour and our long friendship. Let this scene end it. Let us return to the old life and its standards."

The big neck straightened.

"Then go back," he flashed, in tones that cut like steel, "to the wife of your youth and the mother of your children!"

Gordon's fist clenched; he was still a moment, and when he spoke his voice was like velvet.

"It's useless to bandy epithets, or to argue, Mark. I don't reason about this thing. I only feel. My passion is very simple, very elemental. It flouts logic and reason. This woman is mine. I have paid the price, and I will kill the man who dares to take her. Do you understand?"

The banker gave a sneering laugh, and twisted the muscles of his mouth.

"Yes, I understand, and I'm not fainting with alarm. You will be a preacher and a poser to the end."

"I have appealed to your principles and your sense of honour first," Gordon repeated, in a subdued voice.

The one eye was closed with a smile.

"Principles! Sense of honour! What principles? What sense of honour? I agree that, under the old view of marriage as a divine sacrament and a great social ordinance, sacrifice of one's desires for the sake of humanity might be noble. But in this paradise into which you have thrust me, with an invitation on your own door for all the world to enter and contest your position, and with you yourself shouting from the housetop freedom and fellowship - Sense of honour? Rubbish!"

"I can see," snapped Gordon, "that one such beast as you is enough to transform heaven into hell."

Overman slowly pulled his moustache, and a grin pushed his nose upward.

"Exactly. I am the one odd individual your scheme overlooked - a normal human being with the simplest rational instincts, a clear brain and the muscle big enough to enforce a desire."

"The muscle test is yet to come," Gordon coldly interrupted.

The banker shrugged his shoulders.

"I suppose so. And you know, Frank, the fear of man is an emotion I have never experienced."

Gordon bent quickly toward him, his face quiet and pale, and said in muffled accents:

"Well, you who have never feared man, listen. Get out of this house to-night, give up my wife, never speak to her again or cross my path, or else -" a pause - "I am going to disarm you, bend your bulldog's body across my knee by an art of which I am master, close your jaw with this fist on your throat, and break your back inch by inch. Will you go?"

Overman surveyed the questioner with scorn.

"When the woman who loves me tells me to go. This is her house!" he coolly sneered.

Again the voice opposite sank to velvet tones.

"Very well, we are face to face without disguise, beast to beast. You haven't the muscle to take her. She is mine. I gave for her the deathless love of a wife, two beautiful children, a name, a career, a character, and the life of the man who gave me being, who died with a broken heart. For her I turned my back upon the poor who looked to me for help, forgot the great city I loved, overturned God's altars, scorned heaven and dared the terrors of hell. Do you think that I will give her up? I own her, body and soul. I've paid the price."

He paused a moment, quivering with passion. "I know," he went on, "I was a fool floundering in a bog of sentiment. But you - one-eyed brute - you were never deceived about anything. You set your lecherous eye on her from the first and determined to poison her mind and take her from me."

"And I will take her," came the fierce growl from the depths of his throat, "and lift her from the mire into which you have dragged her peerless being."

The man opposite gave a quick, nervous laugh.

"Well, I, who have dreamed the salvation of the world and lost my own soul, may sink to-night, but, old boy" - he paused and laughed hysterically - "I'll pull down with me into hell as I go one Wall Street banker!"

"Talk is cheap," Overman hissed. "Make the experiment. You're keeping a lady waiting."

Gordon stepped quickly to the desk and picked up two ivory-handled daggers with keen ten-inch blades, used as paper knives, and handed one to Overman.

"These little toys," he said, playfully, "were a wedding present from my wife on our second anniversary."

"Which wife?" snarled the big, sneering mouth.

Gordon went on meditatively.

"They are the finest Italian steel - sharp medicine for friends to take and give, but it will cure our ills. I never quite understood before what you meant by the fighting instinct when I used to watch you fasten those little devilish points on your Game chickens. I know now. I feel it throb in every nerve and muscle. The impulse to kill you is so simple and so sweet, it would be a crime against nature to deny it."

Overman threw his head to one side, frowned and peered at the man before him curiously.

"Do you ever get tired of preaching? The articulation of wind is a strange mania!"

"Pardon me if I've tired you," came the answer in mellow tones. "You'll need a long rest after to-night, and you'll get it."

Gordon locked the doors, placed the blower over the flickering embers in the grate, and put his hand on the electric switch.

"I am going to put this light out for the sake of the comradeship and chivalry we once held in common. I could kill you at one blow from that blind side of your head. I'll fight you fair. That is a bow to the higher law in the preliminary ritual of nature. But down below, in these muscles, throb forces older than the soul, that link us in kinship to the tiger and the wolf" - his voice sank to a dreamy monotone. "You sneaked into my home in the dark to rob me of my own. In the dark, we will settle on the price. I paid for this treasure an immortal soul. It's worth as much to you."

He turned the switch, and then darkness and silence that could be felt and tasted - only the thrash of the storm against the blinds without.

With catlike tread they began to move around the room on the velvet carpet. They made the circuit twice, and found they were following each other. They both stopped, apparently at the same moment, wheeled, and again made the round in a circle without meeting, now and then stumbling against a piece of furniture.

Gordon suddenly stopped, held his breath, and waited for his enemy to overtake him. He could hear Overman's heavy breathing at each muffled step. When he approached so close he could feel the movement of his body in the air, he suddenly sprang on him, plunging the dagger in his body, and bore him to the floor, knocking the blower from the grate in the struggle.

Over and over on the velvet carpet, dimly lighted now from the glowing coals, they rolled, growling, snarling, cursing in low, half-articulate gasps, thrusting the steel into flesh and bone, nerve and vein and artery.

Gordon suddenly plunged his dagger with a crash in Overman's shoulder, snatched at it, and broke it smooth at the hilt.

Throwing his opponent to one side by a quick movement, he sprang to his feet, and as Overman rose, fastened his enormous hairy left hand on his throat and closed it with the clutch of a bear. His enemy writhed and plunged the steel twice to the hilt in Gordon's breast before his big right hand found the knife and wrenched it from his grasp.

Then slowly, silently, inch by inch, he bent the banker's body over his knee, driving his great fingers into his throat, until the spinal column snapped with a dull crack.

The limp form sank to the floor, and the two big hands clutched the throat until every finger left its black print as if branded red hot into the massive neck.

A quick knock, and Kate's excited voice called:

"Open this door!"

Throwing the body behind the desk in the centre of the room, he felt for the switch, turned on the light, unlocked the door, stepped back and said:

"Come in."

Kate quickly opened the door and rushed into the room. He locked it and put the key in his pocket without a word.

She turned on him a face blanched with speechless horror as he slowly advanced on her in silence, his eyes wide open, cold and set.

The blood was running down across his cheek in a stream from a wound in the upper edge of his high forehead.

She stood dumb with physical fear.

He came close, in laboured breath, his face still sick and white with the desire to kill.

The voice was hard and metallic with the vibrant ring of steel.

"Say your prayers, young woman," he said, slowly. "You are going on a long journey from whence no traveler has yet returned."

She staggered and caught a chair, trembling and shivering.

"Frank, dear, have you gone mad?" she gasped.

"Yes, I went mad in this house one day at the sight of your devil's beauty, and I have been mad from that hour. Now we

Thomas Dixon

have come to the end."

"You will not kill me?" she begged, in piteous fear. "I cannot die; I am afraid. Surely you love me; you cannot -"

He seized her wrists and she cowered with a scream. He held them in one hand and with the other swept her magnificent hair around her throat, grasped it in his iron fist, and thus choking her, thrust the shivering figure backward into the chair.

She managed to free her hands, threw her arms around his neck, and tried to smother him with kisses.

"Frank, dear, I'll love you. Surely you will not kill me. Have pity for all that I have been to you in the past -"

"Hush," he said softly, putting his big hand over her full lips. "Why such childish terror? Love has its moments of sublime cruelty. This impulse to kill is only the awful desire for utter possession, the climax of love. I'll go with you. Neither life nor death shall take you from me."

With a tremulous moan, she sank into a swoon in his arms.

He loosed the hair from her throat, paused, and looked tenderly at the still white face.

Then he sighed, groaned and kissed her.

"No, no, no, no; not that!" he cried, beneath his breath. "How beautiful she is! I brought her to this. Yes, I was the master of her heart and life. I could have made her anything, angel or devil. I have made her what she is - One last kiss" - he bent and gently touched her lips - "and this the end."

With tenderness he laid her on the lounge, loosed her corsage, smoothed gently the tangled hair from her white face, closed the door, and went to his room.

He bathed the blood from his forehead and bound it with a piece of plaster. His head began to swim. A sharp pang shot through his breast, and he felt he was suffocating.

He began to shiver with the instinctive desire to escape, threw some things into a bag he usually carried, stopped and scowled with uncertainty.

"What's the use? What is there to live for?"

Yet the big muscular hands kept on at their task.

An hour later he struggled and staggered up the hill through the black, roaring storm and rang Ruth's doorbell.

CHAPTER XXX

THE CLOUD'S SILVER LINING

Ruth had spent the Sunday in a desperate struggle with the Governor. Long and tenderly he had pleaded for a pledge that would bind her. He had been sure of the note of hesitation and uncertainty in her voice when she left Albany on the day of his inauguration.

He finally left her with the firm avowal:

"I am going to win, Ruth. You might as well make up your mind to it."

She smiled and said "Good-night."

When she went upstairs a low sob came from the nursery and she tipped into the room.

For the past year Lucy would often sit for an hour at a time in reverie, and then lift her little face to her mother with the question:

"Where is Papa?"

Since their return from the railway accident she had never asked again. She only sat now and looked into her mother's face with dumb pain.

Ruth soothed her to sleep, and was standing by her window trying to look out into the storm, which was lashing great sheets of wet snow against the glass.

The bell in the kitchen rang feebly.

She listened. Some one was fumbling at the front door, but the roar of the wind drowned the noise.

The bell rang loud and clear. She sprang to the stairs and went down with quick, nervous step. She fastened the chain-latch, opened the door an inch, and the dim light of the hall flashed on Gordon's haggard, blood-stained face.

She flung the door open, drew him quickly within, slammed and bolted it.

Throwing her arms around his dripping form, she drew him down and kissed his cold lips.

"Frank, my darling, what is it?" she cried, in breathless amazement.

"You must help me, Ruth, dear," he gasped. "We had a fight. I have killed Overman. If you can hide me for a few days, I can escape. I don't deserve it - but I know that you love me - "

"Yes, yes," she sobbed, kissing his hand, "through life and death, through evil report and good report!"

She put him to bed, washed and dressed his wounds. One of them, an ugly hole over his left lung, kept spouting bruised blood as he breathed. The dark eyes grew dim as she watched it.

"Oh! Frank, I must have a doctor," she said, tremulously.

"No, Ruth; I can sleep now. I'll be better in the morning. A doctor will know me."

"But I have one I can trust," she replied, pressing his hand.

He shook his head, closing his eyes.

"You can't stand up against the wind and sleet. It's awful. You can't walk a block. Don't try it."

She watched his mouth twitch with pain.

"I will try it," she answered, firmly. "Lucy will watch with you till I get back."

When Ruth called and told her, the little hands clasped, a cry burst from her heart, and she kissed her mother impulsively.

While his daughter sat by the bedside gently stroking his big blue-veined hand, Gordon dozed in sleep and Ruth crept out into the wild night on her mission of love.

She was half an hour going and coming four blocks. Three times the wind threw her on the freezing pavements. When she climbed up her own steps her clothing was shrouded in an inch of snow and ice, her cheeks were red and swollen, and her hands were bleeding, but a smile played about her lips. The doctor was coming.

He assured her that the wounds were not fatal, and left instructions for dressing them. A few days of rest and all danger would be past.

Through the night, while the wind howled and moaned and roared, the mother and daughter sat by the bedside and smiled into each other's faces.

The meaning of the tragedy had not yet dawned on Ruth. She only knew that her beloved had come, that she was soothing and ministering to him, and her heart was singing its song of triumphant love. The long night of the soul was over. The morning had come. The storm without was on another planet.

As they watched he began to talk in fevered half-dream, half-delirium words, phrases and broken sentences that revealed the inner yearnings and conflicts of his soul.

"Silly fool," he muttered. "Beauty-marvelous - Ruth-dear dark eyes-I-love-her."

As day approached, Ruth began to dread its message. Already she could see the officers at the door.

When day broke she tried to look out of the window, and could only see across the street. The park and the city below were blotted out. The whole world seemed one white, swirling, howling smother of snow. The wind came in long gusts of shrieking fury. She could count its pulse-beats in the lulls which were growing shorter. And, child of the sea that she was, she knew that the advancing cyclone had not reached its climax. She breathed a prayer of relief. They could not find him to-day.

The cook did not come. Not a milk-wagon or bread-cart echoed through the street. Not a call of newsboy, whistle of postman, or cry of a schoolboy. The house-girl had not come. Ruth descended to the kitchen, made a fire, and cooked breakfasts. With her own hands she was serving her Love, and her heart was singing.

At ten o'clock, she looked out of her window, and the snow was piled to the second story of the houses opposite, which were receiving the full fury of the blast.

The wind was visible. It blew in white, roaring sheets of snow, howling, whistling, screaming, shrieking. Tin roofs, signs, battered chimney-tops, blinds, awnings, brackets, flagpoles, sheet-iron eaves and every odd and end began to crash and rain in the streets and bury themselves in the drifts.

The woman's heart rode on the wings of the storm. Her beloved was hiding safe beneath its white feathers. She wondered if any one else in all the world were singing for joy with its wild music.

For three hours of the morning, struggling men had braved the storm and fought to reach their places of business. Shouts, curses, calls, laughter, the screams of boys, at first; and then defeat, silence and the roar of the wind.

Street-cars were piled on their sides, and the tracks jammed with debris and mountains of snow.

At eleven o'clock, from Manhattan there was no Jersey or Brooklyn. The ferries were still. The great dead Bridge hung swaying in the dark sky, a white festoon of ice and snow, like a jeweled garland swung from heaven to soften the terrible beauty of a frozen world. The waters below were lashed into a white smother of spray. The air cut like a knife with the sand blown from the flying waves of the distant beaches.

Policemen crouched and shivered in barred doorways. The storm had caged every thief, burglar and murderer, as it had sheathed the claws of every bear and wolf on the distant mountain-side.

The snow was piled over the tops of the doors of the City Hall and Court House. There was no Mayor, no court, no jury.

The Stock Exchange was closed, the Custom House and Sub-Treasury silent, and every school without teacher or scholar. Every depot was placarded, and not a wheel was moving. Not a newspaper found its way to a home, or a single piece of mail arrived in New York, or was sent from it, or delivered within its gates. Every telegraph and telephone office was silent and the fire department was paralysed.

The elevated trains crawled and slipped and stalled and fought on their steel trestles till ten o'clock, and the last wheel stopped and froze.

At three o'clock a Staten Island ferry-boat ventured her nose out of her slip. The wind snapped off both flag-staffs and smokestack, hurled them into space, caught her in its mighty claws, dragged her helpless across the bay and flung her on the Staten Island shore.

Wherever men could gather they talked in low, helpless and bewildered tones.

The storm signal, set by the Weather Bureau, was torn to shreds and the wind-gage hurled into the sky as it registered eighty-two miles an hour.

On the mountains of Colorado and over the plains of Dakota it had begun, a fine, misty rain sweeping eastward, throwing out its soft skirmish-line of breezes, drawn by the summons of the Storm King far out on the waste of the sea. And then the king had blown his frozen breath on the earth and the mighty city had been blotted from the map and its tumult stilled in soft white death.

Ruth drew Gordon to the window against which the sparrows crouched and shivered, that he might watch the storm's wild pranks.

"After all," the wounded man cried, "it has been conquered, the rushing, tumultuous city! Beyond the rim of man's map of the world broods in silence the One to whom its noise is the rustle of a leaf and this wind but a sigh of His breath! What can endure?"

His eyes rested on the smiling, lovelit face of Ruth, and he forgot the storm in the deeper wonder of a pure woman's love.

CHAPTER XXXI

A LACE HANDKERCHIEF

The next morning the lulls between the gusts of wind grew longer and the wind-waves shorter. The snow ceased to fall and the shadows on the clouds began to brighten with the glow of the sun behind them.

The city stirred and shook off its white robe of death. The woman looked at the wounded man with a stifled moan.

"It's no use, Ruth," he said, feebly. "I can't escape. I've got to face it."

"What will they do to you, Frank?" she asked, in misery.

"I don't know," he answered, brokenly. "I killed him in the heat of passion in a fight. But I'll be tried for murder."

The officers came and read the warrant of arrest. The dark, tense figure, erect, with defiant face wreathed in midnight hair, stood by his bedside and held his hand.

Her great eyes glowed and gleamed as though a young lioness stood guard over a wounded cub.

Behind the bars in murderers' row the weeks and months were dragging slowly to the day of trial. The rush and roar and fever of the city were now a memory as he sat in brooding silence.

The press was hostile, and reporters worked daily with an army of detectives to find every scrap of evidence against him, and as the day fixed for his arraignment drew near, story after story appeared in the more sensational journals, written with the clearest purpose of influencing the mind of every possible juryman.

Ruth's heart sank with anguish as she read these stories, but they stirred her to more vigorous action. She read every newspaper carefully and followed every clue of reporter and detective to anticipate its influence.

Not a day passed but that she carried to the man behind the bars a message of courage and cheer.

Gordon would sit and watch for that one face whose light was hope until it became the only reality in a universe of silence and darkness. His whole life seemed to focus now on the little face with its dimpled chin and shy, tremulous lips smiling into his cell.

The soft contralto voice, even when it sank to the lowest notes of melancholy, was full of tenderness and caressing feeling. As he touched her tapering fingers on the steel bars and watched the red blood mount until her delicate ears shone like transparent shells in the dark mass of her hair, visions of their life together would rise until the past few years seemed the memory of a delirium.

He studied her with increasing fascination. The illuminating power of restraint had developed new forces in his sensitive mind. How marvelous she seemed, walking toward his cell with gentle yet triumphant footfall, her face aglow with tenderness and love, and how his soul leaped those bars and embraced her!

Many friends on whom he had counted had failed. She had never failed. Her resources were endless, her energy infinite. She would have fought all earth combined without a tremor.

And yet those who came in contact with her felt a gentleness that touched with the softness of a caress.

The day before the trial her face glowed with hope.

"Frank, our lawyers are sure we will win!" she cried, with joy. "Barringer has determined to rest the case on the charge of wilful murder. And if he does the jury will acquit you. There is only one shadow of uncertainty."

The dark eyes clouded and a gleam of fire flashed from their depths.

"I know," he said, sorrowfully.

"We can't find whether that woman is going on the witness stand against you. I've tried in vain to get one word from her lips."

She brushed a tear from her eyes with a lace handkerchief. The man saw it was the mate to the one she had given him stained with her blood the day he had deserted her.

When, she turned to go, he felt for the cot behind him as though blind, fell on his face and burst into sobs.

CHAPTER XXXII

A LIFETIME IN A DAY

The court-room was crowded to suffocation. The corridors were jammed, the pavements, park and street outside a solid mass of humanity.

The prison van plowed its way through the throng. Gordon stepped out, with handcuffs jingling on his wrists, and straightened his giant figure between the two officers who led him.

A cheer suddenly burst from the crowd and echoed through the court-room.

There was no mistaking that cry. He had heard it before. He knew. He had killed a banker. They were glad of it and proud of him. In muttered curses and cheers they said so. He was the champion of a class, and the murder of an enemy had made him a hero. No matter the right or wrong. Down with every banker - what did they care!

Ruth met him in the anteroom, followed him into the prisoner's dock and took her place by his side.

The bill of indictment was read.

"The People against Frank Gordon."

With terrible memories the title rang through his soul. The people, for whom he had fought, for whom he had suffered, worked and dreamed, had put him on trial for his life. What a strange fate! The faces grew dim, and a sense of illimitable and awful ruin crushed him.

A soft hand stole gently into his, and its warmth cleared his brain.

He looked around the room and, to his surprise, saw dozens of people he had helped in his ministry of the Pilgrim Church. Just in front of him sat a woman who, under the inspiration of his preaching, had given her fortune to found an orphanage for homeless girls, and was spending her life in happy service as its presiding genius.

She nodded and smiled, and her eyes filled with tears.

There was a stir in the group of lawyers behind him, and the old woman who had kissed him the day Ruth was watching pushed to his side, seized his hand, choked, and could say nothing. She had come all the way from Virginia to cheer him.

Ludlow, his faithful deacon, he saw, and near him sat Van Meter. The little black eyes were solemn and the mouth drawn with sorrow. Over against the wall, jammed in the crowd, he saw Jerry Edwards, who was still telling the story of his life with reverent wonder and love. He clasped both hands together, shook them over the heads of the crowd, and smiled.

A feeling of awe came over him as he thought of the eternity of man's deeds, going on and on forever, whatever might be his own fate.

He looked curiously at Barringer, the young Assistant District Attorney, who was conducting the case against him. In the dark-brown eyes, keen and piercing, there was deadly hostility. He had become famous as a relentless public prosecutor. He came of a long line of great lawyers of the old South, and the breath of a court-room was born in his nostrils. Gordon was chilled by the cold, clear ring of his penetrating voice.

While the jury was being impaneled, Ruth sat by Gordon, eagerly trying to see the invisible secrets of every juror's soul who faced the man she loved.

The court ruled that Socialists were disqualified to sit on the case.

When the twelve men were selected she scanned their faces with searching gaze for the signs of life or death. Their names all seemed strange. She could make nothing out of them.

The opening address of Barringer choked her with fear. In cold-blooded words he told the jury of the certainty of the guilt of the prisoner. His manner was earnest, dignified and terrible in its persuasive assurance.

For days his awful closing sentence rang like a death knell in her ears.

Four days of the week were consumed by the witnesses for the prosecution. On Friday morning Ruth and her lawyers were elated over the unimportant character of the testimony.

Suddenly Barringer looked at the prisoner, frowned, and said:

"Call Kate Ransom Gordon to the witness stand."

The prisoner went white and lowered his eyes.

There was a stir at the side door. With quick, firm step the magnificent figure crossed the room, with every eye save one riveted on her beautiful face.

She took her seat, and in cool, clear tones told her story.

The prisoner looked up once, and she met his gaze with a

glance of fierce resentment.

She gave the long history of his suspicions of Overman, of their quarrels about him, of his jealousy and his threat to kill him. With minute detail she explained the events of the fatal Sunday, described his entrapping Overman in the library unarmed, and of his murder in the dark. She told how she had rushed to the door and found no light within, and how he had enticed her into the room and attempted to choke her to death.

Finally she explained to the jury that the wounds Gordon had received were not from Overman in a fight, but that he had tried to kill her and commit suicide and had failed.

For five hours she sat in the witness chair and coolly swore his life away, baffling with keenest wit at every turn the shrewd lawyer who baited, harassed and cross-questioned her with merciless vigour.

When she declared that Gordon's wounds were self-inflicted, he stared at her in dazed wonder and gasped to Ruth:

"Merciful God, is she deliberately lying, or does she believe it?"

Ruth did not answer, but slipped her warm little hand in his and pressed it. His fingers were like icicles.

Gordon seemed to sink into a stupor and take no further note of what was going on in the room.

He turned around, placed his arm on the chair, and fixed his eyes on Ruth, looking, looking! As he felt her hot hand trying to warm the chill of death in his own, he followed every movement of a muscle of her face with hypnotic intensity.

When they led him back to the prison van his shoulders drooped with mortal weariness. He had lived a lifetime in a day, and his hair had turned gray.

CHAPTER XXXIII

THE VERDICT

Gordon seemed to take no further interest in the trial. He only sat day after day and watched Ruth. Now and then a faint flush tinged the prison pallor of his cheeks as from some thought passing in his memory.

Barringer's speech to the jury was one of fierce and terrible eloquence. Every art of persuasion, every trick of oratory, every force of personality he used with pitiless power. In ridicule, sarcasm, invective, pathos and logic, his voice rose and fell, pulsed and quivered, or rang with the peal of a trumpet. He held the jury in the hollow of his hand for four hours, while Ruth stared at him with her heart in her throat, every word cutting her flesh like a knife or smashing the tissues of her brain with the force of a bludgeon.

The jury retired.

Through the dreary hours of the afternoon Ruth sat in the anteroom by Gordon's side waiting for the verdict. Minutes lengthened into hours, and hours into days and years, until time and eternity were one, and she lived a life of despair or hope within the second between the ticks of the clock on the wall.

She tried to say a word of cheer to Gordon, and choked. The little chin drooped, showing the white teeth, and she sat in dumb misery like a sick child.

The man looked at her tenderly and said:

"You must be calm, Ruth, dear. Death is a physical incident that no longer interests me, except as it affects you. You are the one miracle of life and death to me."

She pressed his hand and could not answer.

At five o'clock the jury returned for instructions, and she listened with agony to their awful questions.

At six o'clock there was a hurried stir in the court-room. The crowd surged into its doors and packed every inch of space.

The jury were filing in with their verdict.

The judge solemnly took his seat, and the clerk summoned Gordon to stand up.

The giant figure rose with dignity and his steel-gray eyes pierced the jury.

The foreman's lips moved:

"Guilty of murder in the first degree!"

A long breath, a stir, a murmur, and then a broken sob from a woman's heart. Her arms were around his neck, her head on his breast, and her swollen lips in low, piteous tones cried:

"My darling!"

CHAPTER XXXIV

THE APPEAL

Two weeks later the judge pronounced the sentence of death. Again the dark figure was by the prisoner's side, alert, erect, every faculty of mind and body at its highest tension, her cheeks aflame with defiance, her eyes gleaming with hidden fire.

She was sure the Court of Appeals would grant a new trial. She bade her beloved good-by at the gates of Sing Sing, and the door of the Chamber of Death closed upon him.

Day and night she worked with tireless energy. She systematically laid siege to the editors and owners of the papers in New York, and at last won every hostile critic by her patience, her beauty of character, and the infinite pathos of her love.

The moment sentence of death was pronounced on Gordon, Kate sued for a divorce from him as a convicted felon, and it was granted.

The little dark woman became the toast of every hardened newspaper reporter who came in contact with her. The newsboys learned to recognise her from her pictures, and as she went in and out of the court-rooms and the lawyers' offices they would watch and wait for her, doff their dirty caps, smile, hand her a flower, and cry:

"She's de queen!"

When Ruth saw the notice of Kate's divorce, she asked her lawyers to arrange at once for her to remarry Gordon at Sing Sing.

The senior counsel shook his head.

"You must not dare, madam," he gravely said. "If we should not get a new trial, or fail on the second trial, the Governor at Albany is our only hope."

A wave of sickening terror swept Ruth's soul. She recalled King's strange reserve of the past months. His letters were kind and sympathetic, but there was something hidden between their lines that chilled her.

"We must not lose!" she answered, bitterly.

"I don't think we will," the lawyer hastened to assure her. "But we must reserve every weapon."

The Court of Appeals decided in Gordon's favour and ordered a new trial.

As the day approached, Ruth's nervousness increased. His chances were better, but she could hear the awful words of Kate Ransom swearing away his life. Their echoes rang in her soul until she could no longer endure it.

She was at Gramercy Park at last.

When Kate swept proudly and coldly into the room, and extended her hand, she held it in her grasp timidly and nervously.

"I've come to beg you," she said, piteously, "not to say he made those wounds in his own breast. They fought a duel as men have often done. You were in a swoon. You thought he did it himself because he told you he was going to die with you. He did not hurt you. He only laid you tenderly on the lounge, smoothed your hair, kissed and left you. Surely you have brought me enough sorrow. Have pity on me!"

Kate led her to a seat and spoke with quiet decision. "I said what I believed to be the truth. I shall repeat it. I can feel his wild beast's claws on my throat now in the night sometimes and wake with a scream."

"Ah, but he was mad," she cried, through her tears. "He is tender and gentle as a child. Surely you" - she paused and caught her breath - "who have slept with your head on his dear breast know this!"

"It is useless to talk to me," she answered, with anger. "He deserves to die. And it will be a good riddance for you, and for the world. He was stirring the passions of mobs that will yet make work for hangmen."

"But he is not on trial for this," she pleaded, "You should be the last to reproach him with it. Think of all the sacrifices for you - his career, his wife and children, his father, his friends. Surely there is yet one spark of love for him in your heart?"

Kate shook her head.

"Then for my sake, I beg of you - you are a woman. You have loved. Have mercy on me! You asked me once for help - did I fail you?"

The blond face softened.

"No, you didn't. I'm sorry for you. If it were your life, I'd save it if I swore a thousand lies - but for him, the brute - I can feel him strangling me now - you have not felt his hands on your throat."

"No," said the soft contralto voice, "not on my throat; it

　　　　Thomas Dixon

would have been a relief to have felt them there. They were on my soul. But I love him -"

Kate was relentless, and Ruth left, shivering with anguish and angry pride.

The new trial dragged its length to the second jury. Ruth spent and pledged the last dollar of her fortune.

Once more she heard the foreman, in tones that seemed far off in space, say the fatal word -

"Guilty!"

She stood by his side again before the judge and heard the words of death fall from his lips, this time with blanched face and cold little fingers locked in agony.

Again the gates at Sing Sing closed, and a woman turned her footsteps toward the Governor's Mansion at Albany.

CHAPTER XXXV

BETWEEN TWO FIRES

Ruth trembled at the thought of her appeal to King. She knew his iron will, his intense love, and the certainty with which he had long regarded their coming union. His ambitions were still mounting, and daily with better assurances of success. His party had chosen another man their candidate for the Presidency, and had been overwhelmed in defeat, while he had been re-elected Governor by a larger plurality.

He received her with grave tenderness.

"Morris," she cried, pathetically, seizing his hand and holding it, "he is not guilty of murder. Everything has been against him in these trials. They were not fair. He killed that man in what men have always called a fair fight. You are a manly man. You believe in justice. You will not let them kill him!"

She could feel the strong man's hand tremble in hers, looked up into his face, and saw a tear quiver on his lashes.

"Oh! Ruth," he cried, bitterly, "why do you cling to this man? He is regarded as the most dangerous firebrand in America. I could show you hundreds of letters piled on that desk begging me in the name of law and order and all the forces of civilised society not to interfere with his sentence. Come, you know how I love you. This is horrible cruelty to me. The doors of the White House are opening. You know that what I have, am now, and ever may be, is yours. It will all be ashes without you. I offer you a deathless love, honour and glory, and you come here to tell me you prefer a convicted felon in his cell. My God, it is too much!"

The Governor leaned on his desk and shaded his face with his hands.

"How can I help it, Morris, if I love him?" she asked, piteously.

He raised his head, looked away, and softly said:

"Ruth, could you never love me?"

She was silent a moment and her lips trembled.

"If he dies, I cannot live," she gasped.

He leaned close, took her hand, and said:

"I'll order a stay of sentence for three months."

She kissed his hand, and murmured:

"Thank you."

From the telegraph office at Albany over the wires to Sing Sing's house of death flew the message:

"Sentence stayed for three months while the Governor considers your pardon. Faith and hope eternal. RUTH."

The next express carried her to him with the copy of the Governor's order in her bosom.

The warden smiled and congratulated her. She had long before won his heart, and there was no favour within the limits of law that he had not granted to the man she loved.

Ruth looked at Gordon tenderly through the barred opening of his cell.

Her heart ached as she saw the ashen pallor of his face and the skin beginning to draw tight and slick across the protruding cheek-bones of his once magnificent face. Three years of prison had bent his shoulders and reduced his giant frame to a mere shadow of his former self. Only the eyes had grown larger and softer, and their gaze now seemed turned within. They burned with a feverish mystic beauty.

Ruth fixed on him a look of melting tenderness and asked:

"Do you not long for the open fields, the sky and sea, my dear?"

He gazed at her hungrily.

"No. Sometimes I've felt a queer homesickness in these dying muscles that thirst for the open world, but I've no time to think of mountain or lake, or hear the call of field or sea - Ruth, I can only think of you! I have but one interest, but one desire of soul and body - that you may be happy. I would be free, not because I fear death or covet life" - his voice sank to a broken whisper - "but that I might crawl around the earth on my hands and knees and confess my shame and sorrow that I deserted you."

"Hush, hush, my love; I forgive you," she moaned.

"Yes, I know; but all time and eternity will be too short for my repentance."

The woman was sobbing bitterly.

"These prison bars," he went on with strange elation, "are nothing. The old queer instinct of asceticism within me, that made a preacher of an Epicurean and an athlete, has come back to its kingship. Its sublime authority is now supreme. I despise life, and have learned to live. There is no task so hard but that the king within demands a harder. There can be no pain so fierce and cruel but that it calls my soul to laughter. As for Death -"

His voice sank to dreamy notes.

"She who comes at last with velvet feet and the tender touch of a pure woman's hand - her face is radiant, her voice low music. She will speak the end of strife and doubt, and loose these bars. With friendly smile she will show me the path among the stars, until I find the face of God. I'll tell Him I'm a son of His who lost the way on life's great plain, and that I am sorry for all the pain I've caused to those who loved me."

Ruth felt through the bars and grasped his hand, sobbing.

"Don't, don't, don't, Frank! Stop! I cannot endure it!"

The warden turned away to hide his face.

CHAPTER XXXVI

SWIFT AND BEAUTIFUL FEET

For three months Ruth went back and forth from Sing Sing to Albany, battling with the Governor for Gordon's life and cheering the condemned man with her courage and love.

The fatal day of the execution had come, and she was to wage the last battle of her soul for the life of her love with the man who loved her.

It was a day of storm. The spring rains had been pouring in torrents for a week and the wind was now dashing against the windows blinding sheets of water.

A carriage stopped before the Governor's Mansion, and two women wrapped in long cloaks leaped quickly out. The Governor was at his desk in his office.

There was the rustle of a woman's dress at his door. He looked and sprang to his feet, trembling.

He threw one hand to his forehead as though to clear his brain, and caught a chair with the other.

Advancing swiftly toward him, he saw the white vision of Ruth Spottswood the night of the ball when he had lost her. The same dress, the same rounded throat, only the bust a little fuller, and the same beautiful bare arms with the delicate wrists

Thomas Dixon

and tapering fingers. The great soulful eyes, with just a gleam of young sunshine in their depths, and the same flowers on her breast. She walked with lithe, quick grace, and now she was talking in the low sweet contralto music that had echoed in his soul through the years.

"Please, Governor," she was saying, as her hot hand held his, "save my father!"

The man's eyes were blinking, and he put one hand to his throat as though he were about to choke. He looked past the white figure of the girl and saw her mother kneeling in the corner of the room, the tears streaming down her face and her lips moving in prayer.

In quick tones he called:

"Ruth!"

She leaped to her feet and was before him in a moment, with scarlet face, dilated eyes and disheveled hair.

"You've won. I give it up."

Ruth pressed both hands to her breast and caught her breath to keep from screaming.

He pressed the button on his desk. The clerk appeared.

"Write out a full pardon for Frank Gordon, and call the warden of Sing Sing!"

Ruth dropped to her knees, crying:

"O Lord God, unto thee I give praise!"

In a moment the clerk hurried back to the Governor's side and in startling tones whispered:

"The wires are down, sir. I can't get the warden."

The Governor snatched his watch from his pocket.

"There is no train for two hours. Order me a special!"

The despatcher flashed his command for a clear track as far as the wires would work, and within fifteen minutes the great engine with its single coach dashed across the bridge and plunged down the grade toward Sing Sing, roaring, hissing, screaming its warnings above the splash and howl of the storm.

The Governor sat silent with his head resting on his hand, shading his eyes.

Ruth, still and pale, gazed out the car window, and, shivering, closed her eyes now and then over the vision of a cold dead face she feared to see at the journey's end.

They had made fifty miles in fifty minutes, and not a word had been spoken.

The Governor looked at his watch and leaned over:

"Cheer up, Ruth. We are making a mile a minute through the storm, over slippery rails. We will make it in time."

Suddenly the emergency brakes came down with a crash, every wheel was locked, and the train slid heavily on the track, hissing, grinding, swaying, the steel rails blazing with sparks.

The Governor sprang from the car. "We're blocked by a wreck, sir," the conductor said, touching his cap. "The high water has undermined the track on the river bank."

Within twenty minutes the engine in front of the wreck was secured, Ruth and Lucy were in the cab, and the engineer and fireman stood reading their orders.

Thomas Dixon

"Gentlemen, I am the Governor," said a voice by their side.

They looked up.

"This is a matter of life and death. The life of a man - and the life of the little pale woman I helped into your cab. Put this engine into Sing Sing by five minutes to two o'clock and I'll give you a thousand dollars. Five hundred for each of you."

The engineer smiled.

"We'll do it for you, sir, without money. We voted for you."

The Governor pressed their hands.

Down the storm-clouded track the engine flew with throbbing heart of steel and breath of fire like a panting demon. Back and forth over the spongy rails she swayed, her mighty ribs cracking as she lurched and jumped and plunged. But the fireman in his flannel shirt, dripping with perspiration, never paused, as with steady stroke he fed her roaring mouth; and the engineer, with his hand on her pulse, leaned far out of the cab with his eyes fixed on the flying track.

The hour for the condemned man was at hand. He had asked the warden as a special favour to do his duty without delay at the appointed time.

Gordon was ready, dressed with his old fastidious distinction to the last detail of his toilet. He had spent the entire night before writing to Ruth the last chapter in a secret diary he had kept and given to the warden for her.

The warden read the death warrant with halting lips. He had been strangely drawn to this tall young giant with his premature gray hairs. Gordon's words of lyric fire to him of the mysteries of life and death had thrown a spell over his imagination. He was going to kill him now with the horrible feeling that he was his own brother.

"Come, my friend," Gordon said to him, cheerfully, "you promised me there should be no delay. I've a child's eagerness now to push the black curtains aside and see what lies beyond. I've often dreamed and wondered. In a few minutes I shall know. I hear it calling me, that unknown world of silence, beauty and mystery. Let us make haste."

But the feet of the jailer were of lead. He would stop and hold his lower lip tightly under his teeth, as though in pain.

At last they were in the dim chamber that is the vestibule of death. The cap had been drawn over his face and the leather straps buckled on his wrists legs,

The warden put his hand on the electric switch.

There was a shout and a stir without, the thump of hurrying feet, and the butt of a guard's gun thundered against the door.

The warden sprang forward.

"Stop! The Governor!" he heard faintly shouted through the deep-padded panels.

CHAPTER XXXVII

THE KISS OF THE BRIDE

For a quarter of an hour the Governor sat and talked with Lucy, waiting the arrival of Gordon and Ruth. The warden arranged that they should meet in the adjoining room alone.

No eye save God's saw their meeting. Those who waited only heard through the heavy curtains half articulate cries like the soft crooning of a mother over her babe.

When they entered the room and Lucy had clung passionately for a moment to the neck of the tall, gaunt figure, the Governor took his hand.

"I have accepted Ruth's word and yours for the truth in this case, Frank Gordon. I have grown to know that she is the soul of truth. I heard you preach once from the text, 'He saved others, himself he could not save.' I did not know then what you were talking about. I know now -"

"Oh, Morris," Ruth broke in, "we will always love you as the nearest and dearest friend on earth."

"As for you, Frank Gordon," he went on. "I could no longer hate you if I tried. In the presence of a love so pure, so divine as that which hallows your life, I uncover my head. I am on holy ground - I am in the presence of the living God."

He turned away, and Ruth broke into a sob, while the man by her side hung his head and sat down as though too weak to stand.

The Governor lifted Gordon from the seat, seized Ruth's hand and placed it in his.

"I know your heart's desire, Ruth," he said, slowly, "I have an officer of the law here to perform a marriage ceremony. Holding your first marriage a divine sacrament, you once planned a civil one in this grim prison. No matter how I learned this: it shall be so to-day."

The magistrate advanced and pronounced them husband and wife, sat down by a desk, and made out the record.

The Governor rose and handed the official pardon to Gordon.

"To you I give life."

He tore the other paper into two parts by its dotted lines, handed Ruth one half and held the other in his trembling fingers.

"This, Ruth, is your marriage certificate" - he paused - "and my death warrant. Frank Gordon, we have changed places."

Again the woman sobbed.

"You have forgotten something, Morris," she answered, wistfully.

"Yes, I know: myself."

"It is your right to kiss the bride," she said, softly, "and I wish it."

He stooped and reverently touched her forehead. And when he turned away Lucy stood before him, her soft young bosom, neck and face crimson, her eyes dancing, and the sweet little mouth quivering.

"May I kiss you, Governor?" she cried, tremblingly. "You are my hero!"

Her bare arms flashed around his neck, and her warm lips met his.

In the mansion on the hill at Albany, the Governor sat that night in his magnificent room alone until the dawn of day, holding in his hand an old battered tintype picture of a laughing girl standing beside a poor young lawyer.

Choose from Thousands of 1stWorldLibrary Classics By

A. M. Barnard
Ada Leverson
Adolphus William Ward
Aesop
Agatha Christie
Alexander Aaronsohn
Alexander Kielland
Alexandre Dumas
Alfred Gatty
Alfred Ollivant
Alice Duer Miller
Alice Turner Curtis
Alice Dunbar
Ambrose Bierce
Amelia E. Barr
Amory H. Bradford
Andrew Lang
Andrew McFarland Davis
Andy Adams
Anna Sewell
Annie Besant
Annie Hamilton Donnell
Annie Payson Call
Annonaymous
Anton Chekhov
Arnold Bennett
Arthur Conan Doyle
Arthur M. Winfield
Arthur Ransome
Atticus
B.H. Baden-Powell
B. M. Bower
Baroness Emmuska Orczy
Baroness Orczy
Basil King
Bayard Taylor
Ben Macomber
Bertha Muzzy Bower
Bjornstjerne Bjornson
Booth Tarkington
Boyd Cable
Bram Stoker
C. Collodi
C. E. Orr
C. M. Ingleby
Carolyn Wells
Catherine Parr Traill
Charles A. Eastman
Charles Dickens

Charles Dudley Warner
Charles Farrar Browne
Charles Ives
Charles Kingsley
Charles Klein
Charles Amory Beach
Charles Hanson Towne
Charles Lathrop Pack
Charles Whibley
Charles Willing Beale
Charlotte M. Braeme
Charlotte M. Yonge
Charlotte Perkins Stetson
Clair W. Hayes
Clarence Day Jr.
Clarence E. Mulford
Clemence Housman
Confucius
Cornelis DeWitt Wilcox
Cyril Burleigh
D. H. Lawrence
Daniel Defoe
David Garnett
Dinah Craik
Don Carlos Janes
Donald Keyhoe
Dorothy Kilner
Dougan Clark
Douglas Fairbanks
E. Nesbit
E.P.Roe
E. Phillips Oppenheim
Earl Barnes
Edgar Rice Burroughs
Edith Van Dyne
Edith Wharton
Edward J. O'Biren
Edward S. Ellis
Edwin L. Arnold
Eleanor Atkins
Eliot Gregory
Elizabeth Gaskell
Elizabeth McCracken
Elizabeth Von Arnim
Ellem Key
Emerson Hough
Emilie F. Carlen
Emily Dickinson
Enid Bagnold

Enilor Macartney Lane
Erasmus W. Jones
Ernie Howard Pie
Ethel Turner
Ethel Watts Mumford
Eugenie Foa
Eugene Wood
Eustace Hale Ball
Evelyn Everett-green
Everard Cotes
F. H. Cheley
F. J. Cross
Federick Austin Ogg
Ferdinand Ossendowski
Francis Bacon
Francis Darwin
Frances Hodgson Burnett
Frances Parkinson Keyes
Frank Gee Patchin
Frank Harris
Frank Jewett Mather
Frank L. Packard
Frank V. Webster
Frederic Stewart Isham
Frederick Trevor Hill
Frederick Winslow Taylor
Friedrich Kerst
Friedrich Nietzsche
Fyodor Dostoyevsky
G.A. Henty
G.K. Chesterton
Gabrielle E. Jackson
Garrett P. Serviss
Gaston Leroux
George A. Warren
George Ade
Geroge Bernard Shaw
George Durston
George Ebers
George Eliot
George Gissing
George MacDonald
George Meredith
George Orwell
George Sylvester Viereck
George Tucker
George W. Cable
George Wharton James
Gertrude Atherton

Grace E. King
Grace Gallatin
Grant Allen
Guillermo A. Sherwell
Gulielma Zollinger
Gustav Flaubert
H. A. Cody
H. B. Irving
H.C. Bailey
H. G. Wells
H. H. Munro
H. Irving Hancock
H. Rider Haggard
H. W. C. Davis
Hamilton Wright Mabie
Hans Christian Andersen
Harold Avery
Harold McGrath
Harriet Beecher Stowe
Harry Houidini
Helent Hunt Jackson
Helen Nicolay
Hendrik Conscience
Hendy David Thoreau
Henri Barbusse
Henrik Ibsen
Henry Adams
Henry Ford
Henry Frost
Henry James
Henry Jones Ford
Henry Seton Merriman
Henry W Longfellow
Herbert A. Giles
Herbert N. Casson
Herman Hesse
Homer
Honore De Balzac
Horace Walpole
Horatio Alger Jr.
Howard Pyle
Howard R. Garis
Hugh Lofting
Hugh Walpole
Humphry Ward
Ian Maclaren
Inez Haynes Gillmore
Irving Bacheller
Israel Abrahams
Ivan Turgenev
J.G.Austin

J. Henri Fabre
J. M. Barrie
J. Macdonald Oxley
J. S. Fletcher
J. S. Knowles
J. Storer Clouston
Jack London
Jacob Abbott
James Allen
James Andrews
James Baldwin
James DeMille
James Joyce
James Lane Allen
James Lane Allen
James Oliver Curwood
James Oppenheim
James Otis
James R. Driscoll
Jane Austen
Janet Aldridge
Jens Peter Jacobsen
Jerome K. Jerome
John Burroughs
John Cournos
John F. Kennedy
John Gay
John Glasworthy
John Habberton
John Joy Bell
John Kendrick Bangs
John Milton
John Philip Sousa
Jonas Lauritz Idemil Lie
Jonathan Swift
Joseph A. Altsheler
Joseph Carey
Joseph Conrad
Joseph E. Badger Jr
Joseph Hergesheimer
Joseph Jacobs
Jules Vernes
Julian Hawthrone
Julie A Lippmann
Justin Huntly McCarthy
Kakuzo Okakura
Kenneth Grahame
Kenneth McGaffey
Kate Langley Bosher
Kate Langley Bosher
Katherine Cecil Thurston

Katherine Stokes
L. A. Abbot
L. T. Meade
L. Frank Baum
Latta Griswold
Laura Lee Hope
Laurence Housman
Lawrence Beasley
Leo Tolstoy
Leonid Andreyev
Lewis Carroll
Lewis Sperry Chafer
Lilian Bell
Lloyd Osbourne
Louis Hughes
Louis Tracy
Louisa May Alcott
Lucy Fitch Perkins
Lucy Maud Montgomery
Lydia Miller Middleton
Lyndon Orr
M. Corvus
M. H. Adams
Margaret E. Sangster
Margaret Vandercook
Margret Penrose
Maria Edgeworth
Maria Thompson Daviess
Mariano Azuela
Marion Polk Angellotti
Mark Overton
Mark Twain
Mary Austin
Mary Catherine Crowley
Mary Cole
Mary Hastings Bradley
Mary Roberts Rinehart
Mary Rowlandson
M. Wollstonecraft Shelley
Maud Lindsay
Max Beerbohm
Myra Kelly
Nathaniel Hawthrone
Nicolo Machiavelli
O. F. Walton
Oscar Wilde
Owen Johnson
P.G. Wodehouse
Paul and Mabel Thorne
Paul G. Tomlinson
Paul Severing

Percy Brebner
Peter B. Kyne
Plato
R. Derby Holmes
R. L. Stevenson
R. S. Ball
Rabindranath Tagore
Rahul Alvares
Ralph Bonehill
Ralph Henry Barbour
Ralph Victor
Ralph Waldo Emmerson
Rene Descartes
Rex Beach
Rex E. Beach
Richard Harding Davis
Richard Jefferies
Richard Le Gallienne
Robert Barr
Robert Frost
Robert Gordon Anderson
Robert L. Drake
Robert Lansing
Robert Lynd
Robert Michael Ballantyne
Robert W. Chambers
Rosa Nouchette Carey
Rudyard Kipling
Samuel B. Allison

Samuel Hopkins Adams
Sarah Bernhardt
Sarah C. Hallowell
Selma Lagerlof
Sherwood Anderson
Sigmund Freud
Standish O'Grady
Stanley Weyman
Stella Benson
Stephen Crane
Stewart Edward White
Stijn Streuvels
Swami Abhedananda
Swami Parmananda
T. S. Ackland
T. S. Arthur
The Princess Der Ling
Thomas A. Janvier
Thomas A Kempis
Thomas Anderton
Thomas Bailey Aldrich
Thomas Bulfinch
Thomas De Quincey
Thomas H. Huxley
Thomas Hardy
Thomas More
Thornton W. Burgess
U. S. Grant
Valentine Williams

Various Authors
Vaughan Kester
Victor Appleton
Virginia Woolf
Walter Camp
Walter Scott
Washington Irving
Wilbur Lawton
Wilkie Collins
Willa Cather
Willard F. Baker
William Dean Howells
William le Queux
W. Makepeace Thackeray
William W. Walter
Winston Churchill
Yei Theodora Ozaki
Yogi Ramacharaka
Young E. Allison
Zane Grey